THE INVASION

By the same Author
Family Affairs

THE INVASION

A Novel by Jane Williams

WILLIAMS PRESS
Cambridge, MA

ISBN-13: 978-1490962528
ISBN-10: 1490962522

Designer: Susan Woodman

Photographic Credits: Front cover: (foreground) ©Trinity Mirror/ Mirrorpix/Almay (background) Image composite includes Washington Elm courtesy of the Cambridge Historical Society Image Collection 1A.0116 CHS

To JGK & the Raymond Street Writers

Chapter One

In April 1938, a month after Hitler's armies marched into Austria, Mr. Weiss, a groundskeeper at the Parker Farm School, shot himself in the mouth with a 9-millimeter Mauser. Late on a Wednesday afternoon, the night man found him in the utility room. Some said portions of his brain clung like custard to the cold water pipes overhead

That evening, telephones jangled across West Ivers as the news spread, leaving those who thought they knew the man in a state of disbelief.

As room mother to the ninth grade graduating class, Vera Oliver was among the first to receive a call from the headmistress.

"Oh, Miss Graham, the poor man. To be so desperate after all that he'd been through." Vera paused a moment. "What about his wife? How could he leave her like that?" She put the palm of her hand to the hollowness in her chest. "What happened?"

"I don't really know, Vera. When I went with the police to tell Mrs. Weiss she was speechless, numb.

She handed me a letter addressed to Mr. Weiss. I couldn't understand the German. The handwriting was foreign, of course."

"He seemed almost too accepting of his job. Perhaps we should have paid more attention, Miss Graham. We might have stopped him."

"I don't know how," Miss Graham said tersely. "We did what we could."

"What can I do to help?" Vera asked.

Miss Graham fell silent, just the faintest sigh of breath on the other end of the line. Vera knew the headmistress was going through the list of things to do on her clipboard. While Vera sat at attention in the little telephone cubby off the downstairs hall of her house, she imagined the headmistress at her desk, her long legs crossed, her free arm up to her faded blonde hair, readjusting the tortoise shell pins in the bun at the back of her neck. Suddenly the image of the dead man's teeth gaped out at Vera, his steel-framed glasses dangling from one ear of his shattered head. She closed her eyes to push it away.

Finally Miss Graham said, "If you'd call the parents of Katherine's class with the news, that would be a tremendous load off my mind."

"Of course," Vera said eagerly. "I can call the parents of Jenny's class, too, if that would help."

"Someone else can do that." The headmistress paused again, and Vera opened the door of the cubby to let in a little air. "We all know what a good organizer you are, Vera, but you also have a special gift with people," Miss Graham continued. "I've noticed it when you reach out to the other mothers, especially the little shy ones."

"Thank you, Miss Graham." Vera's voice lightened. "I know exactly how they feel."

"It's a lot to ask, Vera, but I feel we owe Mrs. Weiss a visit and I have so much to do. I must collect my thoughts for the memorial ceremony at Friday assembly."

But Miss Graham, I don't . . ."

"You'll be just fine, Vera. I have her address right here. She doesn't have a telephone."

After Vera had pressed her thumb down on the side cradle of the phone, she held the speaking cone up before her lips as if sending out a silent prayer. She was not a prominent member of the school community or a gifted leader like Miss Graham. She felt awkward and inadequate in the face of such a delicate mission. When she finally put the instrument down and stood up, even her lack of height seemed to disqualify her for the seriousness of the task.

She turned to look out the small window of the telephone closet, trying to remember when she had first heard about the Weisses. It was after the January coffee meeting with upper-school mothers. Vera had stayed to clean up. Miss Graham mentioned that she had met another refugee couple the evening before at the Unitarian Church, at a lecture series jointly sponsored with the Hebrew Guidance Society. Mr. Weiss was struggling to explain to a group of antiquarians, in heavily accented simple English, the techniques of furniture finishing in Vienna, where he had been a master cabinetmaker. Miss Graham had been drawn to him for his love of his work. The sallow-looking Jewish woman sitting patiently in uncomprehending silence at the side of the parish hall was obviously the man's wife. Black hat like a pot lid on a tight roll of dark hair at her neck. Beautifully decorated hand-knit cardigan with wooden buttons.

"What meager lives these people come to in their new country," the headmistress had commented when she reached the end of her story.

Vera continued to fold up the tablecloth, tears in her eyes. "And we have so much, Miss Graham."

The headmistress pushed her glasses up the bridge of her nose and turned full face to Vera. Vera could remember clearly the sharpness of Miss Graham's gaze. "We must do something about these people, Vera." Sometime after that Miss Graham appointed Mr. Weiss to the buildings-and-grounds staff of the school, where he took up his work without a word of complaint.

Vera finished her calls and closed the door on the telephone cubby. She was relieved that she couldn't call Mrs. Weiss to tell her she was coming. But this was a job she could no longer postpone. Richard would not approve of leaving the children with Mary, the maid, but he was never there to spell her. Besides, Jenny and Katherine were eight and fourteen now.

Vera put on her coat and hat and called up the stairs to the children to say she was going out for a few minutes to deliver the material for Katherine's graduation dress to the seamstress. As she backed the Buick out of the garage she stopped to think what she would say to Mrs. Weiss. She could hardly pry into the dead man's private life, but to say that she was sorry was hardly consolation for someone left so totally alone. Vera didn't really know what to say. She wasn't the headmistress, she was a perfect stranger to the widow.

The door opened immediately to Vera's ring. Mrs. Weiss bowed slightly, a small woman, already stout, her face crimped in grief. Vera explained she was Miss Graham's emissary and reached for the woman's hands. They sat side by side on the sofa bed in the one-room apartment, knees almost touching, eyes steady on each other's face, Vera searching for answers. But before Vera could speak, the other woman began shaking her head. *"Nein, nein,"* she moaned, hugging herself and rocking gently. *"Er hat keine Heimat."*

Vera recognized *Heimat,* "home." Her great aunt had spoken a little German.

Mrs. Weiss took an envelope from the pocket of her cardigan and handed it to Vera. Vera paused a moment before she took it, afraid of what the letter might tell her, then slowly unfolded it. She recognized the word for mother, *mutter,* and dead, *tot. Sie ist tot geworden,* literally "she is dead become." But how? She could not understand the details. Finally, she put the letter down in her lap. After so much suffering, was this the last straw for Mr. Weiss?

Mrs. Weiss took a handkerchief from her sleeve and blew her nose. "*Er hat keine Heimat,*" she repeated softly.

Vera reached to fold her arms around the grieving woman. "We will help you to make a home here, Mrs. Weiss," she blurted out, and knew she'd overstepped herself.

Mrs. Weiss looked up again into Vera's face. "*Josef ist mein Heimat.*"

Vera lowered her eyes. The two women sat in silence, then the widow turned away from Vera and covered her face in her hands before she wept.

Late in the night, unable to sleep, driven by the rhythm of Richard's breathing from the companion twin bed, Vera dwelt on the bleakness of the widow's plight. Mrs. Weiss had lost everything, yet what of such good-mannered weeping? What did such self-restraint say about the woman? In West Ivers, keeping your feelings to yourself was considered a mark of good breeding, but nothing that bad had ever happened to anyone here. The loneliness the woman must feel brought tears to Vera's eyes, and she reached for a handkerchief in the drawer of the nightstand.

Of course, they should have seen this tragedy coming. At the parents' committee meeting last January, Mr. Lewis, the treasurer, had warned them. Very subtly. But it was just this delicacy that made him one of the members Vera most admired.

When Miss Graham announced that she had

taken on Mr. Weiss without consulting the committee, Vera was relieved that there were no objections about procedure. Most of the members readily agreed that such a gesture was the least they could do. The fellow would be most grateful. They looked at each other uneasily; they were unsure about such matters. Charity was the province of their wives, some of whom served with Miss Graham on Mrs. Parker's University Women's League, welcoming Jewish refugees from Nazi Germany. They'd heard about the problem of housing and the need for warm clothes. Mr. Lewis was uncharacteristically silent, his legs stretched out straight, his head bowed so that his wavy black hair fell onto his forehead. He tapped his fingers restlessly on the tabletop.

Finally, he spoke. "What people who have had their lives pulled out from under them need is hope."

Everyone murmured agreement. "Absolutely, Harry," Miss Graham said, nodding her head.

"Most of us have been the outsider sometime in our lives," Mr. Lewis went on matter-of-factly. "If we're going to lend a helping hand, we must offer real assistance, not just a new overcoat or a pair of gloves. A job is a necessity, but we must not take away a man's dignity or burden him with kindness. What people fleeing for their lives need is to be taken into a community where they can belong."

Miss Graham did not raise her eyes from her clipboard as she spoke. "Thank you, Harry, for your views," she said firmly and moved quickly on to other items on the agenda. Of course, Vera did not question a woman of such wide experience and high purpose, but even then she had felt Miss Graham dismissed Mr. Lewis' comments too readily. A cultivated man like Mr. Weiss would need more than a menial job. Vera knew what it was like to be on the outside. Since that meeting she had wondered what injustices Mr. Lewis had suffered as a Jew before he came to live among them.

At the Friday assembly of the Parker Farm School, Miss Graham rose to stand in front of the big brick fireplace decorated with boughs of mountain laurel and yellow forsythia. She began the simple ceremony with a short statement of what had taken place on Wednesday afternoon and regretted that Mr. Weiss' widow was not up to joining them today. Then, she read John Donne's "No Man is an Island" and explained that Mr. Weiss had come from a famous furniture-making family in Austria, often doing the cabinetwork himself. The math instructor said the Lord's Prayer in German, his young voice swollen with sorrow. In conclusion, the music teacher stepped up to the piano to lead the audience in "Turn Back O Man, Forswear Thy Foolish Ways," adult voices soaring through the final lines, "Earth shall be fair, and all her folk be one," in a brief moment of faith.

Standing at the back of the room along the wall of windows with a small group of parents and other friends of the school, Vera watched as grades I through

IX filed out the side door of the hall, aware that Jenny was one of the few students in her class to be out of line. She shook her head at the thought of her younger daughter and turned to leave by the main entrance. In the hallway Miss Graham stepped forward, raising her voice to be heard above the noise of the janitor folding up the wooden chairs, *crack, crack, crack* like a repeating rifle.

"Thank you, Vera, for visiting Mrs. Weiss. You really have done yeoman service. Not an easy job." She laid her hand on Vera's arm. "But now I want to ask you something else. Will you serve on Isabel Parker's refugee committee? You'd be a great addition."

Vera looked up into the headmistress' cool green eyes. "Mrs. Parker's committee. I'd be honored," she said solemnly.

"I'll tell Isabel to be in touch with you." Miss Graham squeezed the younger woman's arm and smiled, then stepped briskly into her office.

Vera buttoned the jacket of her navy blue suit against the nip still in the air and pulled on her gloves before stepping out of the building. Mrs. Parker's committee, *the* Mrs. Parker, she said over and over to herself as she walked slowly up Parker Farm Road.

The students at the Parker Farm School were dismissed earlier than usual on this Friday, after the big bell rang to announce the end of recess and they had finished their milk and graham crackers. Shedding the melancholy of the morning, they traveled up the hill to the rambling colonials or commodious neo-Georgians that stood in stately progression along the sides of Parker Farm Road. The latest house to be built on the street was the Lewises' showy stucco.

Most of the children had farther to go before they reached home. Some of the older ones were on their bicycles, celebrating the liberation of spring by racing each other along the gravel sidewalks, weaving in and out of the clusters of walkers in contempt of the rules. In a straggly procession the students continued on to the intersection with Great Hamilton Street, where the patrolman, Officer Scannell, raised his hand to command the oncoming motorcars and trolleys to stop. The children hailed him joyously. Some of the younger ones took his free hand as he walked them into the middle of the street, his left arm still held high, addressing the students lagging behind as if he had eyes in the back of his head—"Come on there, Mr. Timothy... Maryanne, darling, hurry along now"—crossing them to the safety of a network of tree-lined streets beyond.

Emerson, Longfellow, Washington, Adams, these were the thoroughfares that constituted the right side of town. Expansive lawns, swampy with the damp of an early spring, hedges of lilac soon to bloom, budding rose gardens. Wrought iron gates, brick walls, urns of ivy at either end of a semi-circular driveway. Mansard roofs, cupolas and widow's walks, an occasional carriage house tucked back in a side yard. Hidden below the fieldstone foundations were the dank, spidery cellars that housed big, black furnaces fed from the coal piled on the stone floors beneath the window chutes. In winter the handymen and caretakers toted coal in heavy square shovels to the mouths of the furnaces, thrown open and gaping red. The woodpiles, the fuse boxes and the web of knob and tube wiring, the copper water pipes, were visible in the furnace rooms. The soapstone wash tubs and newfangled washing machines with rubber wringers stood in the laundry rooms, ready to make the job of Katy or Nora easier on Monday mornings. Half a dozen clotheslines for winter drying crossed wall to wall just below the low ceiling in the room beyond. Many of the larger old houses had larders, root cellars, trunk and storage rooms in their basements as well.

Some students lived on the crisscross of historic streets that bordered University Square; still others took the underground subway into the city and townhouses on the Hill. They would often cut through the elegantly fenced enclave of colonial brick and majestic trees of Boylston University, where in a few years' time distinguished scholars would routinely grant them gentlemanly Cs. Some mothers and grandmothers had attended the women's extension. As these women moved through their lives, ordering the groceries or escorting the children to their appointments, they often looked back wistfully to the challenge of study or the sense of autonomy they had felt when they were college girls.

In the kitchens of West Ivers, at lunchtime on Fridays, the cooks made a nice chicken sandwich on buttered bread, or perhaps egg salad, set out on the dining room table with a glass of cold milk and a plate of cookies and a piece of fruit in season. Often, when they could get away from the hospital volunteers, or the Mothers' Study Club luncheon, or the Home for Little Destitutes board meeting, the mothers would join their children for lunch and read the little ones a nursery story before an afternoon nap or quiet time.

On regular school days the older students stayed at school for hot lunch served in the assembly hall on collapsible Masonite tables set up each midmorning by Mr. Dooley, the janitor. After soccer on the playing fields or dodgeball in the hall when it was too wet, or perhaps an hour of extra art studio, these children would set out for home, green book bags slung over their shoulders, a violin case or a hockey stick tucked under one arm.

Afternoon tea was served in the living room, with a plate of cinnamon toast or little triangles of bread and butter. The younger ones often had milky sweet cambric tea at a neighboring house before listening to the radio, *Dick Tracy* or *Terry and the Pirates*, introduced with a resounding gong. The older ones were excused to put away their things and settle down to their homework. At six o'clock, the children of the neighborhood returned to their own houses to gather around the head of the family, reiterating in the very act of coming together the value of order and responsibility.

This was still a time of the leisurely cocktail hour, when couples or occasionally groups sat down in the

living rooms of West Ivers over martinis or a glass of
sherry before dinner. The conversation was frequently
about the Depression and aching investment losses.
Unemployment. They raised their glasses to the repeal
of Prohibition, and abhorred Frankie and his New
Deal treacheries: the mammoth federal post office
behind the railroad station downtown, the work of
the boondoggling WPA. Packing the Supreme Court
with his chain gang cronies. And imagine appointing a
woman as Labor Secretary in his cabinet. An occasional remark in defense of the administration was scoffed
at as the ravings of a potential Democrat. Unless, of
course, the talk was about Harry Lewis. That was one
thing he hadn't left behind when he moved into the
neighborhood, his Democratic party affiliation. After a
few head shakes, the discussion would move on to the
inadequacy of household help, the sudden dip in the
recovering economy. Would it bring another penny on
a bottle of milk?

The Friday evening of the memorial service began
as usual with the return to house and hearth. And, of
course, there was the relief that comes with any Friday
evening.

But most of the talk—at least for those who had
children at the Parker Farm School—was about the
tragedy and its effect on the students. Some felt it was
an outrage for the man to take his life in such a place.
Others wondered if the school could have prevented it
or at least kept it quiet.

But consider the school motto: *Before All Else Be True*. With that in mind, it was generally agreed that Miss Graham had done her best to dignify the whole ghastly business.

A little later that same evening, on her way home from Molly Norton's house for supper, Jenny Oliver stopped to snap off a few sprigs of Mr. Lewis' forsythia hedge just as Miss Graham was coming up Parker Farm Road. Jenny quickly held the spray behind her back, but the stems were long. There was no hiding it.

The headmistress looked over her glasses halfway down her long nose. "Do you have Mr. Lewis' permission to pick his forsythia, Jenny?"

For a moment, Jenny felt like a criminal. She looked down at her sneakers and scuffed at the gravel on the sidewalk. While she hadn't asked Mr. Lewis, exactly, he wasn't like Daddy, who always said no. Then she remembered the school motto and looked up. She fudged it. "Sort of, Miss Graham," she said.

"There is no 'sort of' truth, Jenny," Miss Graham told her sternly.

Chapter Two

This Friday, Vera sat down with a dry sherry to wait for Richard to return from his law office. She was more restive than usual, skimming through the *Evening Traveler*. Apparently, the Third Reich had officially withdrawn from the New York World's Fair. Adolph Hitler was going to Rome to meet with Benito Mussolini. She tucked herself further into the broad-backed wing chair, accidentally unhooking a garter. As she reached under her skirt to reattach her stocking, she remembered the pleasure of flinging off her corset in the privacy of her room when she was a girl. She must have been a little older than her daughter Katherine. The young today had much to be grateful for. She returned to the newspaper. Smart spring hats and patent leather bags in the department stores.

Richard was late. Was it her imagination, or did it happen more frequently now? And Mary would presently come in to tell her the fish would be dried out. Katherine was doing her homework upstairs in her room, so she could be free to spend the weekend with her friends. Vera and Richard were both proud that their eldest daughter already valued the good opinion of her teachers and friends. The next few years at Miss Emerson's for Girls would prepare Katherine for a fine women's college, and thank heavens Katherine would not have to suffer the indignities of being on scholarship the way Vera had.

Her youngest daughter would be at the Russells' or the Nortons'. Or perhaps sitting at the kitchen table, hanging on Mary's every word. Vera knew that such adoration drove Richard wild. "That maid is filling the child full of nonsense." Vera would assure him that children go through phases and hoped she was right. Jenny seemed such an unpredictable child, moving in and out of her little friendships like a stray cat.

A door opened on the second floor—Katherine coming to join her. She waited expectantly. But the door closed, and Vera stood up, letting the paper fall from her lap, listening to an emptiness moving through the house. It haunted her tonight like the image of that poor man ending his life in a boiler room. Everyone had gone out of their way to be cordial to him. He was always so dignified. Once when she passed him rolling out the barrels of ashes, she greeted him a little too cheerfully. He stopped and gave her a courtly bow. Did that just add to his troubles? He couldn't stand it, being patronized by the West Ivers ladies with their awful noblesse oblige?

As a girl, Vera had tried to imagine what it would be like to kill herself. Playing Romeo in a high school production of the Shakespeare play, she had very much enjoyed the melodrama of the death scene. "Thus with a kiss I die." Once, she had locked herself in the bathroom and stood before the mirror on the back of the door, her squat figure planted in the center of the bathmat. She hoped her pompadour of dark hair gave her height, but the foolish bow at the back of her neck that her mother insisted on reminded her of donkey ears. She scowled at herself, then let the muscles of her face sag in mock despair and raised her pointed finger to her temple, closing her eyes in the finality of the moment.

Suddenly, Vera pictured the refugee again. This time his head was lolling to one side, his shirt front soaked in blood. She moved hastily to the dining room sideboard where she kept her purse in one of the silver drawers and took out a handkerchief to blow her nose. In the silence that followed the snap-shut of the clasp, she began straightening the flatware, tracing the raised edges of the pattern with her finger, polishing the blade of a knife on the sleeve of her blouse. She seldom used the silver service. Only when guests came. It was like money, something she'd never quite gotten used to, as if she hadn't come by it honestly. She closed the drawer as noiselessly as possible. The heavy materials and cushioned furnishings in the downstairs rooms demanded quiet.

When she was growing up north of Boston, the house had been filled with women talking. Mother, aunties, schoolmates, neighbors, her Great-aunt Jenny cooing in her stilted German. "*Nun, nun, Schatze,* there, there, treasure." But now she lived in solitary splendor in West Ivers, on Parker Farm Road. Her husband was a partner in a downtown law firm, she had two children and a lovely house. She didn't have to work. She even had a maid. "What more could a woman want," her mother had scolded when Vera was visiting for what turned out to be the last time before her mother's stroke. Vera had been complaining a little about Richard.

She had excused herself quickly before she said something rude and gone up to her room, slamming the door the way she used to, so that it shook in its rickety frame. It galled her that her mother didn't want to hear anything personal about Vera's life. She had lain down on her childhood bed and followed the familiar water stains across the ceiling. What had once looked to her like mountains or clouds or a streamer of ribbons now looked like her mother's varicose veins.

When she had composed herself, she had washed her face and gone downstairs to the parlor. Her mother looked up from her crocheting and shook her head. "Well, missy, I can't say marriage has sweetened your temper any."

Vera brushed away the memory and plunked herself down again in the wing chair and took a sip of sherry. She picked up the newspaper, then put it down again. Where was Richard?

When she was growing up, marriage had been considered every young girl's hope, always whispered in the hushed tones of a worshipper at prayer. But it was important that Vera be sensible and learn to make a living. Just look at her aunties, her mother cautioned, scraping along in the mills, spinsters to the last. Vera had been confused. Her aunts seemed to lead energetic lives, with their shop talk and choir practice, their many friends and the summer outings. While her mother talked about an office job for her, or perhaps a position in a department store, something respectable, Vera had worked hard to become a scholarship girl at the women's college nearby. She thought dreamily of college theatrics—despite her short stature—or a position on the student government. She looked forward to leading her college class in her cap and gown like the young women she saw marching two by two into the Congregational church at graduation time. When the time came for Vera to receive her degree, her mother had unashamedly wept with pride. Vera thought of a teaching career, but then Richard proposed at the senior ball, and her mother treated him like a godsend.

Vera went restlessly into the hall to call up the stairs, "Katherine, would you like a glass of tomato juice?"

A door opened. "It's so awful. I just can't stand these algebra problems."

"I'm sure you can do them if you put your mind to it. You know you'll be expected to work very hard at Miss Emerson's next year."

The door banged shut, then opened again. "Is Daddy home yet? I'm hungry."

"He's at a meeting, dear. He'll be here soon." Her voice sang the way it did when she mentioned their father to the children.

On the way back to the living room, she stopped to straighten the gilt mirror by the coat closet. She had to admit she enjoyed many things in married life. Her house, for instance, and her children. She was a room mother and the only mother on the parents' committee at the school. Volunteering at the hospital brought her together with women from the old established families of West Ivers, so at ease with themselves and each other. Neighbors like Beatrice Norton and Charlotte Russell. But despite Jenny's friendships with their children, Vera always had trouble telling the women apart. They were tall and willowy, with smooth lustrous hair and fair skin. Looking in the mirror, she ran her fingers over her cheeks. At least her darker complexion meant she tanned well, and Richard had said once that she had nice full lips.

She peered out the window at the street. The Lewises' forsythia hedge was in full bloom, and the yews at the Parkers' on the corner seemed thicker than ever in the evening shadows. But there was no sign of Richard. Or Jenny, who seemed to prefer any place to her own home.

Never mind. She had been asked to join Mrs. Parker's University Women's League, because she was good at running things. Richard wouldn't like that. Only Perfect Little Secretary Miss Sperry had skills beyond the domestic sphere. Sometimes Vera wished Miss Perfect would fall off the top of the Empire State Building. Of course, Richard had made it quite clear that Vera's place was in the home. With the children, like all the rest of the mothers on Parker Farm Road. When Vera pointed out that they hosted the Junior Dinner Dances or the Antiquarian Society teas, Richard nodded his approval. These were proper activities for women of their circumstances. Except Mrs. Parker, of course. She was so grand she could do anything she wanted. And Miss Graham. But she was a spinster. Vera savored the irony as she looked out the French doors into the garden. Richard did not really like Miss Graham. Not feminine enough for him. Leather jackets and those unattractive shoes.

The sky was filled with ribbons of pink clouds. It was well after six. A sadness moved into Vera. She was Richard's wife. But she was not his haven. Nor he hers.

She turned away, inspecting her hands for a moment, as if they held the key to her discomfort. Other women had family diamonds and platinum ring guards burdening their aristocratically long fingers. Hers were short and stubby. She felt the slight bind of the slim gold wedding band on her left hand. Seventeen years now. And she was almost forty. Abruptly, she swung open the door into the pantry.

"Jenny in, Mary?"

"Not yet, Mrs. Oliver, and the fish will be drying out."

"Well, do the best you can."

Chapter Three

Jenny was listening to the radio in Mr. Russell's den.
Sprawled out on the rug with Patsy and Molly, transported into the world of make-believe, they could live
for a few hours free of the bother of each other. Patsy
Russell was eight, but referred to herself as "nine in
two months." Jenny and Molly were always at her
house unless one of them had a dentist appointment or
something. They were a threesome, although to Jenny
they were not quite equal. Sometimes Pearl Lewis
listened to the radio with them. But somehow having
four of them didn't make it any better for Jenny. Patsy
was the oldest and the tallest, and Molly had naturally
curly hair. Jenny was husky. That's what her mother
said. But once, when she couldn't button up the purple
bodice from the Russells' costume box, Mrs. Russell had told her not to worry, she would grow to be
a handsome girl. She always liked Mrs. Russell after
that, even when she wasn't supposed to.

Mr. Russell opened the door just as the sound of
the vibrating gong signaled the end of another episode

of *Terry and the Pirates*. They all sat up straight.

"Time to skedaddle, Jenny, Molly. Patsy has piano practice."

They slipped the stamps they had been trading back into their little wax-paper envelopes. The stamps were from Italy and Ireland and unreal places like Madagascar that they got by sending in the tops of cereal boxes. Jenny and Molly began to gather up their things from the floor.

"Please, Daddy," Patsy whined.

"You know the rules, doodlebug."

Patsy slouched to the door of the den. But when she saw her older brother, Teddy, in the hall, she pulled herself up to her full height and sailed past him into the chintz-covered living room, where her mother sat on the love seat in the bay window. Mrs. Russell was looking at pictures in the *National Geographic* with Howie, all pink and fresh in his Doctor Dentons. The family Airedale lay across Mrs. Russell's long thin feet.

Patsy settled on the piano bench, knees together, skirt pulled down, back straight, the way her teacher had taught her, and launched into "Raindrops Go Pitter Patter on the Walk." Jenny and Molly, wriggling into their jackets, watched from the doorway of the den, unwilling to risk running into Teddy. He was what Jenny's cook, Mary, called a boyo. "Pay him no mind," she always advised Jenny, but it never worked.

When Mr. Russell appeared in the hall with the drink tray, Teddy followed him as far as the doorway of the living room. He leaned against the frame. Mrs.

Russell looked up at her husband with her worried eyes as he set the tray down on the coffee table in front of her. "That business . . . you know, Ed, the refugee man, I think the children . . ."

"They'll be all right, Charlotte, children are sturdy little . . ."

"Blood and gore all over the floor . . ." Teddy began.

"Teddy Russell." Mrs. Russell raised a hand to her cheek. "Really, Ed, where does he hear these things?"

". . . and me without a spoon."

Mr. Russell's face was red now. "You may go to your room, young man."

"Dad!"

Jenny and Molly hurried across the hall and out the front door, slamming it behind them. Molly went back to close it quietly.

At Molly's house, Mrs. Norton was just setting down the plate of crackers on the coffee table as they came in. She steadied herself with one knee on the sofa cushion to reach up under the shade and turn on the side table lamp. The yellow light gleamed around the clusters of plums and grapes appliquéd on the creamy silk shade.

"Shut the door quietly, Molly. Oh Jenny, isn't it time you were at home?"

Mr. Norton followed his wife into their living room, gently stirring a pitcher of martinis to blend the gin and vermouth before he filled the glasses on the silver tray. Mrs. Norton had settled herself on the sofa.

"Hi, Daddy," Molly called out as she tossed her jacket into the front hall closet. "We need to do something, Mummy."

"All right, dears, but be quick about it." Mrs. Norton waited a moment. When she thought the girls had gone up the stairs, she picked up the conversation where they had left off. "You know how strongly Miss Graham believes her pupils should be told the truth, Tom."

Jenny and Molly backed down the stairs and took up their positions inside the closet, Molly on her knees so they could both peek around the closet door into the living room.

"'One learns to find direction from the realities of life,' Mrs. Norton went on, speaking through her nose in imitation of the headmistress. "How often have we heard that one." Mrs. Norton's voice rippled with faint laughter as Jenny and Molly struggled to muffle their giggles.

"Too much, too young," Mr. Norton said and handed down Mrs. Norton's cocktail. He stood at the fireplace and looked at her, his drinking arm resting on the mantelpiece.

"Still she conducted a very moving morning assembly service for the poor man," Mrs. Norton said.

"I bet she did. All poetry and tears." Mr. Norton huffed a little sigh. "In school I itched all over when the master trotted out the poetry books. 'Tiger tiger burning bright, in the something of the night.' That's about all I can remember now, and I still don't have any idea what the hell it's all about."

Mrs. Norton looked down at her lap for a moment. "Awful thought, isn't it, and at Miss Graham's school."

Mr. Norton huffed. "All that hopping and skipping to music, no place for a boy like Pelly, Bea. At six, we were already playing football."

She looked up at him. "Pelly will get plenty of that later on at boarding school. After all, you did."

"Back when being a good sport won you the girl." He smiled faintly.

Mrs. Norton changed the subject. "I feel terrible for that poor groundskeeper. He had to leave everything behind."

"But why do those people have to end up here?"

Mr. Norton moved out of view, and Jenny leaned too far out over Molly's head, trying to see further around the edge of the closet door. They collapsed to the floor with a thud. Mr. Norton appeared in the hall carrying his glass.

"Good God, Molly."

Mrs. Norton came up behind him. "Oh Molly, what a . . . you know you shouldn't listen when adults are talking." Mrs. Norton's voice was sharp. "Molly, you go upstairs where you belong and find Pelly. Katy will have supper ready soon. And Jenny, I thought I told you to go home. It's getting late."

As Jenny picked her jacket up off the floor, the Nortons returned to the living room. "Really, Tom. You mustn't swear like that."

Mr. Norton was shaking the cocktail pitcher. "Here, let's finish this off. It's nothing but ice water."

There was a pause, then Mrs. Norton said, "You know, Molly never snoops when she's with Patsy Russell."

Jenny closed the Nortons' front door as quietly as she could.

Jenny's father was standing in front of the house clutching his briefcase when she came running up the road, the stems of forsythia crushed in her fist. Tall and thin, he always reminded Jenny of a giraffe when he arched over to give her a peck on the cheek.

"That's a nice bouquet you've got there," he said.

"It's for your desk actually." She slipped her hand into his free one.

He smiled down at her, squeezing her hand. "You're my special girl."

Together they inspected her father's array of rose bushes spaced along the driveway to form a hedge. Tiny little reddish leaves sprouted along the blackened stems. Your father's "pride and joy," her mother called them. "First on his list of things he cares about. I come somewhere after spinach." Jenny knew she was up at the top with the roses. She was suddenly aware of the warmth of his grip.

Her father turned his attention to the lawn. "It will have to be reseeded and rolled," he said. Jenny nodded. "I might enjoy doing it myself. I like a little outdoor work, it's good for you. My brothers and I were expected to do the yard work when I was growing up. My mother would get after my father, too, if he were around. But your mother's not one to have her husband in dirty overalls out on the front lawn. 'What will Mrs. Parker think?'" He began to imitate her mother. Then he stopped abruptly and looked down at Jenny, clearing his throat. "Your mother's right, Jenny. We don't want to offend." He paused and Jenny felt she was expected to nod again. "She's a wonderful woman, your mother. Very generous with her time to others." He sounded almost wistful.

"Daddy. Look at the daffodils you planted last year. That one's almost out of its skin." Jenny ran across the lawn to inspect.

Her father strolled after her. "Daffodils grew wild along the creek behind the house in Dayton. A nice simple flower. Your grandmother used to fill the house with armloads. No one else in town had a houseful of flowers. In the summer, it was phlox. She even put them on the counter at Dad's hardware store. Everyone who came in had something to say about that. 'It keeps her happy,' my father used to say, 'and the price is right.' We children were known as Thelma Oliver's saplings." He stood with Jenny, looking at the spread of daffodils under the ornamental maple. "I gave daffodils to your mother when I first met her," he said, "but I had to buy them."

"Did she like them?"

"I think so." He turned away. "Time to go in, darling."

Jenny played follow the leader, stepping in her father's spongy footprints in the grass as they walked to the front door. "I'll have to hire those Italian bandits that work for Harry Lewis to fix up this lawn," he said and took Jenny's hand again. "Come on, we're late. After supper, I believe I'll risk a pipe in my study."

Jenny smiled up at him. "I won't tell Mummy."

The Olivers had baked cod for supper, with parsley potatoes and buttered carrots. While they ate, Richard listed some of the events of his day. Vera picked out a cluster of tiny little bones in the white flesh. She had never really liked fish, but it was what they ate on Fridays because Mary's religion required it. This was too dry. Katherine ate politely, careful not to draw attention so she could follow her own thoughts. Jenny stabbed at her food, morsel by morsel, while both parents struggled to ignore her. A natural break in Richard's report allowed Vera to recount the details of the beautiful ceremony Miss Graham had put together to mark the tragedy at the school.

"Did you like the ceremony, Jenny?" her father asked.

She was concentrating on hiding her fish under some potatoes. "I didn't know the words to the song."

Katherine spoke. "They're quite easy."

"Why did he shoot himself?"

In the silence that followed her question, Jenny looked from one parent to the other.

Her mother said, "Because he was unhappy."

"But, Mummy, everyone said Miss Graham saved him."

"Oh, Jenny," Vera exclaimed sharply. She sounded on edge and tried to soften her tone. "Eat your fish, dear. It's good for you."

Richard stepped in to head off a possible unpleasantness. "A good old simple New England dinner." He pushed back his chair imperceptibly. "You're a wonderful planner, Vera."

This was Vera's chance. She was twisting her napkin under the table. "Miss Graham has asked me to help sponsor some of the Jewish refugee families coming into the university area. It's under the auspices of Mrs. Parker's University Women's League and the Unitarian church group. It wouldn't involve any financial commitment. Mrs. Parker is raising the money. The work is really critical, Richard."

"But we're Episcopalian, Vera."

"Oh, that's not the point, Richard. You don't say no to a chance to work on Mrs. Parker's committee."

For just a moment, Richard felt the tightness across his forehead. He let the muscles of his cheeks sag and waited in silence for the pain to subside.

Vera searched his face, her breath knotted in her throat. "Don't you see, Richard, it's a chance to do something important, to be with the kind of people who matter to me." Richard winced and she leaned forward. "I'll be helping people who will really appreciate what we can do for them." She looked at his doleful face. "Miss Graham recommended me herself."

With exaggerated care Richard folded, then unfolded his napkin. "Mrs. Parker is not such a gorgon, Vera. You can tell her you'll help out another time. You have plenty to do already."

"Miss Graham will be part of it," Vera added.

"No. I have to advise you to say no, Vera. The children . . ."

She did not wait for him to tell her again that the children needed her at home. And it wasn't as if she wouldn't ever be there. "I'm sorry to disappoint you, Richard. I've already told Miss Graham I'd be honored to help Mrs. Parker out. Who could refuse at a time like this?"

The Olivers waited in silence for Mary to clear the table. When it was time for Vera to serve the grapenut pudding, the conversation was about the fancy new washing machine on the blink again. Time for Jenny to get another pair of sneakers, the ones she was wearing were ratty. As each daughter finished her dessert, she asked to be excused. Richard had work to do in his study. Vera went into the kitchen to have a few words about the weekend grocery order before Mary started to clear the table.

Passing back through the heavy swinging door into the dining room, Vera felt lost again in the quiet of the house and stepped quickly into the hall, pausing at the foot of the stairs. Perhaps she would look in on the children. Her eye followed the carpeting to the landing above, where it formed a T and traveled along the upstairs hallway, the crimson color underlining the stark whiteness of the two closed doors. Never mind, she would be tucking Jenny in for the night in another half hour. She turned away and looked over the banister down the lower passageway to Richard's study.

She envied him his capacity to lose himself in his work, and she knew he would politely not welcome her just now. He saw her decision as a defiance, of course. In front of the children. She regretted that part. Suddenly she could hear Miss Graham's melodious voice as she read Donne's devotion earlier in the day. "No man is an island, entire of itself; every man is a piece of the continent, a part of the main." The clatter of plates as Mary cleared the table interrupted her train of thought, pushing the bleakness aside.

Chapter Four

On this same Friday, Harry Lewis emerged from the subway at University Square into the fragile light of early evening, his fedora in his hand. The air was fresh, almost warm; he would walk home. But first, a stop at Newbury Flowers to select a single rose, creamy white. The thought of touching his wife made him smile for the first time since he'd said good-bye to her that morning. He settled his hat on his head.

It had been a hard few days since the suicide at the school. Poor fellow must have reached a level of hopelessness beyond Harry's understanding. Beyond the despair in the face of death that had given the man the courage to flee his country. But that time he had wanted to live. What had gone so wrong for him? Miss Graham had reported to the parents committee that he had received word that his mother had died. But even that death, in circumstances one could only imagine as the worst, did not explain the man's will to die after all he'd gone through to finally reach certain safety. The utter single-mindedness of such an act.

The loneliness. The irresponsibility. The death moved and angered Harry. In similar circumstances would it have been him? The whole business left him with the unsettling sense of a narrow escape.

As he stepped into the florist shop he shook his head as if to empty it. He selected a rose, and waited, staring into the refrigerated case at the tiers of cut flowers while the rose was wrapped.

And then there was the service at the school that he had attended this morning, so absurdly Christian in the attempt to be nonsectarian. Such lack of understanding, insensitivity really, was only Yankee complacency. Almost to a person, the citizens of West Ivers viewed their community as the most comfortable and stimulating place on earth. Harry had no quarrel with that. Most of them had the New Englander's understanding of privilege and the obligation to guide and assist others less fortunate than themselves. But he often viewed their burden of goodness with wry amusement. They were so sure of their own worth and decency when welcoming others into their midst. Yet they remained completely unaware that their heritage was as distinctive and hard to fathom as any other to the outsider. Some years later, he would smile ruefully at his own naiveté, but on this evening he believed there were no villains among the people of West Ivers, only the innocent and the self-absorbed.

Crossing High Street, Harry passed into the grounds of the university through one of the iron gates in the filigreed fence, imposing as much for the exclusion implied as for the protection of those within. His own experience at the university had been intellectually fruitful and socially barren. While most of the Jews at Boylston University tried not to appear Jewish, the fraternal societies were for gentiles only, not open to them anyway. In time, he'd learned to control his anger, although every time Tom Norton, with his smooth pink looks and his club tie, stood up from a meeting table and gave him a slap on the shoulder like the rump of a good trotter, Harry wanted to give him a poke in the eye.

Had he been able to afford the university room and board, would there have been space for the likes of him? He was relieved not to have had to risk it. Each evening, he had returned across the city to the affectionate hubbub of his uncle's family with whom he boarded. Milton Lefkovich had purposefully taken back the original family name lost in the documenting of his grandparents' immigration form. Harry had refused to. The name Lewis was easier in every way— one less chance to be mocked, spoken or unspoken. There were plenty like him, but some of the community had seen him as pushy. No one doubted that Harry was smart. A love of learning was a good thing. Look at the rabbi, who sometimes consulted Harry on the absurdities of goyish culture. Harry liked money. Making money was getting ahead, like his uncle Milton, who owned the furniture store where Harry had sometimes worked. But everyone knew Boylston University was for the privileged, the upstart among them who thought he belonged there, too special to attend shul with his uncle and the rest of them. Too busy to observe the High Holidays. Harry had ignored the occasional gibes of shopkeepers. He was young and ambitious. The Jew's work ethic was the Yankee's. But he acknowledged a difference others didn't: Yankees conducted their business with ruthless courtesy. It allowed them to get away with a lot. Graduation from Boylston had given him a pedigree of sorts. Harry expected to get what he wanted.

Too many people in the West Ivers community were impressed by the wrong things. But then, he was often guilty of the same lapse of common sense. It was hard not to be impressed by so much overwhelming self-confidence that went along with a Boylston education, a little old Yankee money, and the generations of family breeding around here. Sometimes when one of them came into Harry's office at Howell & Howell to work out a recovery strategy on the market or spend down still further the dwindling remains of an old family fortune, there would be a moment of camaraderie following a bout of realization of fiscal vulnerability, like the gratitude and trust a patient feels for the doctor who comes quickly in an emergency. But as the patient feels better his old irascibility returns, and the doctor's advice is just another obstacle to a false sense of recovery.

Plenty of his accounts had suffered in the Crash of '29. Harry had to admire the way some of these people kept up appearances on a shoestring. When he took over the firm a few years ago, he was aware that many of his clients might have preferred to go elsewhere. Natural inertia and loyalty to old Mr. Howell's choice explained in part the reasons for leaving their investments with the firm. But Harry knew that when the chips are down, it's the return that counts, and he had brought some of these families back from pretty shaky circumstances. They could not afford to trouble themselves about birth and bloodline where money was concerned.

He passed through another gate out onto Lower Great Hamilton Street. Across the way, he caught a glimpse of the river beyond a stand of birches, pale beams of the setting sun spotting the ice-blue surface of the water. A trolley car clanged cautiously forward, swaying gently under the load of passengers packed in against each other. Was that Richard Oliver hanging onto a strap? Then the car was past him and suddenly the river came into full view, curving gracefully south at the boat club and gliding in a diminishing line through the great swamp, past the city cemetery to the abattoir rising like a medieval battlement in the distance. Harry paused to take off his hat and topcoat before he descended through a stand of sumac shrubs to the dirt path that paralleled the river all the way up to the town dump. Here the true color of the water was revealed at the river's edge, a murky mud brown, but the gentle sound of lapping against the rocky shore was soothing, and the sight of an occasional rower's shell added detail to the rustic scene.

This was not altogether a safe route to take. Harry would not want the children to stray into the tangle of pampas grass and jewelweed beyond the chain fence at the bottom of Parker Farm Road. Closing the gate, he crossed the school parking lot and stepped out onto Parker Farm Road. He paused to place his hat back on his head and smoothed down the lapel of his gray pinstriped suit in case he met one of his neighbors. As he strolled up the street, he amused himself cataloging the different kinds of money that had settled into the neighborhood. It was like a busman's holiday. There was industrial and commercial money that became family money after two or three generations, like Charlotte Russell's. There was plenty of professional money, too, solid but not substantial. White-shoe boy Tom Norton.

The tranquility of the evening was broken by Mrs. von Kempel's barking dog, fenced in where the crest of earth was blanketed with bluebells. Here was foreign money. Before a scandalous divorce her German husband had captured a corner of the rubber trade. Now Harry caught a glimpse of the boy, Wilhelm, standing there by the outside faucet. Much too old to be poking a stick in the mud that way, Harry thought, and shook his head. He'd managed a good reinvestment of assets for the woman, and he kept close tabs on her account, but she was a frail person without serenity. Mother and son were another kind of outsider.

He raised his hat to the boy and walked on, admiring the last of the purple and yellow crocuses along the foundations, sprouting up in lawns and terraces, wild along the passageway leading to the tennis court. The trees were still uncurling their leaves, the hedges filling out. He paused to admire the carpet of daffodils underneath Richard Oliver's ornamental maple. This was hard-work money honestly come by.

Harry had always enjoyed the flowing of spring. In his youth, his little fluffed-up mother would leave open the windows and the door to the back porch to chase away the winter, often taking a broom to the curtains. The reek of the glue factory down at the end of the street would sweep in, replacing the staleness of boiled potatoes and tobacco. He could almost smell the annual coat of shellac on the common stairwell. And the neighbors' chickens and goats penned up in the scruff out behind the tenements. The common grazing ground of a different New England village that he had been happy to leave behind.

He stepped off the sidewalk to avoid the ancient yews obscuring the elegant old farmhouse that gave the neighborhood its name. This was old money, and the present Mrs. Parker saw herself as the social leveler. The thought made Harry smile. She once told him that his own house lot had been the farm dump. Never mind. This had been the promised land for the likes of him. If not for the poor Viennese cabinetmaker who blew his brains out.

Harry stopped now to admire his own humble abode across the street. He could drive to the city, come home in style, but the walk up Parker Farm

Road made this moment all the more sweet. Sometimes he even admitted to a smugness his mother used
to warn him about. What a place to call home. The
imposing size, the decorative elegance of the stucco,
the putting green lawn, and the dense plantings still
astonished him. At this season, it was his forsythia
hedge that drew his scrutiny, neatly clipped back,
restrained, but in full bloom, the mass of egg yellow
startlingly alive.

Inside her house, Adele sat in the formal drawing room reminiscent of the New York apartment on
the Upper West Side where she had been brought up.
Heavy rich fabrics and Persian rugs. She had changed
for dinner into an emerald-green silk dress, a diamond
pin at the neckline, and black lizard pumps. The high
gloss of her black hair, the faint pink at the rise of her
cheekbones, the fleshy red of her lips disguised the
common sense with which she measured life. She was
aware of how the neighbors viewed her, Harry's wife,
beneath their overly polite behavior. They smiled at
her when they did not smile at each other. What they
did not understand was that the ambivalence was
mutual. It vexed her that their world took advantage
of Harry almost without realizing it. But she suspected
he took a kind of cynical pleasure in their dependence
on him, and she had seen the smooth way he handled
their demands. She would have been happy to buy
in Riverside among the kind of people she could call
her own, near the temple, the better dress shops and

specialty stores and closer to the club where she often played cards and lunched with her friends while they looked at the latest fashions. But there was no point in arguing. This was what Harry wanted.

Adele was glancing through *Life* magazine at the pictures of girls in saddle shoes, or a sea of little flags with the swastika on them in a crowd of waving arms. Horrifying what the groundskeeper at the school was driven to. She was relieved that her mother had not gone back to Prague after her father's death and, instead, had settled near her sister in Savannah.

She could hear the children racing impatiently along the upstairs hall, and she imagined Nanny Pence's disapproving scowl. When Harry came in, the children would be brought down to say good night. Adele stood up and went to the side window, tired of waiting for her husband's return. Then she saw him inspecting his grounds and she softened. He stood tall and muscular, well filled out, square jawed, dark wavy hair. Everything that was masculine except his pretty blue eyes. He had something from the florist's in his left hand.

In a few minutes Harry Lewis was kissing his wife. She didn't like to be kept waiting. After twelve years of marriage he knew that. She said primly, "The children are going wild."

"I know, my dear." He stripped the paper from the rose and handed it to her. She put one hand up to his cheek and smiled that broad red-and-white smile, perfect lips, perfect teeth. He put his arms around her.

"It's getting late, Harry."

Reluctantly he let her go and watched her move across to the hallway to call up to Nanny Pence, then disappear into the dining room.

Moments later, as Adele returned with the rose in a bud vase, the two children came into the room, rushing at their father, who stood his ground, his arms out to greet them. Amid the squeals and hugs, he fell to the rug, gently rolling them to one side, then the other, until he let go and sprawled on his back. Nanny Pence, tut-tutting all the while, tried to gather in the children. She caught up little Harry, a bundle of kicks and screams, but Pearl was too much for her. Adele finally said, "Oh, Harry."

Hugs and kisses over, he poured himself a whiskey. He kissed his wife again. "Have you noticed it, Adele, spring is everywhere. The Russells' lilacs are ready to burst, and the wisteria over the Nortons' door is dripping with buds."

"You came home along the river."

"The mud is oozing in little streams, just like the gutters on Maple Street when I was a boy."

"But the swamp's not safe, Harry."

"It's a wonderful time to be alive, Adele."

"You'd say that if the world were coming to an end." She laughed at him.

Harry smiled broadly before he drained his glass. Then he led his wife in to dinner. They had roast chicken and cake.

Chapter Five

The following week, Vera received a note from Mrs.
Parker in the morning post. She knew it was important
even before she picked up the envelope. Ivory. Good
heavy stock. An informal with Mrs. C. Cyrus Withing-
ton Parker, II, engraved on the front. And inside the
fold in a dash of long bold lines: "Dear Mrs. Oliver,
so awfully pleased to learn from Margaret that you
can see your way to serving on our refugee committee. We gather next on Tuesday, the tenth of May, half
after two in the afternoon, The Farmhouse, 140 Parker
Farm Road." That was it, except for the royal flourish
of the signature, "Isabel Louise Osgood Parker."

Vera studied the note. Margaret . . . Miss Graham,
of course. And Isabel Louise Osgood Parker. Well . .
. Vera May Wallace Oliver. Plain. Even Mrs. Richard
Oliver seemed lackluster.

Vera was acquainted with Mrs. Parker, of course,
everyone on Parker Farm Road knew who she was.
Older than the rest of the mothers, from a distinguished family on the Hill in town, Isabel Osgood

was already socially influential before she married into the West Ivers Parker family. Mrs. Parker was on the board of the Home for Little Destitutes and a trustee of the hospital. At meetings Mrs. Parker sat at the officers' table at the front of the room and sometimes presided. Vera could not recall ever having a real conversation with her, but they greeted one another and commented on the weather as they passed to and from the postbox at the bottom of the road. Silly, isn't it, Vera thought now, as she traveled the same route. We post our notes to each other in the same box, when we could just as easily walk across the street and stick them through the mail slot. But that was not done, she knew, too informal, assuming closeness where there was none.

On the appointed Tuesday afternoon in May, the grip at Vera's stomach was like the squeeze of a claw. She wanted to be accepted, but to endure the awful patronizing—"So good of you to join us, Mrs. Oliver"—would only make her more aware that she was not one of them. For the hundredth time she imagined them greeting each other. Lucy, Elly, Dilly, Beezie. And those healthy laughs. Oh, maybe this was all a terrible mistake. In the bedroom closet she snatched open the hatbox and picked out the navy blue straw, the one with the broad brim. Businesslike. Better than the little saucer with all the ribbons. But was it too summery? The only other possibility was felt. Out of the question. Leaning into the mirror, she set the hat on her head, just a slight tilt, exposing the soft dark waves below the part in her hair. There, that was right. It seemed silly to wear a hat on a beautiful afternoon like this, just to go to a meeting across the street, but who knows who might be there.

As she pulled the front door shut and drew on her gloves, Vera felt a little less jittery. Looking right as she went down the walk, she ignored the scent of lilac everywhere and hurried forward to meet Miss Graham striding up the road from the school, seersucker shirt-dress, stout shoes and her familiar heather-gray lisle stockings, much too hot for this time of year. Hatless. Her arms swinging like a warrior to the beat of her march, her expression calm but with purpose, her briefcase at her right side in her bare hand. She really is like Pallas Athena, Vera thought.

"Miss Graham, Miss Graham," Vera called out, scooting across the road to join the older woman.

Miss Graham halted abruptly, "Ah, Vera." She extended her hand and shook Vera's with gusto. "Margaret, call me Margaret." She placed her left arm lightly on Vera's shoulder. "Come on, my dear Vera, we've work to do. Let's see what Isabel's ladies have for us." Together, they approached Mrs. Parker's house. Vera had never been inside. Surely it must be the most elegant home on Parker Farm Road.

Only it wasn't. That was the first surprise of the afternoon. Passing through the open door, they stepped into a clutter of abandoned slickers and sweaters and galoshes, stacks of books and boxes of Professor

Parker's journals, a bicycle wheel, a bag of balls, stray tennis shoes, all shoveled aside along the walls of the narrow hall to let the visitor pass Indian file into the dining room ahead. In her mind's eye Vera closed the door to the coat closet left open in her own front hall. Ahead of her Miss Graham kicked aside a single roller skate and muttered crossly. As they skirted around the long dinner table Vera noticed the heaps of papers nestled in with the silver tea service on the lowboy. A telescope rested on the top of an ancestral grandfather clock in the corner. The old floorboards of the original farmhouse sagged under a dirty Chinese carpet. Voices swelled up from the doorway beyond. The two women stepped down into the first of the many extensions to the house, a large drawing room, just as Mrs. Parker rose from her chair, long, thin, her silver blonde hair still bobbed. Vera thought she moved as if the wind blew her along.

Mrs. Parker hugged the schoolmistress. "Margaret, always a pleasure."

"You really should get more help around here, Isabel. Hilda's a cook, not a miracle worker."

"Now that all the children are off on their own, I just don't have the time, Margaret," Mrs. Parker said carelessly. "The best thing for you to do is not to look. Do help yourself to lemonade."

What an extraordinary conversation, Vera thought. They might as well be her aunts.

Mrs. Parker turned to Vera. "Oh, forgive me, Mrs. Oliver, Margaret and I have known each other too long. We forget our manners. She's the general around here. Calls the shots." She took Vera's arm and escorted her into the gathering. "I'm so glad you can find the time to join us. We welcome new blood on our committee."

Vera steadied herself and looked around at the faces peering up at her from the comfort of overstuffed couches and chairs. She didn't recognize any of them.

"I'm sure you know everyone. Susan Manly, Agnes Summers . . . oh never mind, too many names. Girls, this is Mrs. Oliver. Mildred, can you make room for Margaret beside you. Mrs. Oliver, why don't you squeeze in next to me. I'm saving that club chair." There was a general shift of hips and backs to bunch up. Mrs. Parker leaned forward to the coffee table to pour Vera a glass of lemonade. "Help yourselves to more everyone." She turned to greet another committee member.

Names like Mildred and Agnes. Fringes and buns, double strands of pearls, a hat here and there, a pair of spectacles perched on a nose. A comforting number of broad derrieres and stubby limbs. Vera was reminded of the Ladies Committee of the Downtown Political Club in her mother's front parlor.

Mrs. Parker was introducing the latest comer. "I've asked Mr. Lewis to join us." For the briefest moment there were a number of almost imperceptible pursed lips and pinched foreheads. Mrs. Parker hurried on. "You all know what a financial wizard he is." Good manners dictated smiles and nods of agreement.

Imagine the cramp in his stomach, Vera thought.

"He will be invaluable," Mrs. Parker went on, directing him to the empty club chair. Mr. Lewis gave a little nod in greeting. Discovering Miss Graham beside him, he took her hand in both of his momentarily. Miss Graham smiled at him. Everyone noticed.

"There," Mrs. Parker went on after everyone was settled. "I think we're all here." She took a deep breath. "Now, to begin, I want to thank you for coming this afternoon, especially Mr. Lewis, who has postponed an engagement to join us."

"I'm happy to help in any way I can, Mrs. Parker."

"Thank you, Mr. Lewis." She turned to address the group. "I believe we, as privileged university women, can work along with the other agencies, both Christian and Jewish, working in response to conditions in Europe." She paused to let the reminder of special status sink in. "Now, since this is our first meeting all together, I want to outline some of the things we can do when . . ."

"The point is, Isabel," Miss Graham interrupted, "they need our help. It is our responsibility to take the refugees in."

"Into our homes?" one of the women blurted out in astonishment.

In the silence that followed, everyone looked away from Mr. Lewis.

"Really . . ." Mrs. Parker began.

"Speak for yourself, Clara," Miss Graham said harshly, "I will be taking the children into the school, on scholarship where necessary."

"But, Margaret, more Jewish children!"

"They are homeless refugees." Miss Graham struggled to keep the contempt from her voice.

"The board will never approve scholarships. You know Jeffrey."

"I have considered that very possibility, and I've decided if that's the case, I will resign." There was an evangelical note to Miss Graham's voice.

"Really, Margaret, you go from one extreme to the other," Mrs. Parker said.

"It's a matter of principle," Miss Graham snapped.

Vera wanted to glance around at the faces of the women, but Mrs. Parker was talking. ". . . only a beginning, but remember when you go through your cedar closets to put away the winter clothes, an outgrown sweater or an old overcoat would make a difference next fall." Vera thought of the neighborhood hand-me-downs she'd had to be thankful for. "And please include the mothers at your lunches. It is our job to make them welcome."

Vera studied Mr. Lewis, leaning forward now, his hands on his knees. How handsome and at ease he looked. And he knew perfectly well he was not entirely welcome. He must be used to it. She wasn't sure if she felt sorry for him in such a circumstance, or cross at him for accepting it. Everyone else was looking at him, too, some furtively, some openly. Whether one approved of his presence or not, just by being a man he was the center of attention.

Miss Graham was urging Mr. Lewis to say something about the importance of sound planning, and Mrs. Parker was calling for volunteers. Vera, straining to follow two conversations at once, overheard Mr. Lewis say, "I'm here to listen, Margaret. I suspect I'll be asked to help." She was wondering what he meant by that when she heard Mrs. Parker call her name.

"Now, Vera, Margaret tells me you're a good organizer."

Vera flushed. Mrs. Parker had addressed her by her given name. She looked across at Miss Graham, who nodded reassuringly.

Mrs. Parker went on. "We will want you, Vera, to look into the other kinds of things these families will need. What are their interests and skills? Anything you can find to bring them into the community. Can you take on something like that?"

Of course, she could. It would be like ferreting out what kinds of books a patient likes to read. Matching up a mother with a grade-room project. Vera nodded vigorously. "I'm sure I can, Mrs. Parker."

"Call me Isabel, Vera. We don't stand on ceremony here, do we, girls?"

They'd taken her in. Just like that.

The committee as a whole would not convene again until the fall. In the meantime a few of them would meet separately to go over preliminary reports, exchange ideas. Vera would be among them. When the meeting ended Mr. Lewis rose to leave, saying he had an appointment in the neighborhood. In the bustle of departure Vera found herself standing next to him. Mr. Lewis smiled down at her as he placed his hat on his head. She felt that brief moment of vulnerability that flashed through her when a considerate man took notice of her. As he passed by he said, "Cheerful girl, your Jenny, Mrs. Oliver. It's a pleasure to have her come to play with Pearl."

Vera smiled in surprise. Whatever did he mean? She thought of Jenny as headstrong, often sullen. She was seized with pleasure, making her a little light-headed. Mr. Lewis was gone before she remembered her manners and could return the compliment.

She said good-bye to Mrs. Summers and Mrs. Manly and hoped she could teach herself to call them Susan and Agnes. Or was it the other way around? But Mrs. Parker, she felt sure she would never be able to call her Isabel. The voice of her mother would warn, "You mustn't be cheeky." Nevertheless, Vera set off down Parker Farm Road, hat in hand, light-footed, giddy with expectation. She could see Mr. Lewis ahead of her going up Mrs. von Kempel's front walk. Keeping an eye on the poor woman's financial concerns. No one ever saw Mrs. Von Kempel in the neighborhood, but Vera supposed it was the shame of marrying a German philanderer and the humiliation of divorce.

The Russells' Airedale was tied up to the gatepost of the passageway that ran between the von Kempel side yard and the vine-covered fence of the community tennis court. When Vera stopped to pat the forlorn-looking thing, she could hear the muted *pop pop* of a

ball hitting the hard clay, then a shriek of consternation as the ball came over the fence in a huge curve,
bouncing and rolling to a stop at Vera's feet. The dog
began to bark. As Vera stooped to pick up the ball, Bea
Norton came running along the passageway, her long
graceful strides a series of shallow arcs like a dancer.
She stopped when she saw Vera, then turned away
abruptly to catch her breath, bending over, her hands
on her knees. Her white skirt rode carelessly up over
the matching bloomers to expose the tops of her sleek
thighs. A little cascade of wavy blonde hair fell across
her forehead.

"Oooh," she exhaled, as she straightened up. "I'm
such a ninny on the court. Honestly, anyone could do
better." She smiled her pretty lips and perfect teeth at
Vera and reached out for the ball with one of her sap-
phire and diamond hands.

Vera was so stunned by the smooth, satin look of
glamour in a tennis skirt, she said, "I can't play at all,"
ingenuously.

"Oh, I don't believe that." Mrs. Norton flapped her
hand. "Anybody can."

Vera shook her head and laughed, embarrassed.

Mrs. Norton gave a little wave with her racket and
disappeared down the passageway. "I bet you can," she
called back. "Thank you so much for rescuing the ball."

Vera hesitated before she continued on her way. As
the only child in a household of women, eavesdrop-
ping had been the natural way to find out what was
going on. "You might hear something you won't like,"

her mother used to caution to her. But emboldened by her success at Mrs. Parker's, Vera stepped up to the fence and squinted through a gap in the vine.

Charlotte Russell was standing in the shade of the grape arbor at the near end of the court, juggling a couple of balls on her racket. If she was not as willowy and tempting as her friend Bea Norton, everyone spoke of her as handsome or statuesque. She was tall and light haired, more decorous in her less skimpy outfit.

Charlotte asked Bea, "Who was that you were talking with?"

"Jenny Oliver's mother, and she was *carrying* her hat!" Bea added the ball she had just retrieved to the two in Charlotte's left hand. "She says she doesn't play tennis. Perhaps she doesn't think it's serious enough for a college girl."

"Or perhaps it's out of her class."

Listening at the fence, Vera scowled and put her fingers over her mouth.

"You are wicked, Charlotte." Bea smiled broadly. "She was coming down the road from her ladyship's, poor little mouse. Dragooned onto one of those committees, I bet. They must be so awful."

Charlotte dropped a ball and gave it a couple of bounces with her racket, dislodging the tape that defined the baseline of her court. "Isabel Parker loves a new cause. Jewish refugees, this time. Like that miserable fellow who shot himself. She couldn't attend the garden club meeting last week, she was so busy." Charlotte crouched to straighten out the tape.

"It's your serve," Bea called over the net.

Charlotte took up her position behind the tape in the far right-hand corner of her court. "Thirty love." She called the score, but as she raised her arms to serve, she lowered it and approached the net. Vera had to move along the fence to another gap in the vine. "Someone said Miss Graham is threatening to take little refugee children into the school," Charlotte said.

Coming around the net to join Charlotte, Bea threw back her head and laughed. "Tom will have a conniption. She'll never get away with it."

"I'm afraid so, dear," Charlotte said. "You know what a bully Miss Graham can be. She took in little Pearl Lewis."

"Oh, surely that's different," Bea protested. "Harry Lewis went to Boylston. He keeps us all out of trouble. His wife is a Schultzberger, whatever that means."

"You know, Jewish, but she is from New York money."

"And poor Mrs. Oliver from nowhere tries so hard to be proper," Bea said mincingly. "I don't think associating with Mrs. P's refugees will help her get her girls on the Junior Dance list."

Her voice. She's imitating me, Vera thought indignantly. I wouldn't dream of letting my daughters go to those dances. She turned to go—but she might miss something.

"If *the* Mrs. Parker says it's all right to hobnob with the poor foreign things, who are we to argue with her?" Charlotte said, tilting her well-bred nose to the sky. "Next thing you know, anybody will be able to get on the dance list. I heard the Webster girl didn't wear gloves at the last one."

"Mother will never believe it." Bea reached for her cardigan and slipped it around her shoulders.

A ball escaped from Charlotte's grip. She bounced it up off the court with her racket to catch it. "Ed saw Harry Lewis coming out of Mrs. von Kempel's house in the middle of the afternoon."

"Well, I suppose where filthy lucre is concerned, it doesn't matter if it's German money," Bea pointed out. "And I can hardly blame her for wanting a little advice, abandoned like that by a husband who was practically a Nazi. And that strange son and awful German housekeeper. I hear even her family won't take her back. And they're from Chicago."

"Well, as Mother says, 'you made your bed, now you have to lie in it.'" Charlotte quoted archly. "Everyone knows if you get divorced, no one can even invite you to their dinner table."

"No one has the Lewises over."

"That's different."

"I like Mr. Lewis, even if he is a Jew who does business with *Frau* von Kempel. He's always very polite to me." Bea protested.

"That's not the point. Why can't the *frau* go to his office, like the rest of us."

Bea raised her eyebrows. "Well, maybe she wants him for something else."

"Oh, Bea, that's not even funny." Charlotte looked down at her little gold watch. "Nora will have tea ready soon." They picked up their racket presses and balls and stepped into the passageway, carefully locking the padlock on the heavy chain. Vera hurried back to the sidewalk just as Mr. Lewis came down the front steps of Mrs. von Kempel's house. She hesitated, caught in a quandary. If she stayed the two women would know she'd lingered and wonder why. If she rushed off, she would offend Mr. Lewis.

Mr. Lewis raised his hat to her. "Hello there, Mrs. Oliver."

Vera smiled awkwardly. The Russells' dog began to bark wildly as the tennis players stepped out of the passageway onto the sidewalk. A pack of girls shot by on their bicycles. "Be careful, children," Mrs. Norton said.

The knot of four adults stood awkwardly on the sidewalk. "Good afternoon, ladies." Mr. Lewis said, raising his hat again

The women smiled back sweetly. "Oh, good afternoon," Mrs. Norton said.

Mrs. Russell unleashed the dog. "Tea time, girls," she called, as the Airedale dashed down the road after the children. She turned to Vera and Mr. Lewis. "They're so free and easy on those bicycles. Forgive us."

"Strange bedfellows," Vera heard Mrs. Norton say as the two women moved ahead. "Everything's changing."

"It's like an invasion," Mrs. Russell replied.

Strange bedfellows. Did she mean Mr. Lewis and me? A little defiant thrill went through Vera. She looked at Mr. Lewis. Had he heard them? But he was looking straight ahead, his face perfectly composed.

Side by side, Vera and Harry Lewis brought up the rear of the procession.

Chapter Six

That June, the Closing Day ceremonies at the school were held outside under sunny skies. Students and teachers filed into rows of benches arranged in tiers around three sides of the square that constituted a common green to the village of school buildings. Everyone was dressed in fresh summer dresses and white pants and shirts, clean white socks, and sneakers. Jenny sat in the front between Pearl Lewis and Neddy Carter. Molly and Patsy were behind her. Across from the students, along the fourth side of the green in front of the playfields, were the parents and grandparents. Jenny waved to her mother in the front row. Pearl pointed out her father standing in the back. He was almost the only man there.

Miss Graham, in her green-and-white print with the cotton lace collar, stepped up to the speaker's stand, a little pinched smile escaping from her serious expression.In her measured tone, she reviewed the school year and talked about goals for the future. "Now we are engaged in a truly cooperative endeavor,"

Miss Graham went on. Neddy Carter took a piece of string out of his pocket and made a cat's cradle. Jenny bent over to retie her shoelace. Then Neddy shoved Jenny in the elbow, and as she turned to shove him back, he snuck a note onto her lap. The teacher at the end of the row scowled at them. When it was safe, Jenny hunched over to read the note: RIGHT AFTER SCHOOL AT MY HOUSE. She turned quickly to nod to Patsy as Miss Graham paused. When Jenny looked back the headmistress was holding the sides of the stand like a shield, gazing up over the tops of the trees. When she spoke, her voice was like a tolling bell.

"In the past months, I have become increasingly alarmed by the restriction of individual liberties in the name of solidarity in many European countries. This aberrant nationalism is teaching strength through physical prowess, courage through force, community through discrimination. And this in the name of purity." Miss Graham raised a fist. There was complete silence. Jenny felt the specialness of the moment even if she didn't understand what Miss Graham was saying. She could tell by their faces that the parents were impressed. Miss Graham shook her head and took a deep breath before she continued. "It is important that we recognize this evil." Evil. But that's like bad men down in the swamp. Jenny tried to listen now. ". . . right to choose, the responsibility to make the whole better than the sum of the parts, to practice the principles of democracy, that *all* men are created equal."

When Miss Graham finished, she dropped her

head like an actress. There was a ripple of applause that began to spread out like the tide along the beach, and Mr. Lewis stood up, still clapping. Miss Graham bowed again and signaled to the music teacher for the orchestra to play.

Songs played and sung, the Maypole danced, the certificates distributed. Tender and lingering farewells brought the school year to an end. While Jenny waited for her mother and sister with her map of Egypt rolled up under her arm, she watched other parents and children herd up Parker Farm Road, carrying their paintings and science projects, a stool made in the shop, a smelly sweatshirt. They called to each other about going to the seashore or the mountains, the best beach or the most faraway view. Jenny groaned. Her family never went *anywhere*.

On the way home, she ran on ahead of her mother and sister, careful not to smudge dirt on the white rubber edges of her new sneakers. She slammed through the kitchen screen door and crashed up the stairs to her room, the way she did when she knew her mother was out. She kicked off her sneakers and climbed out of her plaid gingham dress and got into shorts and a shirt. Clutching her nice old sneakers, she rushed back down the stairs, grabbed her sandwich off the plate in the dining room, and flew past Mary—"Slow down there"—out the back door. The screen door cracked sharply. She didn't care; her mother wasn't there to say, "Be careful not to slam the screen door," and Mary didn't count. Plopping her things into the basket of her bike, she dug her bare feet into the pedals as she charged out of the garage like one of Mary's racehorses she bet on during her afternoons off. It was one of the secrets Jenny kept from her mother. Luckily, her mother and Katherine were walking up the road with Mrs. Parker and Jenny was able to flash by with only a wave, pushing on with a sense of an important engagement. But when she got to Patsy's house, Nora, the Russells' cook, said Patsy had gone to Molly's house for lunch.

Nora smiled sympathetically. "Come into the kitchen, dear. Your mother won't be pleased, you without your shoes there."

That familiar being-apart feeling came over Jenny. She ignored Nora and pedaled up the road, empty now, to Great Hamilton Street, wondering if her mother knew where she was or even cared. At the bottom of the road she paused, straddling her bike while she ate the egg salad sandwich, then got off to put on her sneakers. On the desultory trip back, she tried swoops and circles, but lost her balance and landed on the sidewalk by Mrs. von Kempel's house. The dog began to bark. As she got up she noticed him sitting on the front stoop staring at her. The Beasty. That's how everyone thought of him after Teddy Russell called him that. He had a hollow look to him, everything about him big and spongy and pale. And he had a name that no one had ever heard of. Wilhelm. He never said anything. He just looked. Once, he tried to sit with Katherine and her friends at the Saturday movies, but they got up in a hurry and moved. Jenny's mother was upset that Perfect Katherine could have been so rude. "But Mummy, he's only eleven and he can't be president, ever. He wasn't born in America." Teddy said there was a picture of Hitler in the Beasty's house. Grownups warned he wasn't "all there in the head." Jenny's mother had explained he'd been that way since birth.

Jenny knew to stay away from the Beasty, but for a moment she forgot and stared back at him, wondering what not being born in America felt like. But when he started down the steps, she scrambled up and hurried to push her bike out into the road before she pumped away.

Down at the other end of Parker Farm Road Patsy and Molly were already out on their bikes, and for a while the three girls played cowboys in the school parking lot, herding and charging. When they got bored, they took turns riding up the rise in the hill and coasting down, no hands, no feet. Teddy came out and tried to push a stick through the spokes of Jenny's front wheel. She grabbed the handlebars and swerved aside just as Miss Graham and her assistant, Miss Osgood, came up the road. Teddy and the others went inside, but Jenny sat astride her bike and watched the two teachers. They walked in perfect step, leaning toward each other talking, not even breaking stride when they waved to her. She wondered how it felt being such friends like that.

Long days of high sun brought the flush of roses along Parker Farm Road: Charlotte Russell's stunning display of creamy white double-blossomed damask, Mme Hardy, against the red brick of the house. The romantic scarlet red of the new Blaze climber on either side of the Parkers' front door. The Olivers' low hedge of many-petaled pink Sweetheart blooms that marked the side yard. But with the heat, the seasonal exodus began, at least for the mothers and children, sometimes a nursemaid or a cook. They traveled by rail or car to summer establishments, leaving the management of lawn and garden to the hired man and the simplicities and temptations of solitary life to their husbands, who would join the family for extended weekends until August vacation month.

By the Fourth of July, the Russells were settled in the beach house on the south shore. "It's airy," Patsy told Jenny, echoing her mother. The Norton children went to their grandmother's rambling farmhouse in northern Vermont. Professor Parker stayed on an island off the northeast coast, requiring the motor launch to make an extra trip from the mainland with his boxes of books. The Parker children would join their parents later, for a week or two of family reunion while on holiday from graduate school or professional firms. Isabel Parker would go up between meetings and other obligations. Meanwhile, her younger sister, Eleanor Osgood, free from her teaching job for the summer, could keep an eye on things. Margaret Graham often visited.

The Olivers did not have a second home to go to.
It was not only the responsibility of ownership or the
expense of upkeep; Vera would have liked to chime in
on winter reminiscences about the abundance of the
blackberries or winning the sailboat race. But Richard enjoyed the more leisurely pace of the summer
at home. Empty downtown sidewalks, no lines at the
bank, a seat on the subway, the quiet of the deserted
neighborhood. Although he had learned not to mention it at home to avoid a caustic comment from Vera,
during the summer he was free to show Miss Sperry
his appreciation for all that she did for him and the
firm by taking her out for an occasional lunch or a
glass of sherry. Somehow, Vera had come to feel he
valued Miss Sperry's efficiency at the office more than
her own homemaking abilities. The two were indis-
pensable in the separate spheres of his life, although
perhaps the relationships of his working world seemed
sometimes easier to navigate than the complexities of
home life.

As he joined Vera on the back terrace for a drink
before dinner, Richard often began the conversation
by asking, "Who would want to be anywhere else?" It
didn't irritate Vera so much this summer. She was busy
with committee work. Katherine was at canoe camp
and Jenny was looking forward to going with Mr.
Russell to visit Patsy sometime in August. They would
all go to Squam Lake for a week before school opened
in September.

When the refugee committee met for tea in the Olivers' living room, with the silver service and the thin china cups, Mary always put aside something for Jenny, a few of the lacy sugar cookies or little rounds of bread spread with cream cheese. When she had taken in the tea service, Mary would make Jenny a cup of cambric tea and they would sit at the kitchen table with the pantry door ajar, listening to the sound of cups and saucers, the hum of voices, the bursts of laughter.

Mrs. Parker came one afternoon and brought some of the refugee ladies. From time to time, Jenny passed through the front hall, pretending to be doing something because that Mrs. Weiss was among them and she wanted to know what a "poor bereft" looked like. But they all looked the same. They wore black hats, and they weren't the ones who laughed. They didn't say much either, at first, but they oohed and ahhed at each other as they held up the things they had made to sell at the new store Mrs. Parker and her mother were organizing. The black hats nodded when her mother handed them cups of tea, and they gobbled up Mary's brownies. *"Ja, so the kuchen." "Die torte."* And suddenly. they were speaking higgledy-piggledy all at once about butter and cream and nuts and fruits. The funny shyness was gone. Even Mrs. Parker, in the wing chair, had a recipe for oatmeal cookies. Then, Jenny noticed her mother passing around a pad of paper. "You know, ladies, we don't want to lose track of all these good things to eat. Be sure to write down what you can make."

"We sell the baking, too?"

"Everyone has a secret sweet tooth."

"What of the money?"

"Mrs. Parker has prevailed upon Mr. Lewis to advance us a hundred and fifty dollars for rent and materials." Murmurs of thanks. Mrs. Parker smiled graciously.

After Mary had removed the tea tray, one of the ladies began to sing a soft sad song about a beautiful lady that the man loved from afar, and then two of them sang a duet. When Jenny heard her mother's voice, she squinted through the crack in one of the half-closed double doors to see her posed before the fireplace, her hands clasped at her chest, her head cocked to one side, a funny sweet smile on her face. She was reciting Miss Graham's "No man is an island." The ladies cooed like birds and clapped their hands, and one of them hugged her mother. She had never seen her mother look so small and soft. It alarmed her, and without thinking, she stepped into the room.

"Oh, Jenny," her mother exclaimed. Jenny froze, but her mother was still smiling. "This is my younger daughter," she announced.

All the mouths and cheeks smiled at Jenny. She made a monkey face before she ran away. The murmurs and laughter drove her faster up the stairs. She threw herself on her bed and sobbed into the pillow, hating those women for making her mother so happy.

That evening, when her parents had cocktails, she hung around at the edge of the terrace. "Sit down, why don't you, Jenny," her mother called, but she didn't. They didn't say anything interesting. But when her mother told her father that the ladies at tea had more important things to do than spend their summer days sipping lemonade at the yacht club, it made him cross and silent.

The notebooks and scraps of paper piled up on the dining room table. Her father lost his temper, so her mother had to set up a card table in the corner. It was covered with slips of recipes and hot-looking things like a sweater and some scarves. Jenny was curious to see what was in boxes under the table, but when she peeked, it was just more of the same stuff.

"Vera, please, what is it now?"

"Samples, Richard, for the Back Door Store. It's going to be a kind of social service, a women's exchange and retail showroom."

He shook his head. "I never heard of such a harebrained scheme. You bring these women into our house as if you were running a welfare shelter, and then you think you can just go out and set up shop like a children's lemonade stand. Who's going to pay for it? Have you thought of that?"

"Yes, Richard," she said calmly. "We're not as silly as you think."

He gave her a black look. "Well, not in the dining room, Vera."

Jenny grew tired of her mother's new activities. The wonderful feeling of independence she'd felt at the beginning of summertime had given way to an endless search for something to do. Passing through the whirling streams of water from a sprinkler on the Russells' lawn, picking raspberries along the fence around the Nortons' trash cans. When the gardener came to the Lewises' house, she often visited with him as he knelt weeding the perennials, but the cook always came out, and the gardener didn't pay much attention to Jenny after that.

She visited the school grounds. The crisscross of paths that were so welcoming a month ago seemed to isolate the familiar buildings, dark with silence. When she peered in the window of last year's third-grade room, the rows of desks stood bare and forgotten. Suddenly, she remembered a boy in the first grade who didn't come back. Where do people go when they aren't there any more? An emptiness sprang from the blackboard on the back wall and crashed towards her.

It chased her out across the field and along the line of maple trees that bordered the cemetery. The gray headstones marched up the rise like an army of spooks, and she dashed back along the edge of the dodgeball court, skirting the drainage ditch. As she passed the utility room, she thought of the man who shot himself and dared herself to tiptoe up to look through the window glass of the door. She could just make out the shape of the furnace, a chair in the corner. Did he sit on that to do it? Was some of his brain still on the pipes above? Her throat filled up with a foul taste and she sped down the path into the parking lot, holding her hand over her mouth. Was that the teacher at the end of the causeway to the shop? But halfway along, she could tell that the place was closed up tight. It was summer, and she was alone.

She looked over the railing at the swamp, searching for the big, black spiders spinning their webs like a net across the tips of the touch-me-nots. They ate their babies and their bite could swell you up all white and puffy and close your eyes and make you die. Suddenly, her skin flamed with a skittish tickle. She clawed at the invisible spiders on her bare arms and legs as she ran back down the causeway, eyes shut against the gaping spaces between the planks that would open up and drop her into the black ooze of the swamp. At the parking lot, she bent over to draw a long breath.

He was there when she looked up, his slingshot sighted on her like a hunter's arrow. A half-naked giant, with a round melon head and pasty skin. He was barefoot and the hilt of the dagger at his belt dug into his bare belly.

"Halt," the Beasty commanded. "Put your hands behind your head."

She tried to calm the fear fluttering in her throat, holding her breath until her chest filled up with pain, and she had to let it out.

"Come on," the Beasty ordered. "I told you to put your hands behind your head."

Jenny didn't move.

"Oh, put them up," he begged, lowering his weapon.

He didn't look frightening now, not like the Beasty. "I don't know how to put my hands behind my head," she confessed.

Wilhelm stood up. "Like this." He lifted his arms high and placed the palms of his hands against the back of his head. He looked like a great plump bird about to swoop down.

Jenny stood her ground.

Wilhelm dashed his slingshot to the macadam. "This is no good, you're just a baby." He began to pelt his bare feet with a handful of pebbles.

"I am not," she shrieked.

Wilhelm looked up at her. "I'll show you where the ducklings swim."

"Where?"

"In the pool down by the river."

"I'm not allowed to go on the river path," she told him.

"I know a shortcut. There's a dam. That dead Jew man made it."

Jenny took her time, squinting into the sun, the ribbons of color dancing before her eyes. She knew about the dam. It was for Katherine's science class, but no one had ever been there without a teacher. It would be something to tell about—if she wanted to, that is. She thought of the spiders and bent to scratch her ankle.

"It's easy," Wilhelm coaxed.

She thought, I'd have a secret.

"Follow me," Wilhelm shouted expansively. "We can be pirates on a raid." As he walked by, she inspected the creases of dirt in the folds of his chest. "When we catch the ducks we'll stab them and pluck out their feathers." He brandished his knife in the air, but the blade was only wood like her father's letter opener. She followed him through the gate to the edge of the swamp, fear and excitement beating in her chest.

"We'll give them to the crew for a proper dinner," he was saying, "that's what cook says. 'Sit down, *mein Kind*, and eat a proper dinner.' Do you like dumplings?"

"I don't know."

"You don't know anything." Wilhelm plunged through a break in the weeds. "Dumplings are white and mushy like the stuff in your nose." He disappeared down the incline into the swamp.

The grasses prickled Jenny's bare legs, and the ground gave way to mud. Suddenly, she was over her head between two rows of cattails, the dirty water seeping over the canvas tops of her sneakers. Her mother would be angry. Ahead, Wilhelm paused, then drew each foot high like a prancing horse, plopping and sputtering through the thick ooze, swinging his slingshot like a lariat. He went deep into the swamp and disappeared. Jenny picked her way along, sniffling and coughing, grasping at the reeds. When she looked back, the swamp seemed to close in, the water filling her footprints.

Wilhelm was waiting on the other side, flicking off slugs and snails that clung to a rotten board. They flew

by her face and she felt one in her hair. She dashed
past him back into the jewelweeds. In a network of
webs and hairy black legs and round bodies, a nest of
eggs burst before her eyes and hundreds of black dots
scattered. She waved her arms, beating them off, and
crashed on desperately in a rage of fear and betrayal,
the suction groping at her feet, the mud flying off her
sneakers.

When she stumbled from the weeds, Wilhelm guffawed. She looked back. The trail through the heart of
the jewelweeds was only a trampled patch along the
edge of the path. She burst into tears.

"Crybaby, crybaby," Wilhelm taunted.

She threw herself at his knees, startling him, bringing him down hard. "I'm not a crybaby."

They flailed in the marsh mud, a flurry of limbs,
until Wilhelm, gaining the upper hand, gave up and
rolled away. Jenny jumped free and crouched nearby,
hands on her knees. Wilhelm heaved himself to his feet
and lunged forward, then rolled his eyes to the sky,
letting his tongue hang loose, and held his knife at his
throat in a mock stab.

He looked so stupid that Jenny laughed. "If you
hurt me, I'll run away."

They played together through the afternoon, watching the ducks paddle across the pond at the base of the
dam and waddle up the bank to bathe in the mud.

"My father says they're all Reds at Parker Farm
School," Wilhelm announced.

"You don't have any father."

"I do so. He's just away." The boy turned his back for a moment, then spun around and pointed at her. "You're scared of spiders."

"I am not," Jenny lied bravely. She knew that if he thought she was a fraidy cat he wouldn't let her play with him anymore.

All week long after lunch they meet at the gate at the bottom of Parker Farm Road. They raced water beetles across the pond in the swamp, watched piles of leaves swirl in the water, bombarded each other's sticks with stones. They peeled off the mud caked on their arms and legs in the sun and pelted each other. On the way home, Jenny would leave Wilhelm at the bottom of the road to run through the sprinklers on the lawns of the empty houses. She left her muddy sneakers in the garage and shoved her dirty shorts down the laundry chute. She scrubbed her arms and legs. Mary gave her the eye. "You'll not get away with it, whatever you're up to." One afternoon, the Russells' Nora caught her squirting their hose on her muddy feet.

"Mary told me you come in every day soaked to the skin."

"I got my sneakers dirty."

"You did indeed, missy. Now, you be off home and don't let me catch you dirty again."

On Saturday, Pearl came over to Jenny's on her new bike, a birthday present from her grandmother. They brought it home in the baggage compartment of the train. Overnight. Jenny was impressed. They rode figure eights and no hands all morning, and then they did it again after Sunday lunch. Nanny Pence invited Jenny in for supper. They had stewed prunes. After supper, the daylight hours already shortening, they rode the length of Parker Farm Road for the final ride of the day. On the way back, the dog was barking in Mrs. von Kempel's yard. The Beasty came out on the front steps and stared. Jenny stopped and stood astride her bike.

"Jenny," Pearl called. The dog snapped through the slats in the fence. "Come on, Jenny, the Beasty will get you." After a moment, Jenny got on her bike and followed Pearl.

Every day, Jenny and Pearl rode their bikes up and down the road and along the empty paths of the school, a twosome, at ease, without the pull of Patsy or Molly to split their unity.

In the middle of August Jenny went to visit Patsy. They spent their time at the beach club by the ocean. One afternoon, they saw Teddy and his friends spying over the wall of the ladies' shower stall. That evening, they eavesdropped on a terrible row between Teddy and his father.

"How could you upset your mother like that? Mrs. Ransom and her cousin are your mother's friends. It's shameful and dirty, and I will not tolerate it. You're going to apologize, young man."

"Billy Robins did it, too."

"In my day, boys like you were made to take cold

baths and sent away."

Jenny and Patsy made faces at each other. For once, Teddy looked miserable.

"Teddy looked at a lady naked, and Mr. R says he has to say he's sorry," Jenny wrote in her diary and wondered if Teddy would be sent away.

After Labor Day, the Olivers went to the cabin they rented every year. Jenny and Katherine swam in the lake, and some afternoons, Jenny hung her arms around her father's neck, and he carried her on his back to the float where she could jump off over her head. They ate in the communal dining room at the main lodge, and in the evening, while Katherine was with the older children, Jenny played mumblety-peg under the pines or built card houses on the table in the sitting room. Her parents sat on the porch with some of the other grownups, listening to the news on the radio, the men smoking their pipes. They spoke about events in Europe and their own good fortune. Jenny wondered what was so good about having to go home next Saturday.

That fall, Jenny entered the fourth grade. One evening in the kitchen while Mary was getting dinner, it was announced over the radio that the prime minister of England had met with Hitler. They had agreed to "peace in our time." Jenny rushed into the living room to be the one to tell her parents in case Katherine had heard it on her radio. Her mother said it was a victory for the decency of mankind and poured herself a second glass of sherry. Her father called it a triumph of hope in the face of widespread destruction. She couldn't picture decency and triumph, like statues in the park, but parents often said things she didn't understand. She was just relieved to know that now nothing would change.

On October 2, 1938, a Sunday, a day of rest, German troops occupied the Sudetenland.

Chapter Seven

From then on, events in Europe dominated the news, becoming part of the texture of daily life in West Ivers. Men pored over the morning newspapers when stocks and bonds began to vacillate. Cocktail hour was around the radio now, but the news only added to the sense of disunity. Congressional leaders talked seriously of interventionist or isolationist politics, prompting Harry Lewis to write a letter to his congressman outlining a democracy's moral obligation to support freedom-loving nations. By chance the following day, he was asked to review the prospectus of a small company that had split off from one of the big brass companies. Izrael and Son, Machinists and Die Makers. It might do very well in the event of war, but he set it aside, knowing that the very name would put his investors off.

Ed Russell, who greatly admired America's darling, "Lucky" Lindbergh, wondered if the aviator knew something more than the soft-headed lefties who criticized him when he accepted the Service Cross of the German Eagle from Hitler himself. Respectable members of the New York German Bund cheered goose-stepping Nazis in the newsreels at the movies. The Duke and Duchess of Windsor were welcomed throughout the Third Reich. Bea Norton, looking at photographs of the couple in evening dress or riding habit, or wearing dirndl and lederhosen while picnicking gaily at the Fuhrer's Salzburg retreat, remarked to Charlotte Russell, "You can't beat them for chic."

Richard Oliver, in Washington for a meeting, heard a rumor that foreign governments were recalling their envoys from Germany. Adele Lewis worried that Hitler had begun deporting German Jews to Poland. From Berlin, there were rumors of a night of horror, shops destroyed, synagogues burned, random killings by Nazi youth. Jewish publications in Germany were abruptly banned.

Even the maids, Mary and Nora, heard the wake-up call in the Sunday sermons: "While Men Slept, His Enemy Came," Matthew 13:25, or Philippians 4:9 "And the God of Peace Shall Be With You."

At Boylston University, where membership on the faculty was tantamount to moral leadership, intellectuals deliberated the philosophic dimensions of events abroad at lunch at the Faculty Club or in the evening over a second glass of port.

It happened one week at the dinner table of the Parkers where Vera found herself an anxious guest at the insistence of Margaret Graham, who seemed to have made Vera one of her causes. Fortunately, Richard was out of town. Vera knew he didn't enjoy the posturing of academics—out of touch with the real world, he said. But in a way, she almost envied Richard his previous engagement. While she was thrilled to be asked, she felt awkward in such erudite company.

The party was to welcome the Parkers' houseguest, Herr Doktor Meyer, recently arrived by way of Amsterdam and London. He was a colleague of Professor Parker and one or two others at the table and had been a distinguished professor of medieval art at the University of Leipzig until he was dismissed because he was Jewish.

During the soup course, a tomato consommé, the conversation had been rather desultory, Mrs. Parker dutifully asking the guest of honor about his trip from New York. When he finally finished carving the lamb and Hilda was serving the plates, Professor Parker made his way around the table filling the wine glasses. Polite inquiries turned quickly to a lively competition, the food and beers on a sabbatical leave in Munich, the alarming fitness of the Nazi youth on a hiking tour through the Alps, the dismay of witnessing Il Duce on his balcony in the Piazza Venezia. This in turn led to a discussion about the excesses of nationalism in business and education in fascist countries. As Mrs. Parker served the deep-dish apple cobbler with a liberal dollop of heavy cream, Herr Doktor Meyer himself joined in, posing, unwittingly perhaps, one of those difficult questions that so often turned into the party games of the intellectuals of West Ivers. A young Jewish boy, whose father proudly wears the Iron Cross for valor in the Great War, is barred from a school party for being "non-Aryan." The father blames *Herr Direktor* of the school for failing to recognize his own august standing in the community and sends his son to England for a better education.

"I ask you, my new friends, because I do not know, does it make for a lonely exile for the boy or was the father saving the son's life?" Herr Doktor Meyer hunched up his shoulders and raised his open arms.

A look of uneasiness passed around the table like a secret handshake. The question seemed strangely personal. Vera saw Mrs. Parker glance expectantly at her husband, but the professor looked more than capable of waiting her out in a socially awkward moment.

"Certainly a British education is the best in the world," Mrs. Parker finally said. It was something they could all agree on.

But her sister Eleanor Osgood had to say, "Think of the boy, Isabel, a stranger in a foreign land."

"Perhaps the father was really acting out of concern," Margaret pointed out. "Under the circumstances, it was a courageous act to send his only son away to safety."

"Aren't English schools very snobbish?"

"But they sharpen the intellect," the professor of education on Vera's left said. "And the Jews are very clever."

There was a slight pause. Herr Doktor Meyer raised his heavy eyebrows, prompting one of the assistant professors to reassure him. "The Jewish students at the university are unusually intelligent . . ."

". . . and hard working. They always make the highest grades," interrupted another. "I'm sure the boy will do very well in the English public schools." "Benjamin Disraeli, the English prime minister, was Jewish."

"The Rothschilds and the Warburgs. They've done all right for themselves."

Vera, desperately trying to think of the right thing to say, glanced at Herr Doktor Meyer, but someone had already asked, "Well, what is being Jewish nowadays? Is it a race? A matter of culture? Of religion?"

The elderly gentleman from the history department put down his napkin and pushed back his chair to cross his legs. He scanned his audience as he would in the classroom, then cleared his throat before he began his lecture. "You must understand that Judaism is a developmental religion. Those rituals which stand in the way of full participation in the social and political life of a country are no longer considered expressions of religious truth. The middle-class Jews simply join with the Gentiles. Secularization. Consider the boy's father who wore his Iron Cross, proud to be a German. It's similar to the assimilation that second and third immigrant generations aspire to in this country."

"That's Harry Lewis in a nutshell. His grandfather was a Russian Jew, an itinerant peddler. And look at

Harry. He's just like all the rest of us, only a darn sight smarter."

"And richer," someone added.

Herr Doktor Meyer interrupted, speaking slowly as if he were addressing them in a language they did not understand. "Ah, my friends, you make the lively discussion from the boy and his father, such a small thing. But you must understand there is real evil in the world."

The dinner guests fell uncomfortably silent. Vera supposed this was a social occasion, not a time for threats. The party broke up, and the guests took their leave, giving Mrs. Parker a peck on the cheek or seeking out her husband where he stood like a sentinel beside his guest, who bowed stiffly with each handshake.

Outraged by Herr Doktor Meyer's discomfort, eager to make up for the insensitivity and complacency of her fellow countrymen, Margaret lingered to discuss the elaborate use of color in the Second Golden Age of Byzantine art. After a decent interval, Herr Doktor Meyer bowed to her politely and followed his host up the stairs to his study for a brandy before retiring.

"It never ceases to amaze me, how cold and snobby these university people really are. They rationalize everything," Margaret said, railing a little more than usual.

Vera, already in her coat, standing with Mrs. Parker and Eleanor in the cluttered hallway of the farmhouse, wondered if Margaret's gesture toward Herr Doktor Meyer might have been misconstrued as a little patronizing. Mrs. Parker stooped to pick up a stray mitten or set right a boot while Margaret thrust her arms into the coat that Eleanor held out for her.

"Well, what would you expect, Margaret," Mrs. Parker said, hanging up her husband's mackintosh, which had fallen in a heap. "After all, that's what they do, reason things through."

Vera was digging in the pockets of her coat for her gloves when Margaret said, "They didn't want to explore the feelings of the boy or the motives of the father. It was all a game to display a superior fund of knowledge."

Mrs. Parker laughed. "Too often true."

"It's must hard for these displaced children," Vera said.

"They might at least have thought about the boy," Eleanor added.

"Or Herr Doktor Meyer, for that matter," Margaret pointed out. "But what he said is true. There *is* real evil in the world. Can't they see that? They're supposed to be so brilliant."

"The evil isn't so obvious to many in this country," Mrs. Parker reminded them. "Not yet."

But Margaret wasn't listening. "Don't they care about *truth*?" She threw her head back. "Of all people."

Early in the spring of 1939, the refugee boy from Germany came into the fourth grade of the Parker Farm School. It was in the middle of the morning, because the class was looking forward to recess.

The dodgeball court was finally dry enough to use after heavy rains, and the acrid smell from the leach field had faded so that even the most squeamish were eager to play. In any event, the sight that morning of a new desk at the end of the first row released an energy of expectation and unrest. This would make twenty-one of them.

To begin the day, Miss Zeckner wrote WELCOME GOTTFRIED GOLDSTEIN in her fine script in chalk on the blackboard. But it was the odd-numbered isolation of the desk itself, breaking the symmetry of the classroom grouping, that promised instability, and all through Handwriting and Spelling, the threat seemed to magnify. Jenny doodled on the edge of her paper. Alan Stone, the daydreamer of the class, slowly revolved his six-inch rule in an endless circle. Patsy and Molly had to be separated for passing notes, so that Pearl was asked to change seats with Molly and felt misplaced. Jeffrey Malcolm, a big, blond, restless boy, raised his hand to be excused a number of times. Miss Zeckner herself must have felt the moment would never come.

Months earlier, in a Friday assembly, when Miss Graham had read things about charity and love thy neighbor as thyself and never even once smiled, the whole school knew that something important was going to happen. But refugee children coming into the school to escape something didn't seem very interesting, although most of the fourth graders did know that refugee meant no house, no clothes of their own. Then someone said it meant escaping death, and that was more exciting. No one ever said it because it wasn't something that people talked about, but everyone knew that the refugees were Jewish. That meant not having to go to church on Sundays. But different from the Lewises. The refugees had no money.

"I have met Gottfried Goldstein, he is a fine bright boy," Miss Zeckner told them. "He comes from Berlin, but he has been living in Holland. He is a long way from what he knows. Now he must make a new home."

Jeffrey hoped he wore wooden shoes like the little Dutch boy. Or leather shorts and a feather in his cap, Patsy speculated, like in her *Heidi* book. Molly wondered if his mother wore a long blue dress and a cap like Maid Marion in Robin Hood. "He is not something from one of your picture books," Miss Zeckner snapped at them. "He is a real person, and you must try to think what it would be like to be in his place."

"Do we call him whatever that name was?"

"Does he like dodgeball?"

"He won't know how."

"He is very quick, you will see." Miss Zeckner was a small, plump woman in her late twenties, with wide cheeks and flat, fleshy lips, old enough to be ageless in the eyes of her students. She wore her abundant dark curls closely cropped, in an effort to subdue them. Herself an earlier kind of refugee to West Ivers, she still bristled at the little flare-ups of condescension some of her young charges displayed. Their parents,

more aware of their social responsibility, patronized
in different ways. A warm winter coat, a small gift of
money. She had met such benevolence. One is grateful,
but it can crush a woman's pride. She had been a graduate assistant to a classical scholar at the university
in Munich. When she learned her fiancé was father to
another woman's child, she had fled. As a Jew, she had
been lucky to gain entry into the United States to join
a cousin in nearby Riverside, but Boylston University
did not find room for her. Teaching at the Parker Farm
School had restored her belief in herself. It was the
community that had taken her in, and she was forever
respectful. But it was her first experience with such a
freedom in the classroom. Sometimes a little, how does
one say, rigidity, was necessary. Now she folded her
hands on the top of the desk to signal that-is-enough.
"You hear me, class," she said with great authority.
"It is up to all of you to make the new boy welcome
to the fourth grade." She raised her ruler and snapped
it down sharply on the wooden desk top, wagging her
head at the rows of smooth, pink faces.

The teacher had tacked up a map of Europe on
the beaverboard wall beneath a frieze of pictures of
ancient Greece that the class was studying. Pictures
of heroic statues and figures on ancient vases from
the fourth and fifth century B.C. Zeus, Pallas Athena,
Hermes, Hera. The heroes of the *Iliad*, which Miss
Zeckner had been reading to them at rest time, made
seemingly more authentic by her thick Austrian accent.
In moments of high spirits, the students often hailed

each other by their Greek names, Agamemnon of Mycenae, Ajax of Sparta, Proud Achilles. They attended school assemblies in the Agora, classes in the Parthenon, games on the field of Olympia. In art period they cut out their chitons and painted their shields for the games they would hold. The city of Berlin was nothing more than a teacher's red X on a map.

But shortly before the half-hour this morning, they heard the outside door swing heavily into the latch. Promptly, the teacher directed them to put away their spelling books and pencils—neatly, please, quietly—and sit up straight. They turned to stare through the grid of small panes of glass in the upper half of the schoolroom door. The figures came into view. Miss Graham and Jenny's mother leading. Miss Graham ushered in the visitors, mother and son. Dressed all in black except for the boy's gray pullover sweater, they stood erect, tall and slim, the boy reaching almost to his mother's shoulder. There was an air of great presence about them, solemn but composed. The boy's pale fingers entwined with his mother's black-gloved hand was the only hint of apprehension. She looked like one of the beautiful actresses in the poster illustrations at the movie theater, smooth, delicate face, chin lifted. Only her eyes pleading. For a moment the students were stunned into silence. A pencil dropping to the floor was an explosion.

Miss Zeckner stepped forward, and the little group conspired among themselves, the teacher helping the boy out in her native tongue. Mrs. Goldstein had already mastered a little English. Finall,y Miss Graham addressed the class. "We are so fortunate to have Gottfried in the school. He has come a long way to be with us, and he can teach us many things about other countries and customs. He has been to see Dr. White this morning and he is in fine health. I know you will all welcome him and help him to understand the ways of his new homeland." Bowing and nodding, a pat on the shoulder, a wave of a long hand, and Miss Graham was gone. Jenny's mother led the mysterious Mrs. Goldstein to a seat in the back of the room. Heads swung further right, shoulders turned, to watch their progress until Miss Zeckner cleared her throat several times. Attention.

Alone, the boy stiffened and looked watchful. The students stared at him attentively. He wore shiny black knee pants and woolen stockings that left his knobby red knees for everyone to see. How hot and itchy the stockings looked. Miss Zeckner took the boy's hand in a friendly, vigorous shake and escorted him to the front of the room. His black curls lay in waves at the side of his head. He had big ears and beady eyes.

"Welcome, Gottfried," she commanded, nodding to the class.

"Welcome, Gottfried," they sang out in unison and giggled. "As Miss Graham has told you Gottfried has very recently come to your country." Miss Zeckner paused to glare at the back row of boys who were taking this moment to shove and push their way to settling some dispute. Finally the boys took note of the silence and sat up at attention. "He is a fine quick boy," Miss Zeckner resumed her introduction, repeating her opinion of the new classmate with a warning no-nonsense tone, and then she nodded to Gottfried. He drew himself up and bowed from the waist, his face passive.

He spoke thickly. "Good morning."

The students were puzzled by the almost familiar words, and Jenny looked back at her mother for guidance. Her presence gave Jenny a special feeling of importance on this occasion. She wore the print dress and single strand of pearls of all mothers. Her knees were crossed and she had pulled down the skirt of her dress to cover them. She bent forward a little to show interest or encouragement. But the strange woman's pale face was frozen smooth, even when she nodded occasionally to show she understood, and she wore black clothes as if it were a grandmother's death.

Gottfried was led to the empty desk. His bare knees knocked against the edge and Miss Zeckner called for the spare chair there by the pencil sharpener. Perhaps it was lower. "Thank you, Sammy." There was a lot of shuffling around. "Trade places with Patsy. There's a good girl, it's just for now." Patsy glared and drew herself up at the intruder's desk. Then she turned and flashed him an angry smirk, sitting there in her place.

Recess had come and gone, but there was still time for refreshments, Miss Zeckner promised. Molly was chosen to pass the tray. She watched her feet as she moved between the desks, placing a little paper cup and two crackers on the edge of each. When she reached Gottfried she stopped and looked up. His black eyes stared back. "Goatfred," she said, trying to pronounce his name. There was a ripple of titters. Miss Zeckner stepped in, handing a pencil and workbook to the new boy. She tapped her ruler on the edge of the blackboard and asked the class to please get ready for long division.

From the very beginning everyone called Gottfried "Fred."

Chapter Eight

The Back Door Store opened in May in rooms behind the co-op, with many in attendance, including the wives of the president of the university and the mayor and many of the mothers from the Parker Farm School. Even the headmistress took the noon hour off to be present at the ceremonies. Looking out over the whitewashed walls and blue trim of the display area, where the goods for sale were set out on trestle tables borrowed from attics and cellars and covered with bright colored cloths, Mrs. Parker welcomed the gathering and declared the shop ready for business. The hand-blocked fabrics, patterned mittens and sweaters, crocheted doilies, and leather bookmarkers were snatched up and set aside for birthdays or Christmas. If the markup on bought goods seemed costly, the customer had the satisfaction of knowing it was in a good cause and would do nicely for a hope chest or a wedding gift. Vera and her committee shared the minding of the store with some of the refugee women, and in the happy crush of too much to do, they were soon addressing each other as Susan and Irina, Vera and Ilsa and Rahel.

Charlotte Russell purchased a bright plaid vest for her husband's debut as Sherlock Holmes in the King's Inn Club Spring Revue, and Mrs. Parker bought a hand-knit shawl for her ailing mother to put around her shoulders on a breezy day in the summer garden, or against the draft in the old townhouse on the Hill. Bea Norton chose a box of embroidered hankies for herself and two pairs of children's mittens to hide in the linen closet until Christmas stockings. Mrs. Lewis strolled about the shop inspecting the wares as if she had all the time in the world. Vera watched her with awe. Her expensive clothes, her polished nails, deep red lips, the elegance of the woman, the smoothness, the remoteness. She thought of Harry Lewis' generous humor, his dark, good looks, and how exposed she had once felt when they were alone in Mrs. Parker's front hall. Finally, to Vera's astonishment, Mrs. Lewis picked out a rather old-fashioned set of crocheted silk thread collar and cuffs.

Even Mrs. von Kempel came in one afternoon; at least Vera thought that's who it was. She was wearing a little fur jacket (at this time of year! But then she was said to be fragile) and paid a steep price for six port-wine glasses from the bought goods table. When word got around that they were selling homemade jam tortes and chocolate cakes, Herr Doktor Meyer, visiting the spring term at Boylston University, allowed himself his only nostalgic indulgence, and very soon he returned with his colleague, Professor Parker, who hailed Vera as if they were old acquaintances.

"My dear Mrs. Oliver, this is indeed a pleasure." He extended his hand. "You've met my colleague. Herr Professor Doctor Meyer." Much smiling and shaking and bowing. "You have made my friend at once sad and happy with your delicate pastries, Mrs. Oliver, a state of profound balance." Professor Parker chuckled. Herr Doktor Meyer selected a chocolate cake with a light mocha filling, and the two gentlemen carried it back to Professor Parker's comfortable study in the library. Before settling in, he requested coffee be sent over from the Faculty Club, and they spent an enjoyable afternoon in interesting speculation about the rapid development of the Romanesque in cathedral architecture in France in the middle ages. Not surprising then that at supper that evening Mrs. Parker remarked that her husband's appetite seemed off.

All in all, Vera reflected one day as she was straightening up at closing time, the hundred and fifty dollars borrowed from Mr. Lewis last winter could not have been put to better use. The whole enterprise had the promise of a flourishing women's exchange, nourished by understanding and generosity. She knew the summer exodus would put a strain on business, but she would brazen it out somehow, iced tea on the bricked driveway behind the co-op, light lunch to attract the trade crowd. Whatever happened, she certainly would not tell Richard, and she wasn't going to go running to Mr. Lewis either, like everyone else.

"Keep your fingers crossed," she said out loud, and felt foolish to be talking to the four walls.

The transition of the refugee children into the Parker Farm School was not so smooth. There were fourteen of them now. In most cases, Miss Graham felt it was only a matter of time before those children who had come into the upper school would feel more at home. Most of them had mastered a little English, and in some cases, their French was better than Mme Heffinger's. The refugee children were used to following rules and did well in science and math. Some of them were overwhelmed at first by square-dancing class or bookbinding or woodworking, but these were the very activities Miss Graham believed promoted healthy companionship and personal pride in manual skills. If they seemed hesitant to join in group singing, it was hard to plunge into "Get Along Little Doggies" or "Shenandoah, I Long to See You." Unfortunately, their bewilderment allowed other students in these classes to act up or drift off into their own daydreams. The music teacher had her job cut out for her.

By and large, the regular students were welcoming and friendly, but it bothered the headmistress that as a body, after the initial curiosity, they were content just to absorb these foreign children. They took no interest in their previous plight or what might be learned about the circumstances of others less fortunate. When she mentioned this at the May meeting of the parents' committee, some conceded it was an opportunity missed, others felt that in anxious times like these it was all right to overlook such a developmental experience. The part-time school psychologist, a new addition to the staff, tended to agree with the latter point of view. Studies found that children best absorb change in small increments. Members of the committee paid attention to the expert. Harry Lewis' response was unusually simple. "In a way these boys and girls might welcome the chance to forget." Miss Graham was relieved he left it at that.

The adjustment had been harder for the refugee children in the younger grades, particularly Fred Goldstein in the fourth grade. A strangely grownup boy—so quiet, so self-restrained, so respectful of his teachers—he shied away from other children, avoiding recess play, preferring to draw. Ordinarily Miss Zeckner would not have allowed this, believing with Miss Graham and the sports teacher in the healthiness of physical exercise. He did participate in the classroom preparations for the Greek games, and he was a capable discus thrower. But he was ill at ease with his own accomplishments, hanging his head, averting his eyes. Miss Graham agreed that, without seeming to play favorites, Miss Zeckner would allow him to do what he wanted outside of subject classes.

At first, he drew pictures of mountains and crayoned them purple and gray, with lush green valleys. He had a firm technique, although his subject matter was rather undeveloped for his age. When Miss Zeckner brought this up in staff meeting, Miss Graham reminded her that Fred had not been exposed to the challenging lower school art program. When Miss Zeckner asked the boy where he had learned to draw, cooing to him in their native German, he told her it was what he did when the curfew was declared. She hung his pictures above the blackboard at the front of the classroom in hopes that such attention would bring him out of himself.

On the morning of the Greek games, Fred was one of the first to be dressed in his chiton—he had chosen a sinister black with a geometrical border in gold. While the atmosphere in the room was a mixture of the solemnity of the occasion and the chaos of exuberant high spirits, Fred sat quietly at his desk. Suddenly, he snatched up a box of crayons and quickly produced a series of explosions and fires, balls of red and yellow rolling between burning buildings. Miss Zeckner was alarmed, but she was too busy to spend any special time with him, and frankly, she told Miss Graham afterward, she forgot. She tied up rope belts and pinned back a few mops of hair with the bobby pins she kept in the pocket of her smock. She admired and encouraged, cajoled and scolded once or twice, but her fourth graders were quick to step into their roles at the appointed moment as they lined up, the roughhousing over, no more whispering and giggling. At eleven o'clock sharp the class marched two by two, shields before them, out the back door of the classroom building, onto the walkways painted with little white feet down the middle to remind students to maintain their orderly lines. Warrior athletes turned a smart left at the common and stepped down onto the playfield, forming a semicircle in front of other admiring lower-school children that made up the audience, along with a group of smiling parents and teachers, already applauding. It was the culminating event of the fourth-grade school year.

Miss Graham was there to greet them. She raised her hand for quiet and began. "Hail, fellow Greeks, kings, princes and brave warriors, to the 1939 games here at Olympia." She spread her arms to indicate the fields, the trees beyond, the pale blue morning sky. The class stood stiff and attentive. "Greetings to the loyal spectators gathered here to encourage our brave athletes without prejudice or bias." She gave a little nod in the direction of the expectant parents, then turned to address the warriors more fully, looking sternly over the metal nosepiece of her new glasses. "Brave heroes, men of courage, I salute you, knowing that you have traveled from city states all over ancient Greece to participate together in these great games, the climax of your year of study. We welcome brotherly contest between equals, always understanding that no one man is better than another." When she paused to let this sink in, some of the heroes began to fidget and she hurried on. "Go forth then, O warriors, engage in friendly sport, and may the sense of victory come to all of you." There was a scurry as the warriors took up positions on the field, and Miss Zeckner, raising a stout arm high above her head, held it there for a long moment, then let it drop, signaling the beginning of the games.

The single events went as expected. The girls did very well. Small and wiry, Pearl was not called Fleet-footed Pelius for nothing. She won both the girl's running meet and the mixed relay race for her team. Her face with its halo of dark, curly hair was slashed with a huge smile, and after her victory in the running meet, she stood to one side for a moment, arms akimbo, surveying the audience as they clapped. She gave a little unrehearsed bow and waved at her beaming father. In an unexpected upset in the javelin throw, Daring Diomedes, Jenny, placed second only to Mighty Ajax, Jeffrey Malcolm, the class athlete. As she returned to her place in line, she caught her mother's smile. On the third try, when the math teacher, filling in where he could, went to gauge the final hurl of the discus by Noble Agamemnon, Patsy, it measured farther than Mighty Ajax's last throw, causing a momentary flare-up of independent wills as Agamemnon ducked Ajax's punch to her arm. Everyone was satisfied that Fred as Artful Telemon had at least joined in.

The final event was the wrestling matches. Miss Zeckner had paired up the students as evenly as possible. She stood with her arms crossed beneath her bosom as the contenders took their places. The whole heroic fantasy was almost over, only the awarding of laurel wreaths and the final parade around the field. Watching the struggling pairs, spread out across the field, she was pleased to see that Artful Telemon was taking part without restraint, his arms extended full length, hands on the shoulders of Mighty Ajax. She let her eye move on to the next pair. But instinct told her to look back in time to see Fred break from his wrestling hold and throw Jeffrey to the ground with a wallop. Miss Zeckner rushed forward as Fred crushed the other boy with a brute strength she could not have imagined. He hung over his foe, pinned in his murderous hold, his eyes closed, his face twisted in some torment. "*Halt,*" Miss Zeckner cried out. "*Halt,* Gottfried," she said, pulling him off as he let go of his opponent. "More careful, please."

Jeffrey sprang to his feet, tears rolling down his streaked cheeks. He grabbed at Fred's hair. "You dirty Jewboy," he screamed, "you tricked me."

Fred snatched out at the other's chiton, "You whisper at me, 'Goatfred,' 'Goatfred.' You do not call me 'Goatfred.' "

Miss Zeckner put herself between the two boys, now tearing at each other. Mr. Lewis was suddenly there to lead Fred away.

At the evaluation meeting in the office of the headmistress the following afternoon no one knew precisely what to say. The ashen light of a cloudy day lay heavy on a room already oppressive with apology, Mrs. Goldstein's spiritless poise a measure of the failure they all felt. Miss Graham and Miss Zeckner sat side by side, papers and progress reports in piles on the table before them. Miss Graham was riffling through the collection of Fred's drawings. She had talked to the school psychologist, who brought a new approach to these problems of behavior. She had a pad and pen beside her, prepared to take notes where relevant. Mrs. Goldstein and Mrs. Oliver sat across the table.

"Gottfried is an especially bright and sensitive boy," Miss Zeckner began. "I am very glad to have him in my classroom, Mrs. Goldstein. We welcome him." She looked into the mother's passive face and knew it was too much. Mrs. Goldstein wasn't hearing her. She was preparing herself for another closing of a door. Immobile, her dark eyes watchful. Miss Zeckner had felt the way Mrs. Goldstein looked.

Miss Graham tried next. "I am so sorry for what has happened, Mrs. Goldstein, but you mustn't worry unduly. The school is dedicated to wiping out ugly misconceptions. Because you are the person who knows and understands your son best, we will need your help to guide us as we try to help him adjust." She shifted a pile of papers before her as if she were cutting a deck of cards. She still had to confront Jeffrey Malcolm's parents later this evening. And then, the boys must make their apologies to one another. Before the class or in private? The whole occurrence was a nightmare.

"I want to be of service," Mrs. Goldstein said, but she offered nothing more. Her expression remained wary.

There was an uncomfortable silence, then Miss Graham asked, "Could you tell us a little bit about your journey to this country, Mrs. Goldstein."

Mrs. Goldstein looked at Vera, who nodded her encouragement.

"We take the painting only and board the train to Munich. There we change for Brussels and Amsterdam. We sell the painting to pay."

"And did your husband accompany you?"

"After the burning of the library he was detained. I have not seen him since."

"Does your son talk about his father?"

"No, it is I who speak of him," she went on quickly, the color rising on her pale cheeks. "From our window, we watch the flames. He ran out to save the books. I cry for him sometimes. Gottfried makes the tea, and I ask forgiveness." Mrs. Goldstein was weeping now, shielding her eyes with her hand. Vera offered her a handkerchief but she shook her head and began to scrabble for her own in the pocketbook on her lap. Miss Graham stretched out her hand across the table. Miss Zeckner had turned away.

Suddenly Mrs. Goldstein leaned across the table and snatched the pile of pictures to her. She went quickly through until she came to the one of a series of glowing balls that seemed to be rolling toward the viewer. She jabbed at each ball coming down the paper. "He was on fire. The man he was on fire." She shoved the picture back toward the middle of the table.

There was an awkward moment. Shock. Bewilderment. Vera turned tentatively, remembering what her great-aunt Jenny used to say. Then she lunged forward and put her arms around the weeping woman, stroking her back. Mrs. Goldstein leaned into the embrace. "*Nun, nun, Schatze,*" Vera kept repeating, "there, there, my dear."

"*Danke schoen,*" Mrs. Goldstein said, looking up into Vera's face.

Miss Zeckner turned away again, blinking back the tears. She reached into the tuck in her sleeve for her handkerchief and blew her nose noisily. Miss Graham repositioned the tortoiseshell comb in her bun, scooping up the tendrils of hair with her fingers. She took a deep breath before she spoke. "Thank you for taking us into your confidence, Mrs. Goldstein. We will respect your privacy, of course, but you have helped us to understand Gottfried's state of mind. He has witnessed things many adults will never know."

The sound of the bell filled the office. The school day was over, providing a natural end to the meeting. The women shook hands, remembering to look in each other's eyes, soulful, anxious, understanding looks. "See what you can do," Margaret whispered to Vera. She closed the door and stepped to the window to watch the three women as they slowly followed the little white footprints along the path to the fourth -grade building. She settled at her desk to write up her notes on the meeting. Across the top of the report, she wrote in capital letters: GOTTFRIED GOLD-STEIN IS A CHILD WHOSE BOYHOOD HAS BEEN SNATCHED FROM HIM BY EVIL DESIGN. Some minutes later, when she looked up, she saw Vera and

Mrs. Goldstein coming up the walk. Jenny and Fred preceded them. That's an uncomfortable alliance, she thought. She waved to the little group as they passed beneath her window.

Jenny could hardly bear to sit in the living room with them. It would have been more fun in the kitchen with Mary, even with Fred there, but her mother wouldn't hear of it. When she allowed her to have a cup of cambric tea instead of the usual glass of juice, Jenny knew this was supposed to be a special occasion, and she resolved to concentrate on keeping her knees together to hold the cup. Mrs. Goldstein and her mother talked about the Back Door Store. It was all her mother cared about now. The stock, the running expenses, the sudden slump in the demand for arts and crafts, the popularity of the tea and pastry shop. She addressed Mrs. Goldstein as Ada, and hoped she would call her Vera. "We welcome you, and I need your help."

"But Mrs. Oliver . . . "

"Vera. Please."

". . . I have not the shop skills."

"We are all learning."

"You are too kind."

Mrs. Goldstein was too beautiful, like Pearl's mother, and she spoke so perfectly. Fred sat motionless with his hands on his knobby knees. He wasn't like a boy. He wore a sleeveless sweater on a warm day like Patsy's grandfather and he got along with grown-ups.

Too goody-goody looking. But Jenny knew better. She remembered how savage he looked when he tried to beat up Jeffrey. When her mother asked Jenny to pass the plate of sandwiches again, Fred took the last roll of asparagus. All that was left was bread and butter. As she returned the plate to the tea tray, Jenny snatched up a cookie, dropped it, then picked it up off the rug and ate it. Her mother glared. "You may be excused, Jenny."

Jenny dashed out the door, but her mother called after her, "Show Fred the hopscotch court you made by the garage."

Fred stood looking down at the court, his arms folded across his chest like a judge. Jenny starred at his funny-looking high-top shoes. "You want to play," she asked crossly. "I could show you how, if you asked me." She could be just as stuck-up as he was.

He curled up his lip and said, "That's for girls," and walked away.

Jenny was glad to get rid of him. He'd only ruin things anyway. She played against herself, getting more involved, letting the round stone move ahead of the piece of wood bark, forgetting about stupid Goat-fred. After some minutes there was a strange mix-up of howling sounds like Mary's slide whistle. When she looked up, Fred was standing up in the crotch of the ornamental maple, looking out over Parker Farm Road like a captain in his ship, one arm extended up the trunk of the tree. He made the howling sound again.

She rushed across to him. "My father doesn't like you climbing that tree."

Fred fell silent. He turned toward her but did not look down

"My mother doesn't let me climb that tree," she said emphatically, and waited for something to happen. "She says I'll break the branch."

Fred continued to look through her. Jenny felt her cheeks sting.

She screeched at him, "Come down out of there."

"Oh, never mind, Jenny," her mother said, coming up with her camera already open. Mrs. Goldstein trailed her across the lawn.

"But, Mummy, you said the branch would break, and he's bigger than I am."

"I said never mind, Jenny. Now stand still there at the foot of the tree, so I can get a snapshot of the two of you."

Jenny was so dumbfounded that she did as she was told. Then her mother wanted to take a picture of Fred and his mother, so Fred had to come down out of the tree. As he passed Jenny he hissed, "That is how to yodel." He smiled a crooked mean smile, the kind old Pew gave Billy Bones when he passed the message in Treasure Island. That was more than Jenny could stand. She threw herself down on the grass.

"Get up, Jenny. You'll get grass stains on your skirt."

Jenny looked up at her mother posing Fred and his mother before the front steps. "Now smile . . . Oh, that's lovely." The beautiful, sad woman and her precious son. He was too hateful.

After the Goldsteins finally left, her mother lit into Jenny. "What is the matter with you, throwing yourself down on the grass like that? You'll be ten this summer. You're too old for that kind of behavior. You'll never grow up to be a young lady if you act like that. I was simply mortified." She marched back into the living room.

"He's hateful, Mother. How can you be so nice to him?"

"Honestly, I don't know why your nose is so out of joint. That boy has been fleeing from one place to another for so long, he's almost too well behaved. It's a normal healthy experience for him to be able to play in a tree."

"But, Mummy, he tried to beat up . . ."

"You must try to understand what he and his mother have been through. Mrs. Goldstein is a fine lady. I hope she will join us at the Back Door Store." As her mother placed the dirty tea cups on the silver tray for Mary to clear away, she went on almost worshipfully, "Mrs. Goldstein was once a dramatic actress." She paused a moment. "He's really a sweet boy, Jenny. So shy and quiet."

In protest, Jenny plucked the last lonely cookie off the plate and started to tell about the ugly yodeling thing Fred did, but her mother said, "They don't know for sure, but they think his father is dead."

Jenny had never thought about not having a father.

Her father took trips sometimes, more often now than before. To Washington and important places like that. But then, he always came back. When the trains couldn't run during the hurricane last year, her mother was worried about him. Jenny was afraid too. Maybe he was dead, but really, she couldn't imagine it. She didn't even know what it looked like except maybe the janitor man with a hole through his head and that was too horrible. She didn't say anything about the yodeling. She knew that the right thing to do was to pity someone whose father was probably dead, but how could she? Fred always got what he wanted.

That night before she went to sleep she wrote in her diary: "I have to like stupid Goatfred. But I don't."

Chapter Nine

"It's going to happen any time now. He's all set," Joe Izrael announced. It was the summer of 1939.

"Who?" Harry Lewis asked perfunctorily. He was squatting down with Joe's father, Ira, to inspect the old, broken concrete floor of the machine shop the Izraels had set up after Wellington Brass gave Ira the sack for unionizing. Other organizers managed to keep their jobs, but a Russian Jew with a Polish Jew for a wife was surely a Communist. The irony was that now that labor strikes threatened the big brass companies, Izrael and Son was making dies for them. Brass stampings, things like escutcheon plates and parts for clocks. As primary investor, Harry was eager for expansion.

"Who?" Joe said scornfully. "Hitler, that's who."

For a moment Harry let the announcement hang there. It was the last day of August, when accounts at Howell and Howell were usually reviewed before clients returned from their summer estates. He hadn't put that off to listen to Joe's dark predictions. He spoke decisively. "The French and English have warned that hostile action would mean war."

"Exactly," Joe said emphatically.

Ira flapped his hand at his son as if he were driving away a mosquito. "That one thinks he can see into the crystal ball," he said to Harry, jabbing his screwdriver into the cracks that reached out like fault lines across the floor. Harry looked across at Joe. The Polish Club's scholarship boy to Boylston. Brilliant, of course, but he was an unsettling young man. His intent look and unruly hair reminded Harry of a Russian revolutionary.

"Austria, Bohemia, Moravia gone," Joe declared.

Ira looked skeptical. "This might hold the cooling tanks."

"The Dutch mobilize, and the French. The children are evacuated from Paris."

"But the new furnaces, never." Ira turned to Harry. "We'll need a reinforced floor."

"The Nazis even refer to our own people as 'The Jewish Question.'"

"You have said enough," the father snapped.

Harry stood up. "War in Europe. He may be right, Ira," he said wearily. Then he looked at Joe for a long minute. "But here, everything will be the same."

You had to admire Joe, Harry reminded himself on the drive home. His entrepreneurial chutzpah was what the American dream was all about, and Izrael and Son was the kind of opportunity that Harry wanted to believe in: small scale, forward thinking, the brain child of two eastern European Jews, a father and son. It might have been Harry and his father. In different circumstances. With a different father. No matter, this time he had gotten in on the ground floor. A sound investment. Just to say the words to himself, "my machine shop," or "the plant," was exhilarating.

The motor traffic was heavy this afternoon, and there was a horse-drawn cart inching along up ahead, but Harry had nothing to complain about. There was a smoky blue sky overhead, and he was in the comfort of his old Packard touring car.

This automobile had been the delight of his father-in-law. Harry could still recall the first time he'd been in the passenger seat, luxuriating in the smoothness of the leather, the gloss of the lacquered wooden instrument panel, the well-bred sleek black nose of the hood. He had tried hard not to be impressed. He and Adele weren't married yet, and he knew he was "on approval."

"I think you'll do well for a Democrat, Harry, and that's okay with me," Mr. Schultzberger announced. While Harry was searching for the right thing to say, the older man continued, "I never had a son, but you'll do. It's important to me that you treat my daughter decently, but there's more to it. You're an ambitious yid, taking up with the old Yankees. I like that in you. I've been there and back myself, but I had a father and grandfather before me to do the dirty work, selling arms to the wrong countries, pouring money into shady industrial schemes. By the time it was my turn, I could afford to look good. Maybe you'll vote Republican yourself one of these days."

"Schultzberger Brothers is one of the most respected investment firms."

"I know that, Harry, I didn't have to go to Boylston University. But I want to say a few things before you plunge in all the way. They're always looking at you, especially if you're a Jew making money. So remember to look at yourself. Ask yourself, 'How'm I doing?' and you'll be all right."

Not bad advice, in retrospect, although Harry remembered feeling roughed up at the time. Gradually, he came to realize that his wife and daughters treated Mr. Schultzberger like a pet skunk. Useful in the world of slugs and grubs—even friendly, if you left him alone—but challenge him and he would make an awful stink. He and Harry got on well over the years. When the old financier died suddenly, Harry made a point of buying the Packard from the estate, although the family would have given it to him. It was Harry's tribute to his father-in-law.

As he approached the city, Harry lowered the window all the way and signaled with his left arm out straight, shifted down to wait for the oncoming traffic to pass, then took the turn in first gear. The car roared across the highway onto Center Street, cutting through the town of Riverside, where Adele played bridge three times a week with her friends at the Jewish Women's Club. Occasionally he attended a funeral or bar mitzvah at the Temple Emmanuel on Riverside Avenue. The houses were solid and straightforward, brick and clapboard, staring out on the street with merciless permanence. Wide lawns, ancient copper beech and elm, walls and wrought-iron gates. The familiar symbols of refinement and privilege. But money had made these Jews in Riverside as homogeneous a group as the families of West Ivers, and while Harry was glad it gave them comfort, he was not as easy with his own metamorphosis as some others. He knew it was perverse of him—his mother used to pinch his cheeks and call him stubborn—but he did not want to lose himself in the blending in. He preferred to stick out, not like a sore thumb, precisely, but a lone hand.

As he passed by the old Fort Floyd Arsenal and crossed the bridge into West Ivers, he reminded himself that he must tell Adele about his present adventure. This evening. Just in passing. Under normal circumstances, she would have only a cursory interest in a specific investment he might mention, but this one was substantial, thirty-five thousand dollars, and most of it from Mr. Schultzberger. Adele kept close tabs on what her father had put in Harry's hands for her and the children. He needed to present this undertaking in the best possible light.

Harry pictured himself sitting across from Adele in the living room. He would take another sip of his drink and cross his legs before he mentioned the recent investment. She'd ask a lot of questions if she were in a provocative mood. She was no fool. Of course, he had every confidence in his investment, no matter where the money came from. Why else would he have made it? He did not make mistakes.

He turned onto Great Hamilton Street, the car straddling the ruts of the tracks. This evening he welcomed the long line of slow moving traffic, hostage to the starts and stops of a trolley car up ahead. It gave him a chance to review the events of the afternoon. The plant needed a lot of work, true, but Ira Izrael knew his machining. And in his old-fashioned way, he was as ambitious as his son, Joe. Harry liked ambition in a man. But he would admit only to himself that he wanted to be in charge of this new company. He wanted to do more than move money around; he wanted to be personally involved, make something grow from the inside. He wanted Izrael and Son for himself.

The few clients to whom he had offered the investment turned it down without a second thought. A father-and son-team, two Jews who weren't even born in the United States. A rinky-dink outfit. Too risky. It was just as Harry had expected. But was there something in their objections?

He'd struggled with the issue. He knew he could not take a chance with his own money. He had a family to care for. To have control, he needed a substantial sum. But it was not for himself that he wanted the money. The profit would go back into the company. He mentally squared his shoulders. He would simply explain to Adele that he saw this as a long-term growth investment for her and the children.

By the time he turned onto Parker Farm Road, he had justified to himself one more time his rash and exciting commitment. Taking a calculated risk is how the great fortunes of this country were made. Adele would recognize that. After all, she had always admired her father's boldness. Harry rested his elbow on the open window frame.

As he came down Parker Farm Road, he saw his wife in front of the Olivers' house. Involuntarily he drew in a short breath against the panic of unidentified trouble. Adele was facing toward him, gesticulating, drawing her hands down over her bust, talking to Vera Oliver, who stood motionless, holding the garden hose behind her as if she were trying to hide it. He was astounded. Adele had always made a point of keeping her distance from the neighbors, polite when the occasion arose, but never forthcoming. Something must have happened to Pearl. As he hurried toward them, Adele waved to him.

He greeted her and kissed her lightly on the cheek, then bowed imperceptibly to Vera. "I can see I've stepped into a serious discussion. Is there some way I can help?" he asked.

"I was in the Back Door Store this morning," Adele began, "looking at . . ."

There can't be anything wrong, Harry thought, following the lines of her lips like a deaf man as she formed the words, momentarily overwhelmed by the wish to kiss her. He had to remind himself to listen.

" . . . woman . . . dress, jumper, really, with an apron."

"It's called a dirndl," Vera explained to Harry. "It comes from Austria. Oh, of course, you know Mrs.

Weiss. It's her regional costume. She says sometimes when it's very hot, the young girls wear them without the blouse." She hesitated a moment, and Harry thought she blushed. "But it would really be too much arm."

"It's identical to the one worn by the Duchess of Windsor," Adele said. "I saw a picture of her in a magazine. Charming."

"Your wife has been very kind. And now she has ordered another. Sales at the store have lagged a little bit. It worries the refugee women," Vera confessed. "For some, it's their only security." But she added quickly, "I tell them it's the summer, of course, but these dress orders will help."

Should I offer more, Harry wondered. But Adele was saying, "I'll send Pearl in with Nanny Pence to be measured. I'm sure a dress shop would be a great success. Especially for children."

The women smiled politely at each other, Harry shook Vera's hand, and she thanked him profusely. For what? He hadn't done anything.

As they walked toward their house he said to Adele, "I thought something was wrong when I saw you talking with Vera Oliver."

"Does something have to be wrong for me to talk with my neighbor?" She laughed and took his arm. "When I saw her out there watering that lawn again— she's a slave to a man's work—I thought I'd get a little dirndl for Pearl. I felt so badly for those women at the store this morning. Too many volunteers and no customers. Everything looked so forlorn. I picked out a lovely embroidered table runner to take to Mother next week—those women do beautiful work. As I turned to leave, one of them came out of the back room in this wonderful costume. Powder blue and pink. When I asked if they had such outfits for sale, everyone began talking at once, and in minutes there I was, in with the tea cakes and boiling water, being measured. But they'll need a dressing room if they set up a dress shop. They can't have customers herded into the back room like a pen full of cattle. "

Like the newsreel pictures of prisoners in Spain, Harry thought. The line of marching boots along a cobblestone street in Czechoslovakia, or the fleeting glimpse of droves of refugees pushing their way up a gangplank, clutching all they held dear, the hand of a frightened child, a sack of possessions.

He squeezed his wife's arm to his side as they turned up the flagstone walk that Dominic had recently laid. Picking a dead bloom off the stand of late-blooming white phlox at the gate, kicking aside a pebble in the pathway, Harry let himself be carried along by the waves of Adele's speech. He recalled the chickweed that grew in the scruff of dirt before the tenements of his youth. The inch plants and aspidistras in the shop windows along the avenue where his uncle had lived. He paused at his front door before he pushed down the polished brass latch. Here he was on Parker Farm Road, among the dogwoods and rhododendrons, glossy green now that the flowers were spent, in the rich cultivated soil of comfort and leisure. He was a Russian Jew whose taproot was in a landscape he could not even imagine, a country so hostile to people like himself that only a few days ago the Soviets had signed a non-aggression pact with Nazi Germany. The world jittered to the threat of war. Suddenly, he heard the voice of Joe Izrael, "any time now." As he stepped aside to let Adele move past him into the front hall, he looked out over the lawn and across the fields of the school. He could just make out the line of maples that delineated the cemetery where the Jewish groundskeeper who took his life finally lay at peace.

He ducked inside and slammed the door. Adele looked up at him, surprised.

"Sorry. I was off in another world. It's been a long day."

"Oh dear, I hope you'll forgive me. I want you go over to the Olivers later on. They're going to set off fireworks."

"This isn't the Fourth of July."

"It's a party of some sort for the older girl's new school friends. I understand she's been planning it all month. Jenny invited Pearl weeks ago to join in the fireworks."

"Well, there's no law against that."

"Mr. Oliver's away. I think there should be a man around."

"Vera Oliver won't like you sending me over there like that."

"I'm not so sure. She always looks as if she wants you to rescue her, like the damsel in distress in the motion pictures." Adele tilted her head at him and feigned a simpering look.

They both laughed. Harry said, "Vera Oliver is much too guileless for her own good."

"Just be casual," Adele told him. "Tell her it's your insatiable curiosity."

"I promise I'll keep an eye on things." He kissed the side of her cheek. "Will that satisfy you?"

"Some." She smiled and kissed him lightly on the lips.

Harry decided not to tell Adele about his investment. Not just yet.

After a good meal, Harry settled down in the library to read a recent book, Raymond Chandler's *The Big Sleep*. Clever new detective character. Innocent intrigue. When he heard Nanny Pence at the front door cluck clucking at Pearl and Jenny, he looked up and realized the blue-black of the late summer evening was already seeping into the sky like a stain. He turned out the reading lamp and walked across the hall, tightening the knot of his tie. Then he buttoned his suit jacket and stepped out, closing the door behind him noiselessly, in conspiracy with the darkening night.

Out on the road, he saw the little band of shadows drawing pictures and hurling cascades of tiny stars as they twirled their sparklers before them, setting off new ones as the old fizzled out. The undulating scene was punctuated with shrieks and self-conscious giggles. They were ten years old now. He could make out Pearl, her curly hair flying out as she moved. And Jenny Oliver with her tight bob, and a few of the others from the fourth grade, desperate Fred Goldstein among them. Vera Oliver must certainly have her hands full.

Beyond the group of youngsters were five or six adolescent girls, fifteen perhaps, moving in a circle around the ornamental maple at the far corner of the lawn. They seemed to be performing a dance, two steps to the center, two steps back, as they moved rhythmically from right to left, pale dresses over forming figures, bare legs and white socks emphasizing their virginal young womanhood. They sang a round as they performed their ritual, the pure, young, sexless voices weaving in an out around the lines of the tune:

Come follow follow follow follow follow follow me.
Whither shall I follow follow follow,
Whither shall I follow follow thee?
To the greenwood, to the greenwood,
To the greenwood, greenwood tree.

Harry smiled to himself. Such innocence was almost unreal. As he turned away from the groups of revelers, he noticed the silhouette of Vera across the road near the fire hydrant. She was bending over at the edge of the verge, stabbing the packed earth with the stick end of a rocket firecracker, a paper bag beside her, cones peeping out like baby birds from a nest. She was having trouble making the rocket stand up.

He stepped up behind her to lend a hand. "May I help you with that?"

Vera spun around, her face filled with alarm. "Oh, Mr. Lewis. You startled me." She turned back to her task. "I can't seem to get this to stay in the ground."

"Let me." He bent directly over her, his chest pressing lightly into her left shoulder. She stiffened. As he reached to grasp the stick above her hand he felt her relax into the shelter of his body. Suddenly, Vera let go her grasp, and Harry was able to push the firecracker firmly into the ground.

"Oh, Mummy, we were going to do that." Katherine stood behind them now.

Vera sprang free, flustered, patting her shoulder, adjusting her open cardigan. Touched and a little pleased, Harry stepped back a respectful distance to allow the woman a moment to collect herself.

"Be careful not to break them, the ground is awfully hard," Vera said to Katherine in her usual cautionary tone.

Katherine snatched up the paper bag and began to distribute the rockets to her friends. Harry rejoined the group.

"I'd be glad to help if you need me."

"That's all right, Mr. Lewis."

The older girls set up the rockets like a line of sentinels along Parker Farm Road past the Lewises' to reach the giant yews at the corner of the Parker farmhouse. For a moment, Vera and Harry stood close, watching. Then Vera crossed her arms over her chest and stepped to one side. After a moment, she suddenly thrust her hands deep in the sleeves of her sweater.

"It's awfully kind of you to come out this way."

"It's a beautiful night for fireworks."

"Richard usually oversees these activities with the children, but he's been called away," she explained.

"He's a busy man."

"Justice Department. Confidential," she whispered importantly.

He nodded. "Of course."

The younger children had abandoned their sparklers and were snaking in and out between the rockets, pushing and shoving to be at the head of the line. As they reached the corner of the Parkers' yard, a shadow, taller and rounder than the rest, separated from the dark mass of yews and tried to join the line. The children closed ranks. "Gently, Jenny," Harry heard Vera call out. The shadow moved behind the row of rockets to squat in front of the fire hydrant. It was the von Kempel boy, stabbing at the ground, a knife in one hand, a stone in the other. As Harry approached him, the boy stood up, dropping the stone into his pocket, then tucked his knife under his belt like a pirate. The line of children danced back down the street.

The sky was a black wash now and Harry took charge. He passed the box of safety matches to the von Kempel boy to hold. The boy grinned as one at a time the older girls came up to strike a safety match. Then Harry himself carried the taper forward from the safety line to ignite the fuse, stepping back quickly.

Each flame made a tiny sweep down the fuse to a mounting whoosh like sizzling wind as the rocket thrust into the sky and burst into fingers of light—first yellow, then blue, and green, red, cascading, shooting, swirling, exploding, radiating a six-pointed salute like the Star of David. The children gawked and squealed, shouted, "Look, look!" and covered their eyes, ducking as the diminishing sparks seemed to fall on them. The older girls hugged each other and Jenny and Pearl held hands. Fred Goldstein, standing close to Vera, clutched his thighs below his shorts, digging into his flesh. Vera put a reassuring hand on his shoulder, but with the final sizzle and burst Fred broke loose, dashing after the extinguishing sparks down Parker Farm Road in a wild flight, wailing the broken notes of his yodel.

Harry went after Fred, the von Kempel boy close at his heels, shouting unintelligibly. He passed Harry under the streetlight by the Nortons' house, remarkably swift for a clumsy boy. He was grinning broadly, brandishing his knife over his head, but he seemed more interested in whooping and screaming than in attacking. At the slope of the road in front of the school, Fred confronted him, crouched down and hissing like a cat. The von Kempel boy stepped back, stabbing his knife into his belt.

"All right you two, that was a good run," Harry said, panting to catch his breath. "Now let's shake hands and get back to the party."

The von Kempel boy looked up at Harry, his round face bright with delight. He held his grin a moment longer, then turned and slipped through the Russells' lilac hedge. Harry looked after him, shaking his head. It was hard to fathom the poor boy. He seemed more lonely than threatening.

Harry bent down and reached out his hand. "I won't hurt you, son." He placed his hand on Fred's shoulder. Remarkably the boy did not throw him off. "We can go back now. The fireworks are over." In a few minutes, they came up the road, Harry propelling the boy along, hand caressing his neck. Fred was rubbing his eyes with his fists. There was no sign of the von Kempel boy.

Vera put a protective arm around the boy, murmuring, "*Nun, nun, Schatze*," a little self-consciously. Without a word, Fred slipped off to join the others.

"What became of the von Kempel boy?" Vera asked.

"Darted off as mysteriously as he came."

"He shouldn't have that knife he waves around." Vera said.

"He certainly is an excitable young fellow, but he didn't seem to want to do harm. He stuck his knife like a dagger into his belt and vanished into the Russells' hedge."

"Oh, Ed Russell won't like that," Vera said without thinking. It was so dead right they both laughed. It was one of the many indiscreet views they would share in private.

"I hope this evening won't add to the Goldstein boy's difficulties," Harry said, looking into Vera's face.

Vera held her eyes on Harry's. "I should have realized all those flashes of fire would be too much for him."

"It's only wood, Mummy."

Vera flushed. "Oh, Jenny," she called out in surprise. "You mustn't sneak up like that. What is it you want?"

"The Beasty's knife. It's made of wood."

"Goodness, Jenny, how would you know?"

It was already dark. The older girls began to pick up the debris along the verge. The children said their good-byes and drifted down the road or mounted their bicycles to set off in a pack. It was time to go home. Pearl said goodnight to Jenny, tired of waiting for her father.

"I'll be along in a minute, honey," Harry called after her. He put out his hand to Vera. "It's been a busy night for you."

"I don't know what I would have done without you." She left her hand in his a moment too long.

He looked pleased. "My pleasure."

"Thank you again," she said with uncomfortable formality.

He bowed to her slightly and said, "Goodnight, then." She smiled shyly.

As he walked home, Harry felt a glow of good feeling come over him, not a little because Vera Oliver so obviously enjoyed the protective male role he so easily assumed with her. He thought of Adele's remarks about Vera earlier in the evening and smiled to himself. His wife was smarter than he was when it came to understanding people, especially their neighbors on Parker Farm Road. But he knew Vera Oliver was a smart woman, look at the way she managed the Back Door Store, and no matter how naive she appeared on occasion, she was surprisingly warm in her awkward way. She must be lonely sometimes with her husband away so much.

Coming up his walk, he leaned over to smell the phlox and was surprised that such a delicate trumpet-like cluster of flowers could smell so musky and stale. When he stood up, under the light over the front stoop, he saw it. He held his breath and looked more closely. There was no denying it. Someone had scratched a Star of David on the flagstone. His heart roared. The image was faint, drawn with thin edge of a stone. It must have been the von Kempel boy. Some of his neighbors might like to take a stab at him, he thought derisively, but they'd be afraid to be so childish. The boy only reflected the views of the world around him. Was that why he went after the refugee boy? With such a happy grin. The boy was unbalanced. Harry knew something of the boy's mother's nervous frailties. He threw a handful of dirt on the telltale defacement, then scuffed it in with his shoe. In the morning, he would ask Dominic to turn the stone over and reset it. He would not say anything about this to Adele.

That night, while Harry lay curled around Adele, his hand resting gently between her thighs, Vera lay awake in the shadows of her bedroom, listening for the absent sound of her husband's steady breathing, wondering what he might be doing, suddenly alarmed at the memory of the warmth of another man's breath on her left cheek as he leaned into her shoulder. Almost feeling his caress on the neck of the Goldstein boy as if it were her own. She leapt from the bed to stand at the window, staring unseeing into the night. At last she wept silently for something she did not want to feel, as the school playfields, the cemetery and the city skyline beyond came into focus.

Joe Izrael was listening to the radio while he worked late at the shop on plans for the expansion of the company. The reception on the shortwave band was faint, but he could hear that something was being repeated over and over again. He turned the volume up as high as it would go. There was the screeching whistle of interfering waves and then a steady hum that reached a rumbling thunder. "*UWAGA! INVAZJA! UWAGA! INVAZJA! UWAGA! INVAZJA!*" a voice was screaming. It was Polish.

Chapter Ten

September 1, 1939: HITLER INVADES POLAND.
A date to be remembered.

With the joint declaration of war by England and
France, Americans waited anxiously to learn the position of the United States. When President Roosevelt
announced a policy of neutrality, the stock market
soared with the prediction of a war materials boom.
The startling swiftness of events across Europe—a
Blitzkrieg, a "lightning war"— dazzled the public, and
throughout the autumn and into winter, the citizens
of West Ivers followed the nationwide debate between
interventionists and isolationist, sharpening a growing
edginess in the community.

After Thanksgiving, early this year by presidential
design to stimulate holiday shopping, Isabel Parker
buttoned her cardigan against the drafts of the old
farmhouse despite the central heating and sat down at
her desk to do her Christmas list. With the coal shortage in Britain she'd send half a dozen pairs of serviceable woolen stockings to Dorothy Bent-Wilson,

second cousin twice removed on the English side of her husband's family. Mufflers, hand knit by the refugees, for the children, butter in a can, bouillon cubes for hot beef broth. On the greeting card she wrote: "Wishing you and yours a safe New Year and the hope that 1940 will bring an end to these senseless hostilities. Love to you and Cecil, Rosemary, Ian, and little . . ." What was the baby's name? Isabel had never met the woman; the extent of their intimacy was this Christmas exchange. She inserted a "the" before the word "little" and "one" after. Then she wrote PEACE ON EARTH underneath.

In the $8.4 billion budget submitted by the president to Congress in January, 1940, $1.8 billion was earmarked for defense, a threefold increase over the previous year. Ed Russell, reading the particulars in the *Evening Traveler,* exclaimed, "Look at these figures. And we all know who'll be paying." He stabbed finger into the paper so hard his wife looked up from her marketing list. "That man in the White House will makes paupers of us yet."

Harry, jotting down the same information from the *New York Times,* calculated that the sum was more than 20 percent of the whole. He had always favored helping countries struggling against Nazi domination, but the sorry state of military preparedness in his own country implicit in this ballooning defense budget was unnerving. For a moment, he watched the crowds in the street below his fourth-floor office window, bundled up against the January wind, free to go about their business. And suddenly, he felt an overwhelming gratitude to his country for generations of his family, Lefkoviches and Katzes, thankful to be Americans. He reached into his pocket for his handkerchief and blew his nose.

"Sure," Joe Izrael said dismissively, when Harry tried to explain his feelings a few days later as the two of them went over the books at Izrael and Son. "This is America," he said pointing to the black column of the ledger. "Consider the opportunities in this defense business." He looked up at Harry. "Call it patriotism. After all, it's for the defense of the country."

He's crass, Harry thought, turning away. It's another time, another generation. And then he reminded himself that they were two of a kind, both part of the promise of America.

On a Tuesday in early April, Richard called Vera from Washington to tell her he would be held over for further meetings. After she answered, while he waited as usual for her to run to the upstairs phone, as if his calls were somehow secret, he watched Miss Sperry across the committee room taking shorthand from one of the other attorneys. The hem of her dark skirt was caught up at one knee to show the curve of her leg. He felt a twinge of guilt when he heard Vera's voice again, and he looked at the floor while he explained to her that one of the experts from the trade commission would be in town at the end of the week. Looking furtively across the meeting room at Miss Sperry again, he felt compelled to let Vera in on the issues before the committee. They were technical and detailed, the process slow and cumbersome. "That's the good old democratic way." He gave a laugh, embarrassed at his own banality. Sometimes he enjoyed enlarging on his expertise to Vera—"There's more here than the import tax on bananas. I added my two cents"—because he knew she was proud of him.

His voice sounded youthful and excited. This prompted Vera to ask how Miss Sperry was getting along. As soon as she spoke, she regretted it, she knew she sounded sarcastic. But all Richard said was that Miss Sperry shared an apartment with a co-worker. Lighthearted at this uninteresting piece of news, Vera threw herself into a little anecdote about Jenny and her friends at the movies. It had been raining cats and dogs and it was school vacation. They'd gone to see *Pinocchio*.

"It's a cartoon, Richard. Walt Disney. The puppet's nose grows longer and longer when he doesn't tell the truth. Apparently she said that not telling the whole truth and nothing but the truth was against the law—she must have gotten that from you, Richard. She called it a 'heinous' crime. It's the fifth grade, they want you to know how grown up they are. Then why wasn't Mr. Roosevelt in jail, Patsy asked. You know where she got that; her father is dead set against the man. Jenny insisted the president took an oath to always tell the truth . . . Yes, I know governments have secrets, I said you'd explain . . . Oh, Richard, you could tell Jenny the world was flat and she'd never question you."

He could hear the flutter of pleasure in his wife's voice. "Well, she's about the only one," he said good-naturedly.

"Take care of yourself, Richard."

"I'll see you Saturday."

"I'll feel better when the plane is safely on the ground."

Vera always took Richard's call in the privacy of their bedroom in the hopes of some special intimacy. As she leaned forward to replace the telephone receiver in its cradle on the night table between their twin beds, she wondered what exactly about this present assignment made Richard so alert, almost chatty. At home, when she asked him about his work, more often than not he said he was not at liberty to tell her. It was as if he found the burden of long hours and exhausting travel relaxing. He was always so pinched when he was home. The realization that Miss Sperry would be privy to some of his secrets made Vera feel like a child sitting on the sidelines, watching the others at their games, the way she felt when she passed the tennis court. She missed Richard. She always wanted him when he was away.

At the same moment Richard was thinking about the issue of truth. There was no absolute truth, the "whole" truth, despite Jenny's conviction. He had to admit he had come to admire the president's leadership diplomacy, despite what he suspected was a good deal of political maneuvering behind the scene. The Ed Russells of the world couldn't see beyond the end of their noses, trying to protect what they called "good old rugged individualism." It was money that mattered to men like that, and in Russell's case, he'd married most of it. This war business was far from petering out. Europe's troubles were already good for the American economy.

He saw that Miss Sperry was finishing up her notes, pausing to rub her large, dark eyes. He liked the way the white collar of her dress showed off her full cheeks. He took a certain paternal pride in recommending her for this position; she would be an invaluable addition to the committee's secretarial staff. This was her second round of meetings. He worried that he might lose her permanently to a bigger, less humdrum working world than she was used to in his office at home. She was young at twenty-five—or was it six?—and in this new setting, there was often a soft edge to the usual harsh pitch of her voice. She was smiling, coming toward him now.

"Would you care to join me for a drink this evening, Miss Sperry?"

At the Mayfair Hotel, they ordered cocktails. Standing at the bar, crushed against each other, the brim of her hat against his ear, they were marooned in a sea of servicemen and secretaries and bureaucrats, the piano player skimming the keys behind the din, the cigarette smoke like a sheltering fog. Richard tipped the maître d' and carried their drinks to a tiny cocktail table.

The first time his knee touched hers, he pulled back. "Oh, excuse me, Miss Sperry."

She smiled at him. She was always smiling at him. Admiration, almost adoration. "Oh, that's all right, Mr. Oliver. It's like sardines in here. Someone moves and the whole crowd has to turn over." Her face sparkled with excitement.

They ordered a second round of drinks. Emily Sperry bubbled with an infectious pleasure. The room buzzed with the importance of the moment. As he sipped his martini, his knee relaxed against the leg of this vivacious creature. Richard felt enveloped in a new world of gaiety and glamour. He felt a heady, unfamiliar sexual confidence. He felt desirable.

A few nights later, when the telephone rang, Emily automatically reached out to answer it, but Richard grabbed her wrist and she rolled back to her side of the bed. They both listened for an anxious moment. Reluctantly, Richard picked up the receiver. "No, no, Vera, I was in the bathroom. What's the matter?. . . Oh, for heaven's sake, if the storm is bad tomorrow, I'll take the train. . . . I know, but there's nothing to worry about, now get a good night's sleep."

When the Nortons went to the Russells' house for the ritual Sunday evening drinks, Ed Russell offered to mix the martinis for his guests. Tom Norton, unscrewing the cap on his host's gin, said as a matter of course,

"Thanks, Ed, go ahead and make yourself a whiskey and soda. You know how Bea is about her martinis. She likes them very, very, very dry."

But this time Beatrice Norton did not smile at her husband. "Speak for yourself," she said rudely and settled down on the sofa across the room.

The Russells exchanged looks of surprise as Charlotte Russell got up from the love seat in the bay window to pass the plate of cheese crackers.

"Don't mind my wife," Tom said as he measured a thimbleful of vermouth into the cocktail shaker. "She's afraid I'll join up. Think of those English flyboys soaring around up there, having the time of their lives, like driving a Cord. I have to say it's tempting."

"Don't you dare," Bea protested.

Tom took a sip of his wife's drink before he handed it to her, then one from his own as he sat down next to his hostess. "Don't worry, we've got other fish to fry." He leaned forward conspiratorially. "Now that the rain has finally stopped, I went over to the school this morning to try a little putting on the dodgeball court. That red-faced Irish janitor had skipped out of Mass. He was laying some kind of big canvas hose down the slope by one of the buildings, and the whole place smelled like a latrine. It's not the first time." Tom paused self-importantly. "I thought I might just let our headmistress know that, once and for all, we don't want that squalid stench in our neighborhood."

Ed shook his head in disgust. "You do that, Tom, before she gets that treasurer to bail her out."

"Don't worry about that, I happen to know Lewis has sunk his fortune in that little munitions-making scheme of his."

"He's a disgrace. Like Frankie, giving away what little the country's got. With a name like Roosevelt, I wouldn't be surprised if the president wasn't secretly Jewish. A traitor to his class and his country, playing right into the Nazi's hand." Ed paused. "He's a real S.O.B."

"Ed, really," his wife exclaimed.

The Nortons drained their glasses and went home early, brought together for the moment by a crack in the seamless harmony of the Russells.

On Monday morning, Tom was about to ask his secretary at the bank to take a letter to the headmistress when he was called into a meeting. But Margaret Graham was already out in her old galoshes, hands thrust into the pockets of her leather jacket, crossing the school field with Mr. Dooley. "I appreciate your concern, Mr. Dooley, giving up your Sunday like that."

Mr. Dooley shook his head. "Too much to bucket off this time."

They stopped at the edge of the affected area. "I can hardly smell a thing, Mr. Dooley, only faintly."

"The ground won't take it any more, missus. I had to set up a heavy mud-puppy pump and run the waste down the slope beyond the eighth-grade building." He led the headmistress along the line where the hose had been. At the far corner of the building, a gully had formed midway down the incline from the force of the runoff. A triangle of matted and stained grass fanned out almost to the junipers that divided the school property from the sidewalk beyond. From her vantage point, Margaret could see over the lilacs across Parker Farm Road and into the Russells' front yard. Several years ago, after the hurricane, when the city had once again flatly refused to extend the sewer system to accommodate Parker Farm Road on the grounds of "extraordinary expense relative to per capita use," she had watched the concrete walls of the Russells' newfangled septic system being poured. At the time, Harry Lewis had estimated it cost Ed Russell hundreds of dollars to install the six-foot-square holding tank—about a fifth of the capacity it would take to marginally cover the school's needs.

She considered the situation for a moment. If matters got any worse, some stickler in the neighborhood would surely lodge a serious complaint. She sighed. But then the inordinate expense of replacing the old cesspit would be ludicrous for something so mundane. There were far more important financial issues at stake. Continuing scholarship aid to refugee children, for instance. She turned to Mr. Dooley.

"I think since this is school vacation, you and I can take care of these things without alarming others. We have another week before the children come back. Surely the residue will go away in a day or two."

"If you say so, missus."

"It always has before." She looked directly into the janitor's face.

Mr. Dooley gave no response.

"I tell you what we'll do," Miss Graham said, heading back along the side of the building. "You rake the slope as best you can. With a little luck, in a few weeks the grass will be greener than ever." She gave a little laugh. "And in the meantime, I'll speak to Mr. Lewis when I have the chance."

But the escalation of events abroad through a fearful May and June swept aside all other concerns for the people of West Ivers. The seizure of Norway by German forces, the invasion of Denmark, the surrender of the Low Countries. Terms like "sweat box," "flogging," "tree-binding" appeared in the Jewish press, leaked from a British government report detailing Nazi atrocities. The refugee women working at the Back Door Store recalled relatives and friends, glancing into each other's anxious faces as they stitched up the copies of their native dress or waited on the customers at the pastry counter.

The new prime minister of Britain, Winston Churchill, offered chilling words: "Blood, toil, tears, and sweat . . . victory at all cost. . . for without victory there is no survival." Only heroic Britain stood between the United States and the enemy now. There was already the menace of Nazi U-boats along the Atlantic coast and the German army stood poised across the English Channel. At the university, the professors bemoaned the lack of scholarly access brought about by the war between such great cultures. Humanists among the students, meeting on the library steps or gathered in the dining halls, the ashes from their cigarettes streaking the white tablecloths, lingered to review and reinterpret the Franco-Prussian War or the Crimean struggle, the scope of the Great War in the light of today's alliances. The scientists paused in their laboratory investigations to discuss the use of radar to detect approaching enemy aircraft or the implications of splitting the atom. For a moment, the young hotheads among them promised to join the English and win the war; then feeling powerless, returned to their research. The few remaining German students at the university quietly finished up their studies and returned home.

But not everyone despaired in these troubled times. On Thursday afternoons, after the picture show, Mary and Nora and the other Irish maids gathered at Kathleen's Cakes and Jellies for biscuits and tea. Just among themselves, they had no trouble mocking the English and their big military ways. They shook their heads at the bitter memories. "A taste of their own medicine they're after getting."

In late June, Margaret Graham reluctantly agreed to go to the evening show of *Gone With the Wind* at the University Theater with Eleanor Osgood. It was sure to be a travesty of Civil War history, and she never could trust a man as good-looking as Clark Gable. Sentimental twaddle. But it was the fall of France that made Margaret catch her breath. In the newsreel, she followed the long lines of German troops and their machinery of war. Coming directly at her on the film through the Arc de Triomphe. The sound of boots marching down the Champs-Elysees, as if they were crushing all that was honorable before them. She wept openly with the French men and women on the screen who watched, inconsolable, from the sidelines.

Through the summer of 1940, the whole country listened to the evening news. German dive-bombing *Stukas* whistling terror as they traveled across the channel and up the South Downs to dump their load, day or night. The Royal Air Force night bombing German targets. Reports of German losses over England, 90 bombers shot down in one week in July, 180 on one day in August. The heroism of RAF Spitfire pilots as the Battle of Britain escalated. The eyewitness reports by radio journalist Edward R. Murrow of the death and devastation of a great city, ". . . black columns of smoke from the ashes of London." The familiar tagline at the end of each broadcast, "Goodnight, and good luck," touched listeners across the sea as if it were a final farewell to the civilized world.

At the first assembly of the Parker Farm School in September that year, Miss Graham read Psalm 121, "I will lift up mine eyes unto the hills, from whence cometh my help." The program ended with the whole school singing the first verse of "Jerusalem," the voices almost exalting in the last lines, "and was Jerusalem builded here/ on England's green and pleasant land."

Molly and Patsy were put in separate sections of the sixth grade, but Jenny thought it only glued them more together. Now, when she went to Patsy's house to play, Patsy and Molly often locked themselves in Patsy's room. She would have to sit in front of the closed door and wait. Sometimes when one of them came out to go to the bathroom, the other would beckon her in. But then neither one would keep the other out and that was really unfair. One afternoon when she was sitting in the hall, her knees drawn up under her chin, Mrs. Russell came upstairs with a pile of clean towels. She leaned over and whispered in Jenny's ear, "They are behaving badly, getting your goat like this. Poor little Jenny. But I bet if you go away, they'll come out." Jenny thought for a moment, then slumped off, but she never did find out if it worked, if they unlocked the door.

For a while Molly went to Pearl Lewis' house. Jenny and Patsy found that very mysterious. Then, one evening before supper, when she was listening from the hall, Jenny overheard her father tell her mother that Mr. Norton's bank was loaning money to help finance the expansion of Mr. Lewis' new business. "Money makes strange bedfellows," her father said and laughed. Maybe that explained Molly and Pearl being together, but then suddenly, Pearl was always with her Jewish friend who lived in an apartment with a balcony in Riverside.

When Jenny's father was home now, he and her mother listened to the six o'clock news together. In the morning they exchanged pages of the *New York Times*. At suppertime, they always seemed to be discussing something important, only half-listening when she recited her part of the Declaration of Independence for the Thanksgiving assembly. But after supper they still went their separate ways. Her father to his study or out to a meeting, her mother to read in the living room or to do her telephoning.

Jenny took refuge with Mary, sometimes visiting in her room over the garage. Mary would play the accordion and sing "O Danny Boy" while Jenny lay on her bed looking up at Jesus where he hung on the wall, arms spread out on the cross, a shriveled palm tucked behind his halo.

Suddenly, Patsy and Molly included Jenny again. They did their homework together. They slapped their thighs and galloped across the school fields, whinnying as they went. They dared each other to go under the cemetery fence, then, glancing at the rows of stones that marked the dead, suddenly became self-righteously obedient to the TRESPASSING FORBIDDEN sign. One afternoon in late autumn, they were collecting horse chestnuts from the tree in Patsy's garden, forcing open the prickly burs that still held the fruit, polishing the hard brown shells on the sleeves of their jackets. Snatching off their mittens to feel the smoothness in their fingers, they dropped the nuts into their knit caps as a kind of receptacle. As they lined up their haul at the far edge of the back lawn, Patsy began naming her shiny nuts after illustrious grandparents, special aunts and important uncles, cousins, and even second cousins once removed. Jenny and Molly stopped to watch. As she spoke each name, Patsy nestled a horse chestnut in the stubby frozen grass. Jenny knew Patsy's relatives were all rich and socially "set," as her mother would say, but Molly's were not far behind. One of her great grandfathers might have been Vice President of the United States if some dirty Democrat hadn't snatched it from him. Jenny was choked with panic. She had to squeeze her eyes tight to keep from crying. What did she have? A dead grandmother who was in the train station the day after President Garfield was shot. An aunt in Illinois or Kansas or some other no place. Finally she blurted out, "Mr. Churchill is my cousin. My mother's actually. Very distant."

Molly looked up from her row of glossy relatives. "Who's that?"

Jenny tried to give her a superior smile like Mrs. Parker's and brushed the hair off her forehead. Then she busied herself collecting her nuts in the bowl of her skirt. "He's a very important person in the newspaper," she said brusquely.

"My father says he's a con man," Patsy announced.

"He is not, he's English," Jenny screeched at her.

"You're a liar anyway," Patsy said.

"Liar, liar," they hissed as they charged at her. "Liar, liar," they shouted after her as she slipped through the hedge and ran home.

"'Oh sure, pay them no mind. It was all a lark.'" Mary tried to console her. "Tell them I'll stuff them down the incinerator, if they don't mind themselves."

But even Mary couldn't make it better, because the fact was that Patsy and Molly were right. She had lied. The truth was she was no good at lying. No one ever believed her the way her mother believed Perfect Katherine when she said she'd be at the library when actually she was meeting her friends at the movies. Jenny dragged herself up to her room and flopped down on her bed, burying her face in her pillow. Making up things like important relatives didn't turn out right. And even if Patsy and Molly had believed her, it wasn't the truth. She rolled over on her back. There was nothing really special about her. If Hitler dropped one of his bombs on her, no one would care. She studied the boring pattern of snowflakes on the yellow wallpaper. This would be her whole life now. Locked alone in her room. She wept a little, then slipped into a kind of emptiness, like waking up from an afternoon nap, hot and sticky and tired. She knew, knew for sure, that nothing good would ever happen.

But in January 1941, the president proposed the Lend-Lease Program to Mr. Churchill—a gentleman's agreement, "like loaning your neighbor your garden hose." Then Rosemary Bent-Wilson arrived from England to stay with the Parkers, on loan, so to speak, for the duration of the war.

Chapter Eleven

Rosemary Bent-Wilson's winter coat was so different that Jenny fell in love at first sight. She was shuffling down the path from her house on a shivery winter morning, the buckles on her galoshes rattling like the bones of ghosts. She stooped to snap them tight and her book bag slid forward over her shoulder. When she looked up, Mrs. Parker was escorting someone down the road. The new girl. In a voluminous heavy-knit jacket that reached below the middle of her thighs, giving a flounce effect to the pleats of her skirt sticking out beneath. Rows of white reindeer drifted across a royal blue background, and the buttons were like silver coins. The neck was open around a bright red muffler, and Jenny could see the tattersall flannel lining. With it, the girl wore a white knit hat. A long, dark braid tied with a red ribbon hung down her back. Her gloves matched her muffler, and on her feet she had knee-high smooth black boots. Across her chest was the strap of a canvas satchel that hung at her far side like a soldier's kit bag. Jenny had never seen anyone so elegant.

Weeks later she found out that the sweater jacket had been a going-away present from Rosemary's mother. It was one of her favorite stories. Although Jenny came to realize that Rosemary often fiddled with the truth, this sounded real. "Selfridge's. Young ladies—and *very* dear. Mummy wanted something for all occasions *and* room to grow." Rosemary shivered with pleasure. "Tea at Fortnum's. We'd gone up for the day. We thought the bombs were going get us. It was beastly exciting." What was it like to be in an air raid? Jenny couldn't imagine.

Once, Rosemary pointed out that her whole outfit displayed the colors of the British flag. "Same as the American," Jenny informed her. To Rosemary, British was older and therefore superior, and Jenny almost believed her. But even before she knew these fascinating facts, she longed to have the jacket, unaware then of the loneliness she would feel when it was finally hers.

"Jenny," Mrs. Parker called. She snapped the last buckle and stood up.

"Do meet Rosemary. Rosemary, this is Jenny Oliver. Jenny, this is Rosemary Bent-Wilson," Mrs. Parker said too cheerfully. "Rosemary is going to be in Mr. Johns' class."

Rosemary removed a glove and stuck out her hand. "Frightfully pleased to meet you."

Jenny took off both mittens and waited, unsure of what to do next. "That's my class."

"Oh splendid. Rosemary, you've found a friend already." Mrs. Parker sounded too eager, like Jenny's mother when she was in a hurry.

"My Aunt Isabel—well, to be precise she is only a cousin by marriage, but we have agreed that I shall call her 'aunt'—she has been most kind to sponsor me in your country," Rosemary explained. "She doesn't have any children any more, that is they're grownups now, and then, you see, I'm different. I am English." She gave a Cheshire cat grin, the corners of her mouth lifting the soft pads of her cheeks so that they almost closed her eyes. It was the first time Jenny had ever felt enveloped.

"Hello." Jenny stuck out a hand too late. She felt so awkward, the all-arms-and-legs her mother complained about, the fumble-fingers Katherine called her.

Rosemary smiled again and took Jenny's hand. "'Howdy,'" she said. She laughed a fairy-bell giggle. "They showed a cowboy film on the ship. It was top rate. Mummy would never have let me see it. One of the women wore net stockings and practically no skirt at all."

"Howdy, pardner," Jenny answered from as deep in her voice as she could go, then guffawed at her own cleverness.

Mrs. Parker interrupted. "You don't want to be late the first day, Rosemary."

Jenny fell in beside her exotic new acquaintance, made more thrilling by the acceptance of Mrs. Parker, whom she knew to be very grand. The three of them proceeded in silence down Parker Farm Road.

At the entrance to the school, Rosemary stopped

and turned to Mrs. Parker. She stuck out her hand
again. "Thank you terribly, Auntie Isabel. I shall go on
from here with Jenny."

Mrs. Parker took Rosemary's hand and bent to
kiss her on the forehead. "Are you sure, dear?"

"Perfectly."

"Well, all right, if you think so. I'm sure it's good
for you to be on your own right from the start. I'll just
step into the office to tell Miss Graham you're here."

"That won't be necessary. After I finished the tests
yesterday and she took me to meet Mr. Johns, I promised I would pop in to say good morning. We always
say good morning to the head." Rosemary turned to
Jenny. "Mr. Johns is rather a sweetie, isn't he? He put
his arm around my shoulder when he said good-bye."

Jenny made a face at the thought of being touched
by Mr. Johns. Mrs. Parker looked puzzled. "Did he
really?"

"She'll have me," Jenny reassured Mrs. Parker.

"Yes, Jenny, that's nice," Mrs. Parker said. "Perhaps Rosemary's been on her own rather too long.
Show her how we do things, Jenny."

Right from the beginning, Jenny knew she never
wanted to leave Rosemary's side. But the remarkable
thing was that Rosemary didn't seem to mind. After
she had shaken Miss Graham's hand and that of the
secretary in the outer office as well, while Jenny stood
mute and marveling, they sailed like royalty into the
sixth-grade classroom, a little late, Rosemary extending her hand, nodding her head, melting them with her

smile as she moved through the roomful of sixth graders. Jenny followed behind.

"Here you are at last, Rosemary," Mr. Johns said
when she reached him. "I can see our new member,
Rosemary Bent-Wilson, will be at home with us. Take
your seats, please, class."

Nobody moved.

"As you all know," Mr. Johns went on as if he
were giving an oration like Miss Graham, "Rosemary
has come to us from England, where her countrymen
are fighting like heroes to turn back the Nazi threat to
the world." Rosemary gave a small nod of her head in
acknowledgment. "Jenny, why don't you take Rosemary to her cubby where she can hang up her beautiful jacket."

"Jenny can take her seat, sir. I know where my
cubby is."

Of course, Jenny did what Rosemary said. She
unloaded her book bag on her desktop and sat down,
still in her coat and galoshes.

"Yes, Rosemary," Mr. Johns said deferentially,
"that will be fine." As his eyes followed Rosemary, the
class wriggled and scuffed with expectation. Finally
Mr. Johns faced forward. "Sit down," he ordered.
There was a shuffle of chairs. "Jenny, hang up your
coat. We're wasting work time, class, and it will take
a lot of practice over the next few months to be ready
to draw the map of the United States from memory at
the end of the school year. Now, when you are copying
from the map here at the board, try to keep in mind

the shape of each state and how it lies in relationship to its neighbors. Think carefully how the rivers flow. What does Texas produce, Patsy?"

"Oil."

"Very good. Massachusetts, Jeffrey?"

"Cloth."

"Yes, textiles. Anything else?" Mr. Johns waited but no hand went up. "Agriculture. Remember the apples that go into your Thanksgiving pie. And don't forget the state capitals. We have to know those too. A little memory work in class each week will help you along. Now get out your pencil and paper."

Rosemary gave Jenny one of her smiles as they passed at the cloakroom door. "Over here, Rosemary, please," Jenny heard Mr. Johns say. "I've put your desk where I can be of help to you until you get used to us."

"Thank you, sir."

When Jenny came back into the room, Rosemary was smiling up directly into the teacher's face, her long, dark braid reaching down to her waist. Jenny could tell he wanted to touch it. She was amazed that Rosemary didn't mind Mr. Johns.

Everyone loved Rosemary. With her pippin-pink cheeks and brown hair, the symmetry of the triangular lines of her shoulder blades, her perfect carriage. Her slender legs, narrow ladylike feet and knees, visible between the top of her socks and the hem of her skirt, but not prominent. She had beautiful manners. She spoke familiarly of "my" king and queen. She seemed on the best of terms with the princesses, Elizabeth and

Margaret Rose. "Lilibet can drive a lorry, I saw her picture in the paper." Or, "My skirt is the same tartan that Margaret Rose wears." In the movies on Saturday morning she sang out like a trumpet "God save our gracious king," while the rest of the audience stumbled through "My country 'tis of thee." She spoke with an accent that sounded like the math teacher's clarinet. Above all, Rosemary was English.

All the mothers and fathers on Parker Farm Road found this charming in Rosemary. Once, when Mrs. Russell offered her a second piece of lemon cake— "Poor little thing, separated from your mother like that, another piece will do you good"— Rosemary replaced the teacup in the saucer in her lap and crossed her ankles. "No, thank you, ma'am. I've had quite enough," she said in her regal tone.

"I do love to hear you speak, Rosemary," Mrs. Russell gushed.

One afternoon at the Nortons', while the others were buttoning up to go home, Mr. Norton paused in the hallway, stirring gently so as not to bruise the gin. He smiled and shook his head. "You'll knock 'em dead in a few years, Rosemary."

Rosemary looked up at him and grinned. "Oh, I do hope so, sir."

"That's right, look up to them, Rosemary, just like that. All the boys like that."

She called Professor Parker "Uncle Cy" and he called her "my English Rose." She referred to Miss Graham as The Head when the students talked about her, but she knew better than to embarrass Miss Graham to her face. Mrs. Lewis asked her where she got her Mediterranean coloring, and Mr. Lewis consulted her on the term "spanner."

Jenny's mother was the worst. She acted as if *Rosemary* were related to Winston Churchill. "Terrible, bombing a cathedral like that," she would say as she served the pudding. "I asked Mary to make this especially for you. She used the gooseberry jam." Or, "Your navy has sunk the *Bismarck*, Rosemary." For a time, even Mary admitted the English weren't all blackguards.

Rosemary was good at things like jump rope, jacks, cutting strings of paper dolls, tracing pictures of horses. She could set the table properly, fork on the left, knife on the right, blade turned in. She was always among the first chosen by the captains for teams, and after a while, nobody paid attention to Fred Goldstein racing across the assembly-room floor like a speed skater to be at her side in folk dancing.

She couldn't do math. And she was really not good at remembering things for the memory map of the United States, but then maybe she was right. Maybe it was because she was English.

But really, Jenny wasn't even tempted to be jealous of Rosemary, the way she sometimes was of Patsy, who got to be line leader all the time. Or Fred, who always took what he wanted, like a new piece of chalk or the last cracker on the plate, and got away with it because everyone was afraid he'd have a tantrum. Jenny knew

Rosemary was way beyond her.

And there was Mr. Johns. No one was surprised that Rosemary was his most favorite. He always played favorites, usually girls who were small and pleasant like Pearl or pretty like Molly. Sometimes, one of the boys sneered "teacher's pet" at one or the other of them. He corrected their spelling papers from behind, over their shoulders, his small wiry body almost surrounding them, instead of standing at the right of their desks the way he did with the rest of the class. He noticed their clothes and their haircut, and found their mistakes in grammar amusing, like someone's uncle. He looked at them over the heavy frame of his glasses. He stared right through Jenny. When she thought about favoritism, she viewed it as a mixed blessing. Of course she would like to be chosen once in a while. It would mean that she was considered sweet or agreeable. But then, how could she be valiant like Robin Hood or wily like Huck Finn? Besides, she wasn't pleasant or pretty. She was lumpy, and sometimes she meddled. "Little pitchers have big ears," her father said when she eavesdropped. When she thought of Mr. Johns's body hovering over her, those tiny mouse teeth when he smiled—actually, she wouldn't really like to be noticed like that.

Rosemary claimed she didn't care. "Don't be daft," she said, when Jenny pointed out how he grabbed her hand to demonstrate how to hold the cutting knife in craft period. "He was showing me how to give it more force."

"Not me," Jenny said. He just told me to push harder."

It was a Friday afternoon in March when Rosemary first met the Beasty. She and Jenny were on their way down Parker Farm Road to the assembly hall to attend afternoon dancing class. The sky hung wet and close and piles of dirty snow lay heavy on the landscape. Still they hurried along with an air of anticipation, Jenny's open galoshes rattling. Rosemary carried her party shoes in her kit bag. They were bareheaded to preserve as best they could the perfection of their hairdos. Rosemary's dark hair hung loose almost to her waist, carefully fanned out across the back of her jacket. It was held off her face by a white satin ribbon. Jenny's short brown bob was less noticeable, but Katherine had told her that moisture in the air gave hair body. Jenny was aware of her white knee socks, whereas Rosemary had on the rayon stockings she had purchased at the ladies lingerie counter of the Five-and-Ten. Jenny knew the secret. Rosemary's stockings were held up by blue garters, but that didn't make wearing knee socks any better. When they reached the Nortons' driveway, where they picked up Patsy and Molly, Jenny was relieved to see they had on knee socks, too. They all linked arms and proceeded down the hill, the front line moving into combat.

Dancing school itself made Jenny anxious; going to it was the part she liked best about these twice-monthly forays. She liked the feeling of expectation, the hope that some of the glamour and popularity of the others would rub off on her. She knew that she would be acknowledged by the boys as Rosemary's close friend and ignored by Mr. Knox, the teacher, who preferred those girls he referred to as "young ladies." "Glide, Jenny. Right foot forward. Glide like a soft cloud. No, not like a Mexican jumping bean." Jenny was safe. She would not be asked to demonstrate how to greet the hostesses, or the right placement of white-gloved hands, one on the boy's shoulder, the other in a dirty palm.

As they broke rank at the entrance of the school, Jenny saw the Beasty sprawled out on a snowbank like a great. dark octopus, limbs dangling over the hump of the mound. His damp stringy hair was plastered to his forehead, and he wore a black watch cap perched on his large pink ears. His mittens hung limp at the cuffs of his jacket as he looked down into a box camera he held before him.

"Halt," he commanded.

Molly and Patsy drew closer together. Jenny looked at Rosemary.

"What is it, pet?" Rosemary asked him.

He looked up at her for a moment. "Halt," he said, less confidently.

"I'm waiting here for you to take a snap." Rosemary. said, posing prissily.

He clicked the shutter.

"There you go. Tally ho." She gave a little wave and led the way down the path to the assembly building.

Patsy hurried forward to catch up with her. "That's the Beasty, Rosemary. He's a German." She said it with the air of one in the know.

"We don't like him." Molly shook her blonde curls to make her point.

"Besides, he's tetched in the head," Jenny explained. "And he took your picture."

"In the gloom like this? He probably doesn't even have film in his little box Brownie."

Jenny said, "I know he has a dagger, but it's only wood," but it didn't seem like much.

All through basic steps—"Feet together, forward step, gently with the wrist, men, side step, side step, slide one two three, altogether, *please*"—Jenny watched for the Beasty. Then during the elimination dance, after she was mercifully counted out and Rosemary was soaring around the room with beady-eyed Fred Goldstein, Jenny spied the Beasty treading through the snowbanks from one window to the next, peeping in at them. She wondered if being backward meant you didn't mind being left out.

At the break, Mr. Knox stepped into the hall to switch on the overhead lights and the lady at the piano went to the washroom. Rosemary took this opportunity to show off her red velvet dance dress to the school cook, who was standing at the kitchen door. When the cook turned to admire Jenny's dress, her blue smocked print seemed babyish and made her feel fat. To avert the cook's attention, Jenny pointed out the Beasty, stationary now, his face squished against a window-pane. As the cook hurried over to rap on the glass and shoo the intruder away, Rosemary dropped a slight curtsy to the Beasty. Maybe the Beasty got a picture of that, too. The cook disappeared into the hall, and Mr. Knox came back in time to catch Rosemary giving the Beasty one of her Cheshire cat grins.

"You'll only get into trouble that way, Rosemary," Mr. Knox scolded. "We don't mock people, do we? He'll only take it as encouragement."

Rosemary looked through Mr. Knox and wrinkled up her nose as if he smelled. "Excuse me, sir."

Mr. Knox pursed his lips. "Thank you, Jenny, for bringing this to Cook's attention."

Jenny looked up at Mr. Knox with innocent brown eyes. "I was only trying to be helpful," she said, feeling rather important.

In the grand circle, at the close of the lesson, Jenny was one of the girls who had to be a boy, since there were never enough of them. Each time she passed her, Rosemary grinned hideously like a gargoyle. When they did allemande left, Rosemary whispered, "Perfect Miss Priss." But Jenny didn't really mind, because she knew she had gotten Rosemary's goat bringing her to Mr. Knox's attention.

On the way up the road after dancing class, Rose-mary went ahead with Fred, her long hair perfectly rearranged across her jacket. Jenny was happy to take her time, walking with Patsy and Molly and a few of the boys. But she was relieved to see Rosemary waiting at the foot of the walk.

Rosemary hailed her with a loop-the-loop swing of her shoe bag. "It's not dark yet. Maybe Hilda has some goodies for the goody-goody."

"You're really mad at me."

"Of course not, silly old bear. You're like Mummy when I teased her about getting me out of her hair, shipping me off to America—she's always saying, 'Do get out of my hair, Rosemary, I'm busy' or 'Stop nattering, you're in my hair.' When I fussed about being sent away, she wept. 'You mustn't think things like that, *dahling*. You know how much I love you, *dahling*.'" Rosemary flashed her grin. "She's such a fearful fraud, my mum." She let out a shriek as she dashed off, swinging her kit bag fiercely.

Jenny hitched up her knee socks and followed. Rosemary rarely mentioned her mother, and this was the first time she'd mocked her. Jenny was often critical of her own mother, but she could not imagine being without her. Was Rosemary angry at her mother? Did she ever miss her?

On ordinary afternoons after school, now that the ice was getting too soft to go to the skating club, Rosemary and Jenny went occasionally to Patsy's or Molly's. When spring came and Rosemary dared them to trespass, as a gang they roamed through the cemetery to spy on the lovers wrestling about under the shrubs, while Rosemary explained: "He most surely has his tongue in her mouth. That's when his trousers get big." But then Pearl cried when the boy rolled over on top of the girl, and they had to run. Jenny was sort of alarmed, too—wasn't he crushing her?—but she knew better than to cry. Once, she had overheard Katherine whispering into the phone, "He was all over me." Is that what she meant?

Mostly, if Jenny didn't have to get her hair cut or take a piano lesson, or Rosemary hadn't done her makeup work in American history, they holed up in Rosemary's third-floor room, a cupola with windows all around. They spent the afternoons listing the things that they didn't like about their classmates or teachers and looking at the ads for brassieres and Kotex pads in the movie magazine that Jenny had "borrowed" from Katherine's room. Sometimes, Rosemary would stand before the mirror, tilting back her head to let her hair hang down like the pictures of Linda Darnell or Rita Hayworth, and practice being kissed.

The first Tuesday afternoon in June, Jenny followed Rosemary through the kitchen in hopes Hilda had a left out a plate of cookies or a few slices of bread and butter, then up the front stairs and along the landing on the second floor to the narrow staircase leading to the cupola. Rosemary threw herself and her satchel onto the bed while Jenny checked out the window. She felt like Zeus on his mountaintop. The sun was higher. It made the new roof on the Russells' house shine. The garage doors were open at the Lewises'. That meant Mr. Lewis was at the factory, "hauling in the shekels." Jenny quoted Mr. Russell at the dinner table once, and her mother sent her to her room. Looking further up the road into the Beasty's yard, she could see his German shepherd straining at his chain. Right then, her mother's car pulled into the driveway. Mrs. Goldstein got out of the passenger side. That meant Fred might be at her house after boys' baseball. Her mother would ask the Goldsteins to stay for supper, and for dessert, they'd have tinned raspberries from her mother's precious supply. Her mother would call it "potluck," and Mary would mutter, "Potluck, indeed." People only came when her father was away.

"Can I stay for supper?" she asked.

"I shan't be here," Rosemary said, her nose in a book. "Oh, I shall never remember all those states and capitals for the memory map on Friday. I simply cannot endure it. Those awful lakes at the top hanging down like teats on a goat." Rosemary drew a link of imaginary sacs in the air with her finger.

"Tell me where you're going."

"I'm going to have tea with Wilhelm and his housekeeper, if you must know. He promised me the loan of something."

Jenny lunged onto the bed and grabbed Rosemary's wrist. "You can't do that, Rosemary, he's the Beasty."

Rosemary shook her hand free. "He's just a big baby, not quite right in the noggin. He's chauffeured to a special school somewhere." She pointed vaguely west. "Wilhelm's a sweet thing, really."

"How would you know?" Jenny challenged.

"I was talking with him in his yard yesterday afternoon."

"But we were here yesterday afternoon. I was doing our math."

"I left school early. The dentist, remember?" Rosemary examined her even white teeth in the hand mirror on her night table.

Jenny nodded. "What happened? Why didn't you tell me?"

"On the way up the road from the trolley stop, that dog began barking, so I stepped into the yard and said, 'Do pipe down, dog,' and the big thing stopped his noise. Wilhelm was standing on the steps."

"Weren't you scared?"

"He was quite harmless. He was scraping at a stick with that knife. He had his camera on a string around his neck. He looked like a pudgy giant cabbageworm in his green shirt. He asked me if I liked dumplings."

"Does your Aunt Isabel know you're going to his house?"

"Of course not. She's at Bundles for Britain this evening."

Jenny was frantic. "But Patsy told you, he's *German*."

"I told him his Mr. Hitler had driven me from my country. And when he said I was just like the Jews, I said he didn't even know what a Jew was like. There were two of them in our class."

"Pearl doesn't count."

"Of course, she does."

Jenny made one last attempt. "Dumplings." She made a face. "People don't have dumplings for tea."

"You wouldn't understand, you're American." Rosemary shook her head. "It's high tea. I told Hilda I was going to your house for supper."

Jenny gave up. "I wish you were. Awful Fred will be there."

The next morning, Jenny slipped out early. She opened the door of the farmhouse very quietly, but Hilda stepped out of the kitchen, "She says she's sick." Hilda put her hands on her hips and lifted her eyebrows. "Nothing wrong with her, if you ask me, but the Mr. and Mrs. don't treat her like their own. She gets away with everything." Jenny started down the hall. "No, you don't. You'll be late to school "

All day, she willed the time to pass. When she finally reached the cupola after school, Rosemary was still in bed, with all the windows closed. Her long hair hung loose in clumps of snarls. "The dumplings were mushy," she announced.

Jenny pounced down on the end of the bed. "What happened?"

"I feel slightly woozy. Aunt Isabel wondered if it was something I ate at your house, so don't tell her."

Jenny started to open the window.

"No, I don't want fresh air. I'm trying to stay sick."

"What did the Beasty do?"

"He was a nothing, a beastly baby." Rosemary said peevishly. He followed me about with that camera of his. When we went into the library to get the book he'd promised me, I asked him if there was film in the camera. He didn't seem to understand."

"Did you see the picture of Hitler?"

Rosemary sat up. "I certainly would not go into a boy's bedroom," she said indignantly. "It wouldn't be proper. Besides, he was such a nuisance I didn't have a chance to look. He's worse than my little brother. You'd never know he was fourteen, he's so fat and stupid, like a big booby." She wrinkled up her nose. "Finally, I asked the housekeeper to make him stop pointing the thing at me. She said he was a very special boy and there were plenty of Germans who were nice. That made me think of them shooting at us. My father calls them Bloody Huns," Rosemary whimpered. "Sometimes I miss Fav."

Jenny glanced at the snapshot of Mr. Bent-Wilson on the bureau. He was in his uniform, and he had a nasty looking stick under his arm. Even so, he was Rosemary's father. Jenny didn't really know how to comfort someone, but she reached across to put her hand on Rosemary's shoulder.

"I'll beat the Beasty up for you," she offered. "I wrestled with him once."

Rosemary whispered conspiratorially. "I think he spies on us at school."

Jenny agreed. "Remember dancing class?"

"He knows about the memory map," Rosemary said. "He loaned me his mother's atlas. It has lovely, dark outlines."

Rosemary stayed out for the rest of the week. On Friday, on the honor system, Mr. Johns allowed Rosemary to do her memory map at home.

Later that afternoon, Jenny found Rosemary sitting in the middle of her bed, fully dressed for the first time in days. She was braiding her hair.

"I thought you were still sick."

"When Aunt Isabel came to take my map to Mr. Johns, she said I looked much better. She said I should come downstairs for tea. I thought you could return the book to the Beasty."

"You traced the map, didn't you?"

"It's not my country." Rosemary extracted the book from under her mattress and handed it to Jenny. "Tell the Beasty I'm not allowed to go to his house anymore."

"But Rosemary . . ." For a moment Jenny thought she dared tell Rosemary she was a liar and a cheat, taking advantage of a poor dumb thing. But then she remembered the summer after the third grade, when she didn't want to play with the Beasty any more.

"Oh don't look so shocked," Rosemary said.

"At least I didn't break the honor code." For once Jenny felt superior.

"Honor codes are old fashioned," Rosemary said, tying a blue ribbon to match her dress at the tip of her braid.

They went down to tea. Jenny had China tea with lemon for the first time. It wasn't as good as milk and sugar, but she wasn't going to admit it. Then she and

Rosemary curled up on the plush pillows of the huge, deep sofa while Mrs. Parker read to them from the *Just So Stories.*

On the way home, after she handed the atlas to the housekeeper, Jenny felt sorry for the poor Beasty, always being thrown over like that. She hoped it would never happen to her.

When Mr. Johns tacked up the memory maps the week of Closing Day, Rosemary's was at the front of the room, up above all the others. He shook his head in amazement. "An English girl comes into the sixth grade in the middle of the school year, and at the end of a few months, she produces an almost perfect memory map of the United States."

Chapter Twelve

Nineteen forty-one, the year an anxious country clung to the president's assurance: "We have nothing to fear but fear itself." Taxes went up and up again, government war agencies proliferated, the draft bill was extended. In the morning newspapers, the black-inked mass of the German war machine spread east into Russia and jumped the Mediterranean to North Africa. U-boats plundered the Atlantic shipping lanes, and when a hundred American sailors lost their lives in the sinking of a U.S. destroyer, it struck close to home.

But no one was prepared for the events of the day "that would live in infamy." Radio stations interrupted scheduled Sunday broadcasts to announce the attack on Pearl Harbor, December 7, 1941. The Monday morning headlines of the *New York Times* read: JAPAN WARS ON U.S. AND BRITAIN; MAKES SUDDEN ATTACK ON HAWAII; HEAVY FIGHTING AT SEA REPORTED.

Vera put aside the newspaper and called Richard at his Washington office, feeling the need of human connection that comes with the slow-growing grasp of shocking news—and a little hurt that he had not thought to call her. She was surprised to be told she could reach him at his hotel. "Yes, I was going to call you, but yesterday the entire capital was in a state of chaos. You couldn't get through to anyone."

She thought she heard a toilet flushing in the background. "Are you alone, Richard?"

"There was so much turmoil down at Justice, I decided I'd get more work done up here. Miss Sperry has just come along to take dictation."

The news pierced Vera's heart. She tried to speak evenly when she finally asked, "You mean you and Miss Sperry are working in your hotel room?"

"There'll be more work than ever now, but I'll try to be home in a few days."

Vera had to believe him. He couldn't be doing . . . anything. The image of Miss Sperry emerging from the bathroom in a lacy peignoir hovered before her. Oh, Richard, her heart cried out. But he wouldn't, not at a time of national crisis!

But over the weekend, when she found herself alone with Richard at cocktail time, she couldn't help herself.

"How did your week go?"

"Fine, and yours?"

"Fine."

They sat in silence for a few moments, Richard

sipping his drink, Vera busy with her own thoughts, her body rigid, her brow tight. Finally, she stood up with the plate of crackers as if she were about to pass it to him. "I have to ask, Richard."

He looked up at her with tired eyes. "What's on your mind, Vera?"

"Miss Sperry." She watched his eyes narrow.

"Yes, Miss Sperry." His tone was hesitant.

Vera stumbled on. "She was in your room, Richard. That's not decent."

"These are unusual times, Vera. The work has got to get done."

Are you . . . ?" She raised her eyebrows as if to finish the question.

He put his glass down. "Absolutely not, Vera."

"Really, Richard?"

"You know how I view the truth, Vera." He smiled thinly and picked up his glass.

The parents' committee met at the school on the following Monday. When Margaret arrived with Eleanor Osgood, a little early for the eight o'clock meeting, she was pleased to see that the cook had left a plate of homemade oatmeal cookies beside the cups and saucers on the serving table. Coffee, sugar, butter, all rationed in England. How much longer would there be such amenities in West Ivers? While Eleanor went into the kitchen to bring in the coffee urn, Margaret scanned the room quickly, stepping up to the mantel-piece to set straight the papier-mache Angel of Peace nesting in the hemlock boughs. Then she began to re-arrange the lunch tables into a horseshoe. She wanted everyone to feel a special unity this evening.

Last month's meeting had been a disappointment. After the reading of the minutes which always put her on edge—as secretary Vera read them as if she were reciting an epic poem, but it was parliamentary proce-dure—the discussion had been almost entirely about improving the school's physical plant. This was not a topic that interested her, but as treasurer, Harry carried weight, and his deferential manner made it impossible to restrain him without appearing uncivil.

But tonight, as she set the last chair in place, Margaret's head was spinning with anticipation. Now they were a community unified in war. She had not even admitted to Eleanor that, in a way, she found it a relief. She felt vindicated. For years she had been speaking out about the dangers to democracy, often to people who only tolerated her because they thought her harmless, a humorless old maid.

And then Harry had called yesterday. Pleasant, but more formal than usual? She couldn't really tell. He had been recruited as air-raid warden for the Great Hamilton Street district and requested time to address safety measures at the school. Surely they would all be in agreement on this subject. She knew this meeting promised something better than petty disagreements.

It wasn't often all fourteen members attended. Aca-demics, professionals and businessmen, Vera as secre-tary and Eleanor as right-hand man. Margaret placed her pencil and legal pad at the midpoint on the center table. She straightened the skirt of her gray wool dress and adjusted the green-and-black Liberty silk scarf at the neck, a sleek touch to soften her position of power. Then, she pulled out her hatpin and set her hat down beside her papers. An informal air would be best.

She resisted beginning the meeting with a quote from *Henry the Fifth*, the burying of differences, the rallying of the troops. Instead, she said with simple dignity, "Now we are a country at war. We have our work cut out for us. Before we start I would like to ask you all to join me in the Lord's Prayer." She smiled across one corner of the horseshoe at Harry, particularly somber tonight in his dark suit and navy blue tie. She took the Phi Beta Kappa key strung on a gold chain across his vest as a mark of the seriousness of the business at hand. He nodded his acknowledgment of her remarks without returning her smile and awkwardly squeezed the large scroll of white paper in his lap. There was the sound of cups and spoons being set aside. She bowed her head and began. "Our Father . . ." In ones and twos, the committee members followed her lead, some fervently, others hesitant and embarrassed, glancing furtively at Harry, until he was the only one who remained silent. At the "amen" there was a dead quiet.

"Now," Margaret began, eager to invade the discomfort she had unwittingly brought about, "we have important things to discuss tonight, and too little time. With my apologies to the secretary, I would like to dispense with reading of the minutes. Can I have a motion, please?" Someone obliged and everyone agreed. Margaret smiled at Vera and checked off Item 2 on the list before her.

"I have had many fine ideas from parents stepping up to face the emergency," she went on, "and I hope we will take the time tonight to consider all of them, but first, I want to hand the meeting over to Harry, who will speak to us on less contentious but more alarming matters even than money." She tittered nervously and leaned forward, avoiding Harry's eye. "Everyone knows how much I admire Harry. You will agree with me, he's an excellent choice for his latest job." Her voice twinkled with amends.

Harry leaned forward on his elbows, clasping his hands. He surveyed the faces of his fellow committee members, frozen in expressions of expectation or judgment made or withheld. Finally, he spoke. "Some of you may already know that I've been asked by City Hall to act as air-raid warden for this district. It goes without saying I am honored to serve my country in this way." He paused for a moment. Then he said, "It's no secret that New England and the rest of the East Coast are considered at risk, especially towns like West Ivers, close to the coastline." There were a few nods. "And our proximity to the Fort Floyd Arsenal across the river makes the school particularly vulnerable in the event of an attack."

The curator at the university museum spoke out. "That old arsenal has been an eyesore for years now.

What happened to the motion to tear it down?"

"I agree with you, Theodore, it's hardly a Roman ruin," Harry answered. "But if you've driven by in recent months you must have noticed the rows of tanks and trucks lined up in the parade ground before the main gate. Some of those vehicles have been around for years, but many of them are new. It's clear the arsenal is being used as a storage depot for overseas shipments." There were looks of surprise. "What we can't see is that inside those long, wooden sheds in the back are the holding areas for various kinds of high explosives, incendiaries, shells."

"Did they tell you that, Harry?"

"I knew it already. Some months ago, before the management at Wellington Brass settled their most recent labor dispute, my company, Izrael and Son, was approached to take on some of their wartime production commitments.

"We weren't even at war then, Harry."

"Isn't Wellington Ed Russell's clan?"

"It's his wife's family. Charlotte was a Wellington," Eleanor explained.

There was an uneasy silence. Margaret cleared her throat and looked across at Harry. "We'd all like to hear what you have to say about the school, Harry."

Harry sat back, the long lines of his face pinched. Then, with exaggerated calm, he placed his hands on the scroll in his lap. "Before I go on with my proposal to ensure the safety of the school, it's important that everyone on the committee know just where I stand.

Izrael and Son is one of the companies, including a division of Wellington, now making dies for many of the types of ammunition stored at the arsenal. We consider it helping the war effort."

"You people sell bullets?" someone asked incredulously. "That's amoral."

"There is a war on." Vera tried to sound supportive.

"That's all right, Vera." Harry spoke irritably, without looking at her. "It's not worth acknowledging."

"We really must move on." Margaret reset a large bone hairpin into her bun.

But Harry held up his hand to her. His eyes narrowed and the corners of his mouth tightened. "I don't want any misunderstandings, Margaret. Izrael and Son manufactures the steel dies for shells." Harry spoke deliberately. "We are a small company. We're not set up to stamp out the casings or produce the gunpowder and bullets." Everyone began talking at once.

"But is it right to make a profit from such things?"

"Well, the Wellingtons aren't precisely in business for their health."

"But that's an old Yankee outfit. They've been around since before the turn of the century."

Before Harry could speak to this, someone said, "Old money doesn't count anymore. It's really a crime, but somebody's going to make a packet on this war business."

"There's some truth to that," Harry said matter-of-factly, "but the difference is between a fair charge and profiteering. Competitive pricing is not criminal."

Then quite suddenly, to Harry's relief, the debate took a different direction.

"The real crime is storing such things near a school for children."

"The arsenal is less than a mile away as the crow flies."

"There ought to be a law against it. It's terrifying."

"It's very frightening." Harry took up the point quickly. "And in the event of an attack, I should warn you we really have only a rough idea of what to expect. Bombs, incendiaries. I'm told there's a very simple device known as a 'calling card,' phosphorus on a small card. I've forgotten my chemistry, but I think it's white phosphorus that ignites in the air; it would kindle tinder nicely. It's also poisonous. I don't know precisely how these things are distributed, low-flying planes perhaps? We've got to learn to identify enemy aircraft and help build up our air defense."

Words like "incendiaries," "ignite," "kindle." The committee was frozen in silence. For the first time Harry relaxed. Once again Margaret hurried in to say, "Shocking. It makes it all too real, doesn't it? But I want to reassure you. Harry tells me Civil Defense is first and foremost concerned for the safety of the children."

"Yes, tell us what can we do," Vera prompted.

"Thank you, I'll need the help of all of you. First I want to go through the procedures set up by Civil Defense." Everyone prepared to takes notes. Harry spoke easily now. "In case of attack, when the observers positioned along the coast spot enemy air craft, the alert will be sent to Civil Defense Headquarters at City Hall and sirens will go off all over the city. The alert will also be broadcast on the radio. The word YELLOW will mean the planes have been spotted and are an hour or more away. If it's RED, the bombs are imminent—minutes maybe. The civil defense manual says these incendiaries usually come ten or twenty at a time and suggests you scoop them up with a long-handled shovel and bury them in a bucket of sand." He looked up from his notes. "If any of you can do that, more power to you."

There was a flurry of protests. "But such a raid would be under cover of darkness. The children would be home in bed."

"Not necessarily."

"But here?"

"West Ivers? It's incomprehensible."

Harry pushed on. "The safest place to be in the event of an attack is below ground. If this is not possible, the next best thing is to crouch under a table or stand in a doorway or against a supporting wall away from windows."

"But Harry, the school." Margaret was alarmed. "Almost all the buildings have large section of window glass."

"Yes, Margaret, because of the architecture of the school, I consider it best to evacuate the school buildings in the event of *any* kind of alert. If it's a yellow

signal and we can get the students home, that would
be best, but if that's not possible, I propose the basements of Parker Farm Road as shelters. From the looks
of it some of them are built like fortresses. Poured
cement is fine, that's what I've got, probably you too,
Vera. But those old fieldstone foundations will do just
as well. Rocks like that shift position and hold rather
than cave. I'll need the committee's approval to make a
thorough inspection and see which spaces are safe for
children."

"It won't be very comfortable," Vera said, thinking
of her laundry and furnace rooms. Damp and bleak.
The sirens, the bombs. She imagined herself huddled
with Richard and the children against the wall
between the two rooms, or crouched under the folding
table in the laundry.

"Won't the neighbors resent the intrusion? Children in wet galoshes tracking snow through their
houses, marching up and down the cellar stairs. My
wife certainly would."

"During an attack?"

"You have our full support, Harry." An impas-
sioned Margaret spoke up. "Knock on any door and
tell them we sent you. Our first concern is for the
safety of the children."

After the unanimous vote to approve Harry's
plan was recorded in the minutes, Harry asked that a
letter of explanation and endorsement be sent to the
neighbors. He handed Margaret the list of names and
addresses.

"These are not all school parents, Harry," Margaret said.

"I can require them to comply by invoking civil-defense ordinances, but we don't want it to come to that. It will be easier now with the backing of this committee. Perhaps it would help if one of you came along with me." He glanced around the table—too many unresponsive faces. Then he reached for the white scroll. "I don't mean to scare you unduly, but it's rumored that Axis sympathizers are flashing messages to U-boats from the peak of Mt. Monadnock in New Hampshire. I thought I'd show you this." He unrolled the poster across the table and held it up. "I'm going to put one up in my machine shop." It showed a red, white and blue Uncle Sam holding his finger to his tight lips. A SLIP OF THE LIP MAY SINK A SHIP, it read across the bottom in bold letters.

"Oh, wonderful," Margaret exclaimed. "Eleanor will tack it up on our bulletin board."

Harry allowed himself a wry smile as he rolled up the poster and pushed it along the table toward the headmistress.

"Thank you, Harry, and thank you for that clear presentation. While the prospects are grim, we are in good hands. You have my full support." She smiled back at him, relieved to have gotten to this point without further discord from some of the more conservative members of the committee. She ostentatiously made a check on her list. "Now I'd like to take up the matter of . . ."

"Excuse me, Margaret," Harry said, "while I still have the floor. One more thing, if you don't mind."

Margaret looked irked. "We have quite a few more items on the agenda, Harry."

"It will only take a minute," Harry went on. "I want to bring the committee up to date on the waste problem." There were a few groans.

"Why don't you and I talk about it after the meeting?" Margaret said.

But Harry persisted. "I've had a chance to speak with Mr. Dooley. He agrees with me. What we have is hardly a 'system' at all. It's really nothing more than a cesspool."

"I'd really rather not have you questioning my employees." Margaret held her eyes on Harry's for a moment, then looked down at her pad. "It's true, occasionally Mr. Dooley does a little pumping."

"This is important to the whole school body," Harry said.

"We have to follow parliamentary procedure." Margaret tapped her pencil down on the tabletop.

"This is not a meeting about finances, Harry," someone said sourly.

"Let me explain, and I'm sure the committee will agree, we must allocate . . ."

Margaret interrupted him. "We have limited funds, and the physical safety and mental health of our students comes first."

"Very heartfelt, Margaret," Harry snapped, "but more to the point, one of these days, you won't be able to hide a sewage overflow. The authorities will close down the school."

"That's not possible. It's unimaginable." Margaret was indignant. She adjusted the scarf at her neck. "Should something happen, you can rest assured I'll take responsibility, Mr. Lewis," she said, packing all the authority she could into her pronouncement. "And now, if you don't mind, there are important matters to discuss."

The committee members followed this exchange with astonishment, stunned at the icy tone in the voices of the two former allies. Few would argue with the headmistress's concern for the children, and several had felt for some time that Lewis had gotten too big for his britches. But most could not ignore the threat in his warning. After all, Margaret did not have much of a head for the practical and the mundane. No one broke the few seconds of throttling silence before Margaret returned to the business of meeting. They covered a few items in a desultory way—a first aid course at the school, the wisdom of tracking the events of the war on a map in the central hallway—when Margaret could no longer ignore the fatigue in the room. It had been a hard evening, and the unity of the group had been disturbed. For the life of her, she could not keep Harry Lewis in check. Reluctantly, she acknowledged defeat. The meeting was adjourned. The committee members gathered up their papers, collecting in cliques of two or three, speaking in hushed tones. Two men at the coat rack broke apart and headed for the doorway when Harry approached.

"Pushy fellow," one of them said.

"No surprise," the other replied.

Harry and Vera had often walked up Parker Farm Road together after these meetings, but until now, they had been joined by Mrs. Parker, who had recently resigned from the committee to devote herself full-time to war work. Now, as she slipped into her coat and adjusted her hat, Vera was suddenly aware that most of the conversation on these walks had been between the other two, Isabel Parker continuing the business of the meeting or remarking on some item in the news. Even with nothing to say she was never at a loss. And Harry always responded with a murmur or a comment in that courteous way of his that often made Vera wonder what he was really thinking.

But after tonight's meeting, the air still filled with contention, the prospect of walking up the road alone with Harry was daunting. The same committee that had always worked as one was suddenly splintered, and Vera felt torn between loyalty to the headmistress and the school's principles and a growing sense that Harry's lucid pragmatism was more in keeping with her own approach to things. She admired Margaret Graham for her idealism—everyone did—but she had lost some of her majesty in Vera's eyes, stooping so low as to humiliate a man of Harry's integrity.

Vera did not tell people how much she admired Harry, "a prince among men," her mother used to say of their minister. She was not fool enough to lay herself open to ridicule. It was childish of her, but there had been times, walking between those two people of grace, Mrs. Parker and Harry Lewis, who always treated her with consideration, when Vera had felt she was princess to a king and queen.

Now it was up to her to make easy conversation on the way home, to dispel the dark afterthoughts of the meeting. "Small talk." She used to laugh when her mother said men liked that in a woman, but Vera had been young then. Nowadays she encouraged her daughters to polish the skill. It would smooth their way. But, of course, Jenny . . . Suddenly, Harry was standing before her. Vera tried to smile as she drew on her gloves. They stepped through the door into the cold, dark night. Her heart sank, but she would do the best she could.

She congratulated Harry on his appointment as district air-raid warden and remarked on how interesting the work must be. She asked him what he thought of President Roosevelt's address before Congress, and when he said he had been impressed, she said that Richard had said the same thing. She even pointed out the delicate beauty of the blue spruce silhouetted in the light from the Nortons' front porch Harry stood in silence for a few moments as if admiring the tree.

"It was a difficult meeting," he began, turning to face her in the thin light. "I appreciate your support. Perhaps I was too aggressive."

"Oh, you were . . . very forceful," Vera said,

searching for the right word.

He was smiling at her now. "I confess I really was trying to bully Margaret into taking some action. Of course, it's important that we take this civil-defense business seriously. And I admit a new septic system is not going to protect democracy, but it may be a more realistic concern for the school than the likelihood of enemy air raids."

"I think most people understood you were just being practical."

"Not all of our fellow members on that committee see things as we do, Vera, and a few of them are downright bigots. I hope the fact that you understand what I'm talking about doesn't get you in trouble with the rest of them."

"Oh, don't worry about me," she said too cheerfully. The thought had never crossed her mind, but she was touched by his concern for her. "Where I came from a girl was an upstart for even wanting to go to college. If she didn't get married she went into the mills."

"Sometimes I get impatient with the high and mighty. Too grand to deal with the crux of the problem. We're two of a kind, you and I. Look what you've accomplished with the Back Door Store."

Vera was delighted. "It's the refugee women, really."

"I know better," he said lightly, putting his hand under her elbow and proceeding to walk her up the hill. "And I would like you to be the one to come with me on my tour of the neighborhood cellars," he continued, bowing slightly, as if he were asking her to dance. "I'll draw up a list of a few basic requirements. Access, space, so forth. And if you like," he added, "I'll designate you my deputy warden."

Vera was thrilled. I'm thrilled, she wanted to shout, thrilled that you chose me. Too thrilled, she told herself. She mustn't undermine his trust in her by dithering. Men like Harry did not like that in a woman. Good sense prevailed. "Isn't Professor Parker going to be precinct warden for Parker Farm Road?"

"You know that already?"

"Jenny learned it from Rosemary."

"Professor Parker is a man with his head in the clouds. Don't misunderstand me, he'll be fine patrolling for cracks of light in the blackout. But he's not the man for this mission." Vera caught Harry's smile in the street light. "You and I will keep an eye on him. Sub rosa, of course."

"Of course." They had entered into a conspiracy.

They walked on in easy silence. When they reached Vera's house, she saw the two metal trashcans for the morning collection across the front path, making it awkward for Harry to escort her directly to the door. It flustered Vera. It would upset the courtly routine. And of course, it would not be so at the Parker house.

"Jenny should have put the trashcans by the driveway," Vera said bluntly.

"It's good for the children to take on a few household chores." Harry tipped his hat and Vera went up the walk. At the door she turned to see him standing there like a parent lurking in the background at Halloween. She hurried to put her key in the door, eager to be where she could soften any awkward reality in the events of the evening as she committed it to memory.

She opened the door on the sobs and shrieks of Katherine from upstairs. Jenny was sitting on the bottom step in her pajamas.

"What happened?" Vera rushed to pass Jenny, who leaned her knees aside, then followed her mother.

"Charles is going into the navy."

"Oh, for heaven's sake." At the landing, Vera stopped to catch her breath and take off her coat. She left it hanging over the banisters and went into Katherine's room. The girl was in her pajamas, her body thrown across the bed, her face in the pillow, her bare feet hanging over the side. She smells so young, soap and healthy skin, Vera thought, as she took off her hat and sat down. She began to rub the small of Katherine's back, around and around until the sobs subsided into heaves and sighs. When Katherine rolled over, she closed her red and swollen eyes. "Charles says he's going to enlist in the navy. Right after vacation. He says he doesn't want to be a foot soldier."

"Charles is only a freshman at Boylston. When he's with his parents in New York for the Christmas holidays, he'll change his mind. He's too young."

Katherine opened her eyes and looked up at her mother. "He's nineteen. He's a year older than I am." She began to cry again. "I only just started to like him, Mummy. When he was at boarding school he was so juvenile. Maybe he'll be an officer. He'd look so hand-some."

Vera was thoughtful for a moment. Boys like Charles considered war heroic. Look at Mrs. Parker's eldest. He couldn't wait. Now he's somewhere in the Far East with the British. But she knew the refugee women were frightened, all the old memories. Yesterday one of them asked her if she thought they would have to flee again. She told her of course not. What else could she say? She took a deep breath before she spoke. "I suppose there will be lots of men who will want to join up now, full of patriotism and good intentions."

Jenny nestled down on the bed beside her sister, and Vera laid her other hand on Jenny's hip. When Jenny was born, Vera had given Katherine a nurse's costume. She looked so sweet and purposeful in her blue cotton cape and little pointed cap pinned onto her bobbed blond hair. She carried the little black bag everywhere. Richard had just been made a junior partner, and Vera felt so lucky that they had finally settled on Parker Farm Road. For a few years she had felt that her life was worthwhile and that nothing need ever change.

She felt the warmth of her touch on the bodies of her children and looked around the room for further comfort, the flowered wallpaper, the starched white curtains, Katherine's slippers on the floor by her vanity table. Suddenly, Vera recalled the lines of a favorite hymn from her childhood. She hummed softly, saying the words to herself. "Now the day is over, night is drawing nigh, shadows of the evening, steal across the sky." How did it go? "Grant to little children, something safe in thee . . ." And she wondered if abandoning faith in God, along with the lace curtains and the Saturday night bean suppers of her unworldly upbringing, had been a prudent thing to do.

Chapter Thirteen

It was weeks before Harry and Vera could get together
to visit the basements of Parker Farm Road, despite
a sense of urgency. Vera had the extra responsibilities
that come with the holidays, bringing with them a
special false gaiety this year, as if entering into a tradi-
tion would hold the imagination at bay, at least until
people had a chance to catch their breath. Friends and
acquaintances, their arms full of packages, greeted one
another with cheerful voices and grim faces as they
passed in the square. The tree lights seemed more brilliant, the carols with their stories of miracle,
charity, and hope, more poignant.

As warden, Harry had other precincts in his
district to organize and he was up to his neck in the
details of the new construction at the company site,
the further expansion already months behind sched-
ule. And then Adele, disturbed by an encounter at the
school, unexpectedly made last-minute plans for the
family to spend the school holiday with her mother in
Savannah.

A few days before the school vacation, Adele had made one of her infrequent visits to the school to deliver her daughter's snow pants in case Pearl went to the skating rink after school. On her way out, following along the path between the buildings, she looked in a window of the assembly hall where the first grade was rehearsing their nativity pageant. Young Harry, in blue gown and yellow halo, was among the children up on the stage. Adele stepped through one of the side doors into the hall and asked the teacher if she could speak to her in for a minute.

"Certainly, Mrs. Lewis. Keep your places, children. I'll only be a moment." The two women stepped to one side.

"I apologize for the interruption, Miss Tenley, but I'll have to ask you to excuse my son from the pageant."

"Of course, Mrs. Lewis. I didn't realize he had an appointment today."

Adele shook her head. "It not right for him to be an angel in a Christmas play."

"But he looks so darling, Mrs. Lewis."

"Miss Tenley, please," Adele said abruptly. "I want him excused from further rehearsals."

"If that's what you think is best, Mrs. Lewis, but . . ."

"I feel very strongly about this, Miss Tenley. The school should recognize that not all the children are Christians."

The teacher stood in stunned silence.

"Since this is the last period of the day, he can come along with me now."

Miss Tenley turned back to her actors, who were staring at the two adults, mystified and curious. "Harry, your mother wants you."

The boy looked bewildered, then stepped down from the stage obediently. As his mother removed the halo, she whispered in his ear, "Little Jewish boys don't believe in Christmas." The child's protests were suddenly muffled as his mother pulled the gown up over his head.

Miss Tenley said gently, "I'll take that, Harry," reaching for the costume.

The boy whimpered all the way home, but his mother promised him a lollipop in the shape of a horse before he brushed his teeth that night, and in the end, she agreed to let him attend the pageant. When the day came, he sat in ignominy with the kindergarten class.

The incident prompted a certain speculation. Was it that Mrs. Lewis felt an angel was not an appropriate role for a boy? No, she said it was the Christian nature of the traditional scene that she objected to. Well, none of them ever objected before. She thinks she's so special. She's too good-looking.

It caused some disagreement in the bosom of the Lewis family, as well. Harry looked pained. "Of course, my dear, you are his mother, it is your right, if you feel it is your duty." There was a sharp silence. Harry recrossed his legs before he reached for his whiskey.

Adele sat opposite him on the far side of the fireplace in the matching Chippendale chair. She looked smooth and groomed and pouty. Finally, she said crossly, "Well, at least you agree with me there," and looked away from him.

"I always want to back you up, Adele, you must know that. But in this instance, I . . . "

"But, but, but." She shook her head.

"The commotion, Adele. Does the boy know what it's all about? After all, you allow the children to set up a tree in the basement."

"Harry, that's a pagan ritual."

"But, Mummy!" Startled, they both looked toward the doorway. Pearl stood at the threshold in her plaid bathrobe. "We already stick out enough."

"But, sweetie, we *are* different. Will you and Daddy never understand, they're not your people."

"Most of them don't care, Adele."

"How can you say that, after the way that Graham woman humiliated you at the last meeting? They rely on your good judgment, and then when you tell them something they don't want to hear, they turn on you."

"I've had my disagreements with some of them, but we get along." Harry put out his arms to Pearl. "Come on in, honey." Pearl leaned against the side of her father's chair, fiddling with his lapel, while he continued. "The best of them are good honest people who want to help others."

"I like Miss Graham," Pearl added coyly.

"Then one of you might point out to your precious

do-gooders that not everything is Jesus Christ and jolly Christmas."

Pearl shook her head vigorously. "'Merry,' Mummy."

Adele stood up. "You two deserve each other," she said as she left the room. Harry put his arm around his daughter's waist.

"But she was wrong, Daddy. It is 'merry.'"

"She knows that, honey." He was thoughtful for a moment. "I'll tell you what. You can come along with me when I go to the shop on Saturday. The men don't get to see a pretty little girl at the factory very often. We can stop at the diner on Route 9 for lunch."

"Mummy might not let me."

"You leave that to me."

"Do I have to have a boiled egg?"

"You can have anything you want."

Pearl smiled. "Can I ask Jenny?"

When Jenny mentioned Pearl's invitation, her mother looked up from her book, startled. Jenny was barefoot, dressed in a pair of her sister's oversized pajamas, which gave a reassuring frumpy look. Nothing much showed.

Jenny could tell from her cheery voice that her mother was trying not to be cross. "Oh, what a nice thing for Mr. Lewis to do, and I know how busy he is. He's such a rare man. Too bad it's this Saturday. You'll be with Rosemary at old Mrs. Osgood's party."

"I can't go to Christmas tea on the Hill. Just Rosemary can go. Mrs. Parker says her mother's too sick."

"I'm sorry to hear that, but you'll have a nice time with Pearl. Now how about putting on your bathrobe and slippers?"

"To go to a factory, Mother!"

"Of course not, Jenny." Her mother was exasperated. "You'll catch your death going around like that."

Jenny ignored her. "When I wanted to go to the World's Fair with the Lewises you wouldn't let me."

"That was years ago, dear."

"You didn't know him then."

Her mother blushed. "It's true, I hadn't worked closely with Mr. Lewis."

Jenny gave up pestering her. "I'll go with Pearl, but I'd rather have gone with Rosemary."

"You'll enjoy yourself, dear." Her mother's face softened, and she looked out absentmindedly across the room. "Mr. Lewis is such a fine-looking man."

"MOTHER," Jenny screamed and threw her arms across the pudgy swelling of her breasts as if to crush them. "Why do you always say things like that about Mr. Lewis?"

"Really, Jenny, I . . ."

"All he *is* is Pearl's father. He's not some god." Jenny whirled around, still embracing herself, and stormed from the living room. She felt hot and her head ached. When she finally reached Rosemary on the telephone to report that her mother had said she liked Mr. Lewis' looks, Rosemary was unimpressed.

"Perhaps she has a crush on him. My mum always

has a crush on someone. The greengrocer. Or Colin, the dustbin man, she called him 'my dirty sweetie,' just for a lark. She's probably got one in some gorgeous uniform, that's how she gets things done around the house."

Jenny shook her head at the telephone. "It's not like that."

"What does it matter? Nothing's going to happen. You get so nervy about things ever since you got the curse."

"All you think about is now you can have babies."

"Oh, really, Jenny, don't be so juvenile."

"You sound just like my mother. I hope you have a horrible time on the Hill."

"*Toi aussi.*"

On Saturday, Harry drove out to the company site in the Packard, the two girls in the back seat like dowagers on the way to the symphony, hat and coat and gloves, even a sealskin lap robe between them against the drafts that seeped in around the window frames. Jenny's galoshes lay in a heap on the floor. Harry had let Pearl get away with rubbers. When he opened the heavy metal door of the diner where they stopped for early lunch, the smell of cabbage and onions hit him like a heady rose, but he waited patiently, sitting across from the girls in the booth, while they read each other every line on the menu before they gave up. He ordered them each a chicken sandwich and a plate of nice stuffed cabbage for himself. They had no trouble choosing dessert, and both of them attacked the rich chocolate pudding with energy. Why should he be surprised to see so much of her mother in Jenny? Dark complexion, the earnest demeanor, and the same naiveté. Mother and daughter shared a kind of polite constraint, as if neither of them expected much for herself.

He began to review the progress on the second addition to the plant in his mind. The push was on before prices went up and materials became hard to get despite priorities. The outside shell was finished off, the roof completed. The board and batten alternated with panels of windows to give as much natural light as possible, but they'd have to black them out when they went into around-the-clock war production. The new wing was set T-shape to the east side of the old, red-brick machine shop, in line with a previous addition on the west side that housed the cooling room and the furnaces. This would allow the north end of the old building, with the office, a small drafting room, and the stock and shipping area, to be separate from the machining operations. Harry took great delight in the irony of the new cathedral design.

"Fit for a cardinal," he had remarked to Joe Izrael. "All that's missing is the stained glass and gold dome. We'll stick a cross on the roof to fool the Germans."

"If it were the Pope, he'd invite them in to make soap out of us."

The new building would almost double their space to four thousand square feet. At Joe's rough estimate of fifty-four square feet apiece, lathes, milling machines, two drill presses, two surface grinders, a bench grinder, and the saws, they were adding another six lathes for dies to the twelve lathes they already had.

"What are the rough numbers on dies per day to pay for all this, Joe? Norton thought he was doing me a favor when he negotiated five years on the loan."

"Business is good, and it's gonna get better, believe me, Harry. That Norton fellow will be gnawing at his liver he didn't invest for himself. 'Be Prepared,' that's the motto, and I was a good scout, eh, Pop? We can handle five or six more lathes, easy, maybe more, as well as the general machining. Half a dozen more employees, at least. Who knows how many with a war to fight."

"Slow down, big shot," Ira said. "I already have thirty-five men under me."

"Listen, this mobilization will get everyone out of the red."

"And pretty soon, there'll be nothing worth spending your money on."

"Hey, Pop. I didn't start the war."

It was after two in the afternoon when Harry and the girls stepped through the side door of the big silent shed. It was a half-day, and Harry knew by now the workers were on the loading dock having a little celebration. He was glad to have this chance to look around without the construction men everywhere. He closed the door against the cold and ran his hand along the first of the interior sidewalls to be completed. The girls dashed across the floor, unbuttoning their coats as they went. They twirled and fell into each other's arms and then spun off again, liberated from sitting in the car. But Harry stood for a moment, looking across the virtually vacant shell to the wooden crates lined up in the corner. The new lathes. As soon as the wiring was finished they'd be ready to go into production.

Whenever Harry stepped into a vast empty area like this, he felt the tension of space holding him back like the long, measured walk down the empty football field after he had been warned that the team did not welcome Jews. Or the customs shed in New York where he received the coffin of his father, who had died of a heart attack on a visit to the family village in the Ukraine. The first recognition of the coffin, abandoned along the far wall of the great empty hall, had disappointed Harry. It was so ordinary and small, the smooth wood shaped like the hull of a boat, the steel plate dead center on the lid. But he remembered that the journey across the shed was like wearing a yoke. A tug forward, the pull back. The name on the plate, small script letters, like a mail slot. He had wanted to knock on the lid so his father would open the door.

Now, as he started to walk across the concrete floor of the new factory, suddenly the children came up behind him, Pearl grabbing at his hand. The three of them approached one of the crates, bending to look through the slats, like viewing a exotic caged beast.

This monster had a solid, dour look to it. The head stock, tool holder and tail stock were painted battle-ship gray. The bare steel of the guiding ways was coated in thick brown grease.

Jenny stuck her finger through a slat. "What's that icky stuff?"

"Cosmoline," Harry said knowingly. "It protects the lathe against rust." He gave a slap to the broad surface of the wooden slat.

The children skipped off. He surveyed the place more carefully. The chains for the newfangled fluorescent lights hung from the ceiling. That was Joe, everything the latest. The heating pipes were in place, but the last he'd heard, the radiators themselves were held up. Shipping priorities. Two new loading trolleys had arrived without wheels. Rubber shortage, Joe said. His father made do with some old baby carriage wheels.

Clever old craftsman, Ira Izrael, they couldn't do without him. But he ran the floor on a kind of caste system. The toolmakers were the aristocrats, the clubmen. The other machine operators came pretty close. But Ira hardly acknowledged the men in the cooling room, despite the fact that he kept a keen eye on them. He viewed life much like Harry's Parker Farm Road neighbors did, as a holding pattern. Harry preferred to see it as an opportunity.

He looked across at the girls, swinging at arm's length around one of the thick structural columns. "Come on, Pearl, Jenny. Let's see what the men are up to."

They walked through the machine shop, skirting the stolid machinery at rest now, aware of their human mobility, their cleanness, Jenny and Pearl stepping gingerly in the expectation of industrial dirt. They stopped to peer in at the doorway of the cooling room, the huge tanks like flat-bottomed tubs, the fluids still murky with diminishing heat. The furnaces hulked in the rear. As they approached the connecting door at the far end of the machine shop, they could hear voices. Harry opened the door and looked in.

The workers, still in their heavy boots and smocks, sat in twos and threes on shipping boxes or the platforms of the loading trolleys, the Irishmen passing around the communal whiskey bottle, restricting themselves to a swig or two in the presence of the bosses. Harry noticed the few Jews among them drank black coffee, including Ira and Joe. The young Pole on one of the milling machines had joined the two older Polish die makers to welcome a young compatriot who had just come on in the furnace room. They stood to one side, tossing back a shot of Vodka in one gulp. It wasn't often these men had such luxuries; they were far too costly. It was Joe Izrael's experiment in labor relations. He was restless and full of grand ideas these days, cramped by his machining expertise and management skills that classified him a key person in industry, denying him heroism in army intelligence or a naval command. College degrees were a dime a dozen. So despite his father's outrage—"Drinking in my plant. Never"—Joe had insisted that it was an office holiday, an investment in loyalty beyond shared job skills, and would pay off when stepped-up production demands would require closer worker cooperation. "What's the matter with a little democracy, Pop?"

Harry called in from the doorway, "We're here," and looked back at the children, crowding in behind him. Then he took off his hat and said, "Here we go, girls." Pearl led Jenny into the shipping area.

There was a scurry of movement as the men hid the bottles and pushed back from the packing case that served as a table. Someone produced bottles of golden ginger ale and cups and plates of little cakes and shortbreads. Ira gave Pearl a little squeeze—"So much a young lady now"—and pinched Jenny's cheek. Harry introduced them around the circle. "This is my daughter, Pearl, and her friend, Jenny Oliver. Don't let us interrupt your good time."

The men nodded and smiled and said, "Quite a miss, you are," and "I have one at home just like you." Joe poured the girls each a ginger ale and began to pass around the cakes and cookies. Others moved in to help, and the talk resumed. One of the older men stepped from behind the storage shelves with a little balsam tree on a stand, hung with slivers of steel shavings like drops of crystal. At the tip was a five-pointed star.

"Christmas is for children. Lord love the pair of you," he said and set the little tree on the packing case.

"Oh, how beautiful." Jenny stepped forward to touch one of the ornaments. It twisted and swayed.

Pearl looked up at her father for an instant, then into the broad Irish face. "I'm Jewish," she said solemnly. "My mother says we don't believe in Christmas."

The room fell silent and Harry placed his hand quickly on his daughter's shoulder. "Jenny's right, it's beautiful. Thank you, Michael. That was very thoughtful. What a craftsman you are."

"To be sure, Mr. Lewis, it's one that knows her mind," the old die maker said kindly. Then he turned to Pearl. "You see, miss, I'm a Christian," he said, "and it's my holiday. I'll need your help to celebrate with a bit of a cake." He offered Pearl the plate. She took her time choosing.

Later, as Jenny walked home from Pearl's house carrying the tree with the neat ornaments, she thought the whole afternoon was like an exotic adventure to a foreign land, as if she'd stepped into a geography book. The luxurious lap robe across her knees. The sticky red leather seat in the diner that squeaked when she slid off. The huge, tall emptiness of the new factory, like the pictures of those churches that Mary believed in. The bigness of the men that faded when Pearl made her strange announcement. The awful tightness of the moment creeping up her body. But now that it was over and nothing bad had happened, she was impressed that Pearl said the truth like that. She'd always thought that being Jewish meant trying to hide it. Since they couldn't really, Jews had to be particularly nice to everybody, like Mr. Lewis.

Her mother was enchanted with the tree that Jenny thrust at her as she came through the front door. So simple and imaginative, with its little Star of Bethlehem. Hope in troubled times. She set it at once on an oval piece of mirror glass in the center of the dining room table. When her mother asked about the visit to the factory, Jenny told her, "Pearl said she was Jewish."

"Well, I suppose she is," her mother said, taken aback.

"Did Rosemary call?"

Finally, Vera and Harry met one January afternoon in the new year at the bottom of Vera's front walk to make the rounds of the neighborhood basements and consider suitable air-raid shelters for the schoolchildren. The first thing Vera mentioned was the charming little tree.

"A nice old man made it for the girls," Harry exclaimed, his sturdy rubbers crunching on the skim of hard snow packed down by the plow. Vera walked beside him, bundled up against the cold, holding her clipboard close to her chest. It was a heavy gray afternoon. "I'm afraid Pearl was not very appreciative, but Jenny made up for her," Harry went on. "She was a very polite girl, and we enjoyed her company."

"I'm glad to hear it, but I have to laugh," Vera said. "She can be pretty surly at home."

Harry smiled. "I'm not so sure I was wise to take them to the plant."

"Oh, I'm sure they found it quite interesting," Vera

said eagerly. "Jenny was very enthusiastic. She told me all about it." She knew her little white lie sounded false, too gushy, but Harry didn't seem to notice.

"Well, I don't believe in keeping our children from the real world," he continued. "Parker Farm Road is as good a way to begin life as I can imagine, something you and I didn't have. But I thought they were old enough to see how other men make a living." He was silent again. Vera stopped to pull up the collar of her navy blue overcoat under the brim of her hat. Harry waited for her in silence, then returned to his musings. "But they change, children do. Pearl has always been the most satisfying person in my life, pleasant and obedient. So affectionate." He smiled at some private moment. "I have always loved her as an extension of myself." He noticed Vera's puzzled face. "Oh, don't misunderstand me. My wife is the dearest thing to me, the air I breathe." In the pause, Vera felt Harry's words like cool silk against her skin, a caress meant for another woman. "And my son," Harry continued, "well, where I come from the son is the little king. But Pearl is growing more outspoken. I miss the easiness."

They walked on in silence. Finally, Vera said, "Pearl's twelve, that's all." Shifting moods, that was something she knew about. "I felt the way you do a few years ago, when Katherine was going through a stubborn stage. She's eighteen now, a senior, and I have to say with all her broken hearts she's a delight."

"Is she really eighteen already?" he asked politely, and Vera realized she'd broken into his reverie.

"Pearl is such a nice girl," Vera said, trying to lead him back.

"I worry about what's ahead for all of them," he said, turning up the Russells' front walk and removing his hat before he pressed the bell.

The inspection went well. Most of the homeowners had left word with the maids to show them the outdoor entry or lead them through the kitchen and turn on the light at the top of the cellar stairs. Harry examined room dimensions, recessed windows, overhead wires and pipes; Vera noted down easy access, position of the light switches, whether or not there was a toilet. Most of the basements had been cleaned up, trunks and odd boxes of old china or outgrown baby furniture safe in separate storage space, the coal dust confined to the furnace room, wood piled out of the way of outer entries and connecting passageways, the door to the laundry room shut. The Russells' main basement room had a rug on the floor. The Nortons' had a set of garden furniture grouped as if for a summer cocktail party. At Vera's house, Mr. Lewis thanked Mary for running up to the second floor to demonstrate the laundry chute for him. He told her he wished he'd thought of that when he built his house. At Harry's house, Vera was treated to a brief lecture about his new furnace. Each agreed the other's space was more than adequate. At the Parkers' there were accommodations for several classes of schoolchildren, two basement rooms. The playroom had an upright piano.

As they went from house to house they discussed the report they would submit to the committee. Numbers, sitting arrangements, icy steps in winter weather. Was it too much to request keys to back doors? Perhaps Miss Graham would devote one of her Friday assemblies to a practice run-through before scheduling a surprise air-raid drill. Or, indeed, experiencing the real thing. They exchanged grave looks.

When they reached Mrs. von Kempel's house they could hear the dog barking inside. The housekeeper opened the door.

"May we come in, Miss Braun?"

"I am to allow you, Mr. Lewis," the housekeeper said. The dog snarled behind her.

Vera and Harry stepped up into the front hall where the housekeeper stood pointedly before the heavy mat at the side of the door, until they caught on and bent to wrestle off their outdoor footwear. In her haste Vera twisted the rubber heel of her overshoe and it would not peel off. She had to put her hand on the wall to support herself as she tugged, feeling clumsy and exposed. Harry knelt to help her, setting her overshoes neatly on the mat beside his rubbers, as if they had always rested side by side. As the housekeeper led them through the house to the kitchen, muttering about children with dirty shoes, both Harry and Vera unbuttoned their coats in the oppressive heat of the house, and Vera slipped her gloves into her pocketbook. As she followed behind Harry, she noticed the huge tapestry along one whole wall of the hall.

Some medieval scene in dark reds and blues. The dour portrait of a man in frock coat over the mantel in the living room. Heavy draperies at the windows in the dining room. Everything immaculate. It all seemed lifeless. In spite of herself, she tried to catch a glimpse of the picture of Hitler, but then she remembered Jenny had said it was in the boy's room, and that would be upstairs. The housekeeper was explaining to Harry that Mrs. von Kempel had suffered another "spell."

"I'm sorry to hear it."

"Gone visiting the clinic in one of her moods." The housekeeper sniffed. Vera said, "Of course," as if she understood.

The kitchen was more comfortable. It smelled of simmering stock and Vera could see signs of the boy everywhere. A jacket hanging on a hook by the back door. A box of colored pencils and some crayons and a pad of writing paper on a child's desk near the window. One of the Hardy Boys books. Was that the wooden knife she'd seen him brandishing the evening of Katherine's party two years ago? It did seem sad to think of a fifteen-year-old boy still playing with children's toys.

"He's a good boy," the housekeeper said as Vera looked around the room. "Very obedient."

The cellar door stuck, and Harry had to open it. The dog rushed forward to nose into the darkness, then halted at the top of the stairs. The housekeeper flicked on the light. "I do not go down. It is not for the children either," she said.

Without saying a word, Vera and Harry peered
down and looked at each other in agreement. The
light was dim, and it smelled rank. The plumbing and
heating pipes ran along the low ceiling forming a grid
like the roof of a cage. Still, they went down the stairs,
Harry ducking his head, and Vera moving cautiously
to avoid the spider webs overhead. At the bottom,
she halted on the dirt floor, as Harry stepped into the
unfinished space. The furnace, the coal pile, an old
clothesline strung at the entry to a crude enclosure
with a workbench and a soapstone sink. An old laundry area. He wondered what the housekeeper did now
for washing facilities? He thought he felt the string
cord of a ceiling light brush over his hair as he moved.
"Nothing here for us," he reported to Vera. Turning
away, he noticed the red light bulb and the pans. "It
looks like someone's been using this as a darkroom."

As Vera stepped further into the cave, the squalid
stale smell enveloped her and the ragged stonewalls
seemed to move in. She stopped to compose herself.
Out of the corner of her eye, she glimpsed a moving
shadow hugging the base of a sidewall, and suddenly a
mouse dashed across the floor at her feet. She cried out
and put one hand over her mouth, swallowing hard to
suppress the rise of vomit in her throat, reaching out
blindly with the other. As Harry came towards her, she
dropped the clipboard and grabbed him around the
waist, then buried her nose in his chest, dislodging her
hat. He held her in his left arm while he reached up
to grope unsuccessfully for the light cord overhead. In

the dim illumination from the cellar stairs, he adroitly removed the hat pin from the back of her head, but before he could catch it, the hat fell at their feet in the dirt. "It's all right," he murmured, "everything is all right." She closed her eyes and lingered, listening to the rhythm of his soft voice, feeling the bulk of him in her arms, the smell of him earthy and suggestive.

She felt him reach up again and then was momentarily dazed when the light suddenly went on. "Forgive me," she said, drawing away quickly and looking up at him. "I really don't know what came over me," she protested. "For a moment, I felt I was going to be smothered."

"It's an awful place." He stooped to retrieve the clipboard and her hat.

"Thank you, Harry," she said, dusting off her hat. "I wouldn't want you to think I'm one of those women who goes to pieces when she sees a mouse."

"Not for a minute, Vera."

She laughed nervously and patted down her hair, setting the hat back on her head.

As she turned to go up the stairs, Vera put her hand out on the wooden wall panel to her left. She felt the curl of the stiff paper under her palm. When she looked more closely she saw the photographs. The housekeeper, the German shepherd. Someone bending over in an awfully short tennis skirt. A girl in a familiar knit jacket. In the schoolyard. Coming up Parker Farm Road. Dozens of them. In some, her hair is in a braid. In others, it sweeps over her shoulders like a cape. In the one in a bathing suit, she's wearing a cap, but she's posed in front of a lawn sprinkler with her head tilted and her hand on her hip, like one of those pinup girls. How could it be? It was Rosemary Bent-Wilson.

Chapter Fourteen

"There you are, Rosemary," Jenny's mother exclaimed, coming through the kitchen door.

They were making soda bread, Rosemary stirring a pinch of salt into the mixture of flour and bicarbonate of soda, while Jenny measured out a cup of buttermilk. Across the table, Mary was doing the potatoes for dinner, letting the peelings drop onto a sheet of newspaper spread out on the blue and white checked oilcloth. All three looked up abruptly as the door swung shut with a clap.

"Mr. Lewis and I have been looking into neighborhood basements," Jenny's mother went on. "Air raid shelter for you schoolchildren. You would know all about that, wouldn't you, Rosemary?" She smiled, resting a hand on Rosemary's shoulder. "Mr. Lewis found what seemed to be a photographer's workroom in Mrs. von Kempel's basement. I just wanted to make sure everything is . . . Is there anything that's happened that perhaps you're not quite comfortable with, Rosemary?"

Jenny's mother didn't usually address Rosemary the way she would one of her refugees. She usually spoke to Rosemary in a sort of chummy way, as if they were in some pickle together, and together they would triumph. In fact, her mother's tone of voice to Rosemary often made Jenny furious. She felt left out. As if she couldn't succeed at anything. But this time, her mother's tone was definitely care-for-the-less-fortunate. Beady-eyed Fred Goldstein and his mother, people like that.

Her mother looked earnestly into Rosemary's face. "Are you all right, dear?"

"Perfectly fine, Mrs. Oliver." Rosemary's clipped speech always made her sound virtuous.

"I'm glad to hear it." Jenny's mother pulled off her gloves. "I only have a little time before the meeting of the Back Door board, but I thought you girls might join me for tea. Perhaps you wouldn't mind bringing the tray into the living room, Mary. I think there are some cookies in the tin. Plenty of milk for the children, but I'll have a slice of lemon."

"But Mummy, we're busy," Jenny pleaded, rising to one knee and stretching her arms out across the table to a pile of potato peelings like someone begging for alms.

"Don't be so melodramatic, Jenny," her mother said crossly.

When Jenny sat up there was a trail of flour on the oilcloth.

"Dear me, you are so exasperating, Jenny." Her mother unbuttoned her coat. "Rosemary can come keep me company while you finish up. And try not to get flour all over your sweater."

Rosemary flashed her quizzical look and followed Jenny's mother. As soon as the door swung shut Jenny cautiously pushed it open again. Her mother was putting her things down on the dining room table, her coat draped over the back of a chair.

"Don't you be snooping," Mary warned, as the door closed behind Jenny. She hurried across the hallway to catch a glimpse into the living room, pressing herself against the wall in her usual spot at the foot of the stairs by the double doors.

Her mother pointed to Rosemary to sit down. "Tell me, dear," she began, adjusting the hem of her skirt, "are you sure everything is all right"?

"Ever so, Mrs. Oliver." Rosemary looked perplexed.

"Perhaps I should have left this to Mrs. Parker. You do understand, it's for your safety."

"Oh, Mrs. Oliver, whatever are you talking about?"

"I'll just have to tell you, dear. I saw pictures tacked up on the wall of Mrs. von Kempel's basement, Rosemary. Pictures of you. One in a bathing suit."

Everything was frozen in a moment of silence. Rosemary flicked her braid over one shoulder and began fiddling with the ends. Then she said gravely. "I promise you, Mrs. Oliver, I never went into the cellar."

"You were in the house?"

"It seemed polite, Mrs. Oliver. Wilhelm asked me to tea."

"Your aunt knew, of course."

Jenny held her breath. Finally, Rosemary answered really sweetly, "Oh, yes," as if it were the truth. "When I got there he acted really dim, pointing that camera at me. He finally stopped when the housekeeper wagged her finger at him and said, '*Nein, nein,*' something, some funny word."

"But that doesn't explain the pictures, Rosemary. They're in all seasons."

"The one in the bathing suit is in your yard, Mrs. Oliver. Last summer. He popped his head over Mr. Oliver's roses."

"Good lord. But the pose, dear. You mustn't be vulgar."

"I was only joshing him. He's such a laggard. But he might be a German spy, because he knew about the memory maps in the sixth grade last spring."

Mary swung through the door with the tea tray, giving Jenny one of her black looks. Jenny stuck out the tip of her tongue, then followed Mary into the living room.

"And he knew about Katherine's party, Mummy," Jenny chimed in. "Remember he was behind the Parkers' bushes?"

"Thank you, Mary. Really, Jenny, you should be ashamed of yourself." Her mother began to pour the tea. "Offer your guest a cookie. You should know enough to respect Rosemary's privacy."

Rosemary rubbed one forefinger along the other to make the tut tut sign and flashed her grin. Then she turned back to Jenny's mother. "Sometimes I see Wilhelm in the strangest places. Remember that time Patsy told her mother about the man in the lilacs?"

"And Patsy was driven around the neighborhood in the patrol car," Jenny added, pinching another cookie off the plate on the tray.

"Last spring, will I ever forget it?" Her mother shook her head. "We were all so upset. Now you see, Rosemary, how careful you must be."

Rosemary leaned forward in her chair. "Well, I'm not positive," she whispered confidentially, warming up to the story. "But I think that was him. Patsy swore the shadow had a big round head."

"But didn't the policeman ask you children if you'd seen anything unusual?"

Rosemary looked at Jenny. "Did he interrogate you?" she asked.

"No," Jenny said truthfully. It was Rosemary herself who had answered the policeman's questions.

"That's odd," her mother noted. "He said he had. The report said the police search found nothing unusual except footprints from a heavy boot. But they weren't in the Russells' hedge, they were in the alley by the tennis court. Some vagrant. I remember the report recommended cutting the vines back."

"Oh that was only one of Mrs. von Kempel's gentleman callers. Mr. Lewis goes there once a month." Rosemary leered at Jenny, who couldn't help giggling.

Her mother was astonished. "Girls. Really. That's enough. Mr. Lewis goes there to look after Mrs. Von

Kempel's business affairs. She's a very frail woman."

"Sorry, Mrs. Oliver. Anyway, remember Jenny? Patsy was doing her important relatives thing that day, and I said I wouldn't bear to hear it one more time. That's when Patsy decided she saw him in the lilacs. She really is pathetic."

"You said you had a wonderful time at her grandmother's house," Jenny challenged. "You said it had been 'enlightening.' I heard you."

"I shouldn't like to hurt Mrs. Russell's feelings," Rosemary replied easily.

"If you didn't mean it, it's a lie."

Jenny's mother looked at the clock on the mantelpiece. "Sometimes it's just as well not to say something so we won't hurt someone's feelings, just as Rosemary says." She set down her teacup and stood up. "My meeting at the Back Door Store is in twenty minutes." She paused a moment. "You girls must realize that the von Kempel boy is older than he seems," she said. "You must be careful, especially you, Rosemary. These obsessions that boys have as they develop . . . grow up . . . can lead to . . . to upsetting things. You'll understand when you're older." She stepped into the dining room and put on her coat and hat, then drew on her gloves. "And no more pictures, Rosemary," she called back across the hallway.

"Your mother was talking about babies," Rosemary said as the two girls went through the swinging door back into the kitchen.

"I know that." Jenny began to beat the ingredients

in the mixing bowl as if she were cranking up an old car.

"Easy there," Mary said.

"Did you really see someone coming out of Mrs. von Kempel's house?"

"I thought I saw a man in a soldier's uniform going down the alley."

"I bet you made it up. Besides, you lied about telling your aunt."

Mary stepped over to the table, wiping her fingers on the apron of her green and white uniform. "Rosie girl, you shouldn't tell fibs to Mrs. Oliver."

Rosemary looked up at Mary, her great dark eyes puddles of concern. "She'd tell Aunt Isabel and it would come out that Jenny knew all along, and then Jenny would really be in the soup. It was just a little white lie, really."

"To save our Jenny, was it? I'm on to you, you little English devil." Mary brandished the paring knife at Rosemary and returned to the sink to wash the potatoes. Rosemary stuck out her tongue at Mary's back, and Jenny made a fist at Rosemary. Her love for Mary was unconditional. Rosemary sneered back as she poured the mixture into the buttered loaf dish. Jenny ignored her. She carried the mixing bowl and measuring cups to the sink, where Mary had set the potatoes in cold water. The girls watched as Mary drew a cross with a knife in the surface of the batter, then placed the baking dish in the oven.

That done, Mary untied her apron. "His nibs is

home from the wars early this week"—she winked at Jenny—"I'll be getting into my best bib and tucker."

When Mary had gone upstairs to change into her black dinner uniform, Jenny poured two glasses of milk and snuck out two oatmeal cookies from the jar in the pantry. They settled at the table.

"Does Mary always call your father 'his nibs?'" Rosemary asked.

"Sometimes she says 'himself,' but not in front of Mummy." Then Jenny added quickly. "Don't you dare tell."

"I don't really like your precious Mary anyway."

"That's because she likes me better than you."

"Only because I'm English." Rosemary dunked her cookie into her milk. "Fav says the Irish are just bloody micks and should go back where they belong."

Jenny shook her head vigorously. "I don't care what your father says, Mary's my friend," she snapped. She could feel the color rising in her cheeks. "I don't want her to go anywhere. She'll never go back. Where would she go?" She shot the question at Rosemary, tears forming at the corners of her eyes.

"Home to Ireland, silly. They're neutral, you know."

"What's that mean?" Jenny was suspicious.

"They're not in the fight against Hitler. They're practically traitors."

"She is not. She's our cook. I don't want her to leave. I love Mary better than Katherine. Better than Mummy, sometimes."

"Really, Jenny, you are too funny. That's as if I said I loved Aunt Isabel's Hilda better than Fav. That's ridiculous."

"I didn't say better than Daddy," Jenny sniffled.

"You mean 'his nibs' don't you?"

Jenny stood up and folded her arms across her chest, glaring at Rosemary. "Sometimes I hate you, Rosemary Bent-Wilson."

Rosemary raised her eyebrows. "Sometimes you're a silly old bear, Jenny Oliver." She smiled her cat smile and picked up a potholder. She opened the oven door to have a peek, then set the pan down on the gas range. "Do be a love and fetch the butter."

Vera and Harry completed their report, "Recommendations for Evacuation of the School in Case of Air Raid," in time for the next meeting of the parents' committee, and Miss Graham and Miss Osgood unfolded the plan to the school at Friday assembly. The matter at hand was grave enough for Miss Graham to forgo the usual reading. While she explained the alert system and evacuation procedures, the importance of speed, Miss Osgood followed the written instructions on the blackboard with a pointer.

All the students were unusually silent and fidgety, squirming restlessly on the rows of wooden benches arranged in a semicircle like a Greek amphitheater. In the past few weeks they had grown accustomed to the even voices of unnamed anxieties, the warnings, the subtle supplications. Parents spoke solemnly of blackouts and air raids, then donned warden's helmets or went off to roll bandages for the Red Cross. Some older brothers and cousins were already in uniform. The whole adult world had suddenly joined in a single endeavor beyond their childhood realm, and there were so many new rules.

Miss Osgood flipped the board around on its swivel pin while Miss Graham cleared her throat. She continued, her voice low and grave. "In the unlikely event of a RED alert"—Miss Osgood pointed at Roman numeral II-- "the big bell will ring continuously until the buildings are clear. The school must be evacuated in six minutes." Miss Graham paused. Miss Osgood kept the pointer at 6.

Miss Graham repeated, "The building must be cleared in six minutes."

Basement assignments were posted on the back of the second blackboard. At the close of the assembly, the school sang "A Mighty Fortress Is Our God." Everyone was relieved when it was over.

At first, there was a general feeling of anticipation and speculation among Miss Osgood's seventh-grade students. When would the raid come? In time to miss math? Their class had been assigned the Parkers' playroom. Isn't there a piano? Yes, but the rules said they had to sit along the wall. Patsy would try to arrange to be next to Jeffrey Malcolm. What about Fred and Rosemary?

As usual, Miss Osgood chose Patsy as line leader in the event of an alarm. For a moment, Patsy looked her usual smug self, but much to everyone's surprise Jeffrey was designated to bring up the end of the line. Patsy said Miss Osgood did it on purpose; she was dried up like an old prune. Rosemary agreed with Patsy, but Jenny kept her thoughts to herself. She liked Miss Osgood.

"She thinks they'll kiss in the dark," Rosemary whispered.

"But the lights will be on?"

"Not when the bombs knock out the electricity."

Jenny was suddenly frightened. Rosemary knew about these things.

The following Monday, the students were told there would be a mock alert sometime that week. For days they were on edge, jittery, like a herd of sheep in a holding pen. Then, just before assembly period at nine o'clock on Friday, they heard the every seven-second ring like a majestic church bell. "YELLOW alert," they called joyfully to each other as they retrieved their coats and jackets.

Rosemary lured Jenny on. "We'll meet at my playroom. My Aunt Isabel got us Chinese Checkers and a new Parcheesi board."

"Quietly, children. Quiet, please."

Reminded of the rules, the seventh graders stood attentively by their desks, ready to go directly home. But when they were actually dismissed, they were cautioned to go only as far as the main entrance and then return to the classroom. This was only a trial run. There would be another rehearsal in a few minutes before the school day resumed. The second time felt more like a betrayal; all they had missed was assembly. Rosemary and Jenny and a few others could not resist breaking clear at the main entrance, dashing up the road as far as the streetlamp beyond the Nortons' and then back down again like a flight of grackles. After that, nothing more happened, and the students no longer studied the poster of Uncle Sam with his forefinger to his lips on the bulletin board in the assembly building, or flattened themselves against the inner walls as they lined up to go to lunch.

Then, one chilly Wednesday morning during art period, the big bell began to ring vigorously, rapidly, steadily, and Miss Osgood appeared out of nowhere, her hair flying, still buttoning up her tweed coat. The students stood transfixed before their easels, messages of fear and confusion exchanged in their glances. Everyone started talking at once.

"Children, children. Be sure to put the lids on your paint pots and your brushes in the soapy water jars," Mrs. Eldridge was calling above the din when Miss Osgood interrupted her.

"Quickly to the cloakroom," Miss Osgood ordered. "Put on your jackets and hats as you form your line."

"Cleanup, children," Mrs. Eldridge ordered imperiously.

"RED alert, Muriel," Miss Osgood threatened.

They were electrified by the word RED and the show of temper between teachers. Obediently, they followed Miss Osgood out into the brittle cold air and along the path to the main entrance, listening to the gunshot crack of their footfalls on the frozen-stiff wooden planks of the boardwalk laid down against the snow and ice. As they marched, they buttoned up their coats and searched the pockets for their mittens. Where the pathways across the school property came together and widened into the main walk like streams into a river, lines of students converged, turned and filed past a resolute Miss Graham on the steps of the assembly building, then up to the sidewalk and Parker Farm Road. The headmistress raised her hand or nodded her head in encouragement. When one of the little children whimpered noisily and chaos seemed close at hand, she stepped down to lead the boy to the head of his line, linking his hand with his teacher's.

Out on the road, Miss Osgood's seventh grade hurried up Parker Farm Road beside other classes, pressing forward in loose formation like an army in flight. Jenny followed Rosemary in front of her, concentrating on the prancing reindeer encircling Rosemary on the back of her sweater jacket, elated at first that in an emergency she did not have to wear her galoshes. Then younger children fell behind and were ushered down into the safety of nearby houses. As Molly watched her little brother file into their basement, she put her fists to her eyes to hold back the tears. When they reached the streetlamp at the corner, they were surprised to see Mr. Lewis. Pearl reached out her hand, but while her father smiled at her, something about his preoccupied look made her hand fall. Some of the children searched the pale gray sky; others listened for enemy sounds above the steady crunch of feet on the thin layer of packed snow in the road. Fred walked with his eyes cast down. When a patch of ice roared like a rocket off a garage roof, Rosemary put her hands over her ears. Jenny cupped her mouth in her mitten and tried to swallow away the lump that had lodged in her throat. When at last the seventh graders reached the Parkers' basement, Jenny felt rescued from her scary imaginings.

Miss Osgood led the way down the cellar stairs and into the laundry room where some of Miss Merriweather's ninth grade were still passing into the furnace room on the way to the old trunk room on the right, shedding their jackets in the welcome heat. The furnace itself, packed like a casualty in white asbestos bandages, roared. Miss Osgood switched on the lights in the playroom and nudged the bucket of sand aside to let the children pass, then closed the door. "It's awfully hot in here," she remarked, "but of course we can't open the windows. Look on the bright side, it's better than the cold." The students welcomed their teacher's familiar optimism and settled on the bits of worn carpet laid along the inner walls, sitting cross-legged, shimmying out of their coats in the comforting warmth. They looked around at the upright piano, at the card table and chairs, the bookshelf of games, at the fire logs laid in the brick fireplace on the far wall. Except for the table tennis set, it might have been a father's den. Only the heavy black canvas covering the recessed windows was a reminder. They prepared to wait.

After they were settled and Miss Osgood had taken off her coat, hanging it over the long-handled shovel by the bucket, she passed among them, crouching down with a reassuring word or bending over to pat a shoulder. The girls began adjusting knee socks, repositioning barrettes. The boys gave each other body punches, then someone spluttered out a tense giggle. When Molly asked how long it would be and Patsy said, "Shhh," Miss Osgood smiled vacantly and shrugged her shoulders. They fell quiet again.

"Everyone comfortable?" Miss Osgood asked too cheerfully. "I want to congratulate you, class, moving right along the way you did. We beat the wretches to safety, didn't we." She undid the bottom button of her cardigan sweater at the waist of her skirt. "We're like the crusaders. We're hot and weary from our long journey. We'll rest here safely before we move on to reach Jerusalem."

She looked at the sea of wan faces and tried again.

"You know what the Union soldiers did in the Civil War to keep their spirits up while they marched?" A few nods. "They sang rounds. We all know 'Row row row your boat.'" She began to sing in a quavering soprano, then some of the girls joined in. "Let's start again. You take the first line, Pearl, with Patsy and Molly. Jenny and I will come in on the second." In a moment or two, others joined in. By the time they heard the first faint sizzle like a hot griddle, Rosemary was teaching them "Oranges and Lemons." "'When will you pay me . . . Say the Bells of Old Bailey.'" The two voice parts on the third line halted to listen. Nothing. Some of the singers went doggedly on. "'When I am rich . . .'" There it was again. Through the wall. Louder this time. Miss Osgood cautiously approached the door, shovel in hand as if she were going to stun a great beast. The swish erupted into the terrible hiss of danger. White smoke billowed into the playroom as Miss Osgood grabbed the sand bucket and plunged into the murkiness of the furnace room in search of the incendiary. Jenny squeezed Rosemary's arm. The whole basement filled with the noise of shrieking children, one group echoing the other.

And then, as fast as it had engulfed them, the smoke dropped onto their hair, sweaters, shoes in drops of water. Miss Osgood came back into the room smelling of damp wool, Miss Merriweather's ninth grade crowding in behind her.

"Steam from the furnace. That's all it was," she said joyfully. "I thought I was going to be shoveling up a bomb for a moment. Steam, Elizabeth," she called to Miss Merriweather, coming last into the playroom. "I knew it was too hot in here. Damn it all, you can bet it was Cyrus, my brother-in-law," she explained, forgetting herself in her relief. "The handyman's joined the army and what does a professor know about running anything."

From where she stood on the sidewalk in front the school, Margaret watched the last of the lines of children disappear up Parker Farm Road. She lingered for a few minutes, hugging herself against the cold, exhilarated by a sense of accomplishment. Six minutes to the second on her wristwatch. They were ready for the enemy. She took a deep breath and savored the burning of icy, clear air in her lungs. When she finally sauntered up the empty road to rendezvous at the streetlamp, in her head she heard the steady, solid, sober-minded, reliable beat of a Bach chorale in the cadence of her tread and felt in good company. Together she and Harry politely declared the surprise air raid drill an overwhelming success. Then she began the final phase of the operation, going from house to house to announce the All Clear. As she approached the basement steps of the Parkers' house, she heard the sound of children singing. "Now Thank We All Our God," perhaps. She listened more closely as she opened the door into the laundry room. "'Chattanooga Choo Choo,'" blasted out at her. She could hear Eleanor's high soprano in the lead. "'Ohhh won't you choo choo me home.'"

Suddenly, it seemed everything happened just to torment Jenny. One afternoon at school, while she was waiting for her mother to finish her volunteer job selling defense stamps at the table in the main hall, she overheard Miss Osgood whisper to her mother ". . . Fred Goldstein, in particular." Jenny knew her teacher was complaining about her because she couldn't stand Fred, even if he was a Jewish refugee. Miss Osgood looked up and saw her. "Oh hello, Jenny, I'll only keep your mother a minute." Jenny pretended to look at the drawings by the younger grades tacked up along a nearby wall. ". . . and ever since the fright of the air raid, I just feel the tension mounting in him." Miss Osgood shook her head and sighed. "Oh Vera, it's the bitter truth of war. It's snatching away the children's youth." Jenny thought about what she'd overheard and wondered how knowing the truth made people old.

Jenny was glad when Katherine was at her after-school airplane-spotting class and her mother had to go to an evening meeting of the Civil Defense volunteers with Mr. Lewis and Professor Parker. On those days, she got to eat supper with Mary in the kitchen—except when her father was home. She sat in her mother's place at the dining room table so she could step on the buzzer for Mary when it was time to clear the table.

"What are you studying these days?" her father asked.

"Medieval stuff." She put her shoes on the front rung of the chair and leaned forward over her plate. "Daddy, can they put those Japanese people in jail?"

Her father looked at her in astonishment. "How do you know about such things?"

"On Fridays, we have current events now. Miss Osgood reads to us from the *New York Times*."

"Quite the little scholar, tackling the *Times* at your age." He chuckled. "Miss Sperry always says you're a chip off the old block."

"What's she got to do with putting those people in jail?"

"It's not precisely jail," her father said cautiously. "It's an internment camp."

"That's what Hitler does to Jews."

"This is different," he said evenly. "The Japanese are our enemy now. It's very complicated. You mustn't worry yourself, honey."

Jenny slumped back in her chair. They ate in silence. After a while, she pushed the brussel sprouts to the edge of her plate with her fork. Finally, she asked, "Is it secret or something?"

"In a way, yes, Jenny. Wartime secrets. Keeping them from the enemy. What if some of these people are spying on our government?"

"But it's their government too. Why would they do that?"

He gave Jenny a stiff little smile. "Why don't you ring for Mary?" But she didn't. Her father sighed. "It may be difficult for you to understand, honey. You see, the climate of opinion in this country is against the Orientals at this time."

"What's that?"

"How people feel collectively, as a community. In some areas they are moving German and Italian legal aliens away from military zones. But the real fear of invasion is from the Japanese on the West Coast."

"You mean like Pearl Harbor?" she asked.

"I'm afraid so. It's certainly more realistic than this hysteria of your mother's and Harry Lewis about air raids. You can't launch a bomber off the deck of a U boat. In any case, while the president may be acting on prejudicial evidence when he orders the roundup of the Japanese, there's no doubt it's a popular move. When I was downtown today I saw an Oriental man on the street with a button that read *I Am Chinese* pinned to his lapel."

"How come we have meat and Rosemary's mother doesn't?"

"That has to do with availability. It's complicated."

"Why."

"They're at war. Now that's enough, missy. Ring the buzzer."

Reluctantly, she inched down on her spine to the edge of the chair and reached with her foot for the buzzer

In an instant, Mary came through the swinging door. "Quite the little smart one, aren't we now," she said, taking Jenny's plate.

Jenny scowled at her. "They put you in a camp for spying."

Mary made a mock-horror face. "Is the little madam going to serve the pudding, or will I?"

"Serve the dessert, Mary," Her father said, shaking his head. "I don't know what's been going on around here, but I would say the climate of opinion is bordering on impertinent."

"Sorry, Mr. Oliver."

"That means they'll put you away."

"Now Jenny, that's enough. You're not to be rude to Mary."

Mary pursed her lips at Jenny and passed through the swinging door into the pantry.

"I swear she'll get her notice, talking up that way," Jenny's father muttered.

They were silent for a moment.

"Does that mean they will take Mary away?" Jenny asked anxiously.

"No such luck."

"I won't let them," Jenny said defiantly. "You won't let them, will you, Daddy," she pleaded.

He leaned over to put his hand on her knee. "I'll say this for you, Jenny, you never give up."

At lunchtime, Fred often sat with the girls now, his shiny, black eyes turned like beams on Rosemary. Jenny felt Rosemary slipping away from her. She was snappish and argumentative. One Friday after current events, when Rosemary was going on again about how much better parliamentary government was than democracy, Jenny reminded her that Miss Osgood had said that under the American system everyone was equal because there was no room for a monarchy. All of a sudden, Rosemary stood up, her favorite custard untouched. As she proceeded majestically toward the kitchen area, Fred raced after her and grabbed her tray, walking beside her, balancing the two lunch trays.

Jenny was left to pick at her pudding.

Rosemary had just gotten boring, all she did was talk about Fred, Fred, Fred. Jenny hung around her house after school to show Rosemary she had things to do. She finished her homework in a hurry, so she could listen to the hit tunes on the radio after supper or talk with Mary in the kitchen. She tried to follow the news in the paper the way Katherine did, and sometimes she snooped in her sister's room to look at the maps and pins that were supposed to explain what was happening thousands of miles away in places she had never heard of and couldn't begin to imagine. She knew about Singapore, though. That was where the Parkers' son Cyrus Junior was when the Japanese soldiers marched in.

One evening. when she was missing Rosemary so badly that she went down early to sit with her parents before supper, she was surprised to find there was no one in the living room. She crept to the end of the hall where she could hear them through the gap at the study door.

"What were you doing going through my desk, Vera?"

"Snooping, Richard, I was snooping. The jeweler called to say the clasp on the bracelet was fixed. I knew whose bracelet it was. I found this little billet-doux yesterday when I was getting your suit ready to be pressed. 'Thank you for two beautiful years. E.' " Her voice was shrill.

"Vera, give me that."

"You told me no," her mother cried out. "The great defender of truth. You lied to me, Richard."

"It's just a token, Vera. Nothing's happened. She doesn't mean anything to me. It's all in your imagination."

"Working in a hotel room. That's not my imagination."

"Space is tight in wartime, you know that."

"I know that you lied to me, Richard." She raised her voice. "You want Miss Sperry, I'll get a divorce." She was screaming now.

"You don't mean that, Vera." He sounded shocked. "Think what you're saying." Jenny could hear her mother's sobs in a moment of quiet. "You're upset, Vera," he went on. "You'll calm down in a minute."

There was a hideous silence. Then a crash. "You didn't have to throw my pipes on the floor like that. You're out of control, Vera."

Her mother howled, "Don't touch me." The door flew open, and Jenny ducked into the dining room as her mother raced up the front stairs.

In the kitchen Jenny put her head down on the table and wept.

Now when the maids came downstairs in the late afternoon to prepare supper for the families of West Ivers, before they added the onions to the stew they'd braised at noon or scraped the carrots, they pulled the heavy dark blackout curtains across the windows. In the evening the wardens dressed warmly against the

icy temperatures of the New England winter and put
on white helmets and arm bands to patrol the streets
of their neighborhoods, looking for infringements of
the national blackout. They had read their guerrilla
warfare manuals—how to deliver a karate chop-—in
case they encountered an infiltrator in the shadows, and they carried police whistles, some of them
stamped "Made in Japan."

On Parker Farm Road, when everyone had settled
for the evening, sometimes Jenny would turn out the
light in the upstairs hall and lift the edge of the dark
green shade that hung like an eye patch across the
windowpanes. Kneeling on a chair she watched for
the solitary figure of Professor Parker to pass by on
his route from the turnoff at Great Hamilton Street
where his beat began to the far end of the road and the
grounds of the school.

As she waited, she patrolled the street with her
eyes. The pole of the streetlight by the Nortons' house
was a solid dark pencil line in the murky moonlight.
There was still a streak of yellow from the Russells'
house beyond, where the fancy new Venetian blinds
were supposed to keep out the light. They were more
elegant than Jenny's mother's navy blue cotton behind
the glass curtains in the dining room, but they didn't
work. Patsy would not like it when Professor Parker
gave her mother a second warning. Up the street in the
other direction, Jenny could see the dark hulk of the
Parkers' third-floor cupola reaching above a skeletal
elm. Rosemary would be sitting on her bed, cozy in the

hidden light, painting her toenails a lurid red or standing before her mirror trying out the orangey Tangee Natural lipstick she had stolen from the five-and-ten. The theft still bothered Jenny. She had refused to go with Rosemary, not because she knew it was wrong, but because she was afraid of being caught. She was ashamed of her own timidity, but she was even more concerned that Rosemary could still be found out and taken away to jail miles beyond the end of the trolley line. What would they give her to eat? Could she visit her? Would Mrs. Parker fix things with the police like she could everything else? Jenny wished they would take away Fred instead. As she waited for Professor Parker, her worries seemed to multiply.

At last, he came into view, sauntering along as if on a midnight stroll rather than a mission of wartime, the ashes from his pipe glowing each time he drew on it. It seemed a violation of the rules. Wouldn't the enemy see it? When she went to bed, she left the door ajar so she could hear the drone of the voice on the radio downstairs. Her father was home more often now. Her mother was prickly with him, but he was nicer to her. Jenny liked to imagine them sitting together on either side of the console radio listening to the news, talking over the day's events. But when her parents turned the radio off, as she lay awake examining the threatening shadows in the triangle of light cast across the ceiling from the fixture in the hall, Jenny strained to hear the murmur of their voices. The silence frightened her. Sometimes she cried herself to sleep.

Chapter Fifteen

The Home Front. The greatest salvage and recycling
drive in the history of the nation, launched in a frenzy
of public unity, galvanized the country into action.
Morale was high. The patriotic imagination of New
Englanders was caught by the reenactment of the
1775 hauling of a captured British cannon from
Ticonderoga to the siege at Charlestown. Retracing
the route, a flatbed truck carrying a reproduction of
the cannon passed through cities and towns, prompting the citizens to donate commemorative statuary
and historic weaponry from the town green or village
common to crush the Nazis. At the central railroad
junction in Vermont, when they finished scooping the
scrap into container cars, the yardmen threw their
shovels on top of the load for good measure. In Massachusetts, under a sign that read:

"This SCRAP to LICK the JAP"

Dismantling of this "EL" is being expedited

For the best interest of national defense,

the governor, in a pinstripe suit and a hard hat,

put a cutting torch to the filigreed fence at a stop on the elevated line. Behind him loomed the dome of the state house, once gold, now gunmetal gray.

Old radiators, boilers, lawn mowers, crank handles, tire chains, furnace grates, doorstops, toys, garbage pails, bedsteads, any kind of scrap iron and steel would go to make the machines and arms of warfare. "About 50% of every tank, ship, and gun is made of scrap iron and steel," the campaign posters stated. Parker Farm Road emptied out garages, cellar storage areas, even the garden tool shed. When he received his commission as lieutenant in the Army Accounting Corps, Tom Norton donated an old set of golf irons. The call went out for copper and brass as well. Ed Russell parted with the radiator from his father's 1912 Ford Model T, which had been mounted like an icon on the wall of his garage.

Old batteries and lighting fuses, bicycles tubes, rubber tires, garden hoses, rags, carpets, Manila rope, burlap for bombs and Jeep tires, parachutes, gas masks, and barrage balloons. The Russells' Nora and the Olivers' Mary poured off the fats and saved the grease for the missus to turn in at the butcher's for future use in high explosives. Tin cans and tin toothpaste containers. Even the inside foil wrapper on a cigarette package counted. The neighborhood children went from house to house towing Pelly Norton's red wagon to collect old phonograph records when the movie theater in the square offered a free ticket for every six discs turned in. The shellac could be reused. In the late summer Margaret Graham and Eleanor Osgood collected milkweed pods on the Island to pad life jackets.

Shortages. Real and imagined. People began to hoard. When stockpiling created a shortage of sugar, it was the first commodity to be rationed, eight ounces per person a week. While black markets sprang up in every city, in West Ivers the refugee women of the Back Door Store—used to deprivation and eager to show their loyalty to the country that had taken them in— were quick to adapt to baking their special delicacies with corn syrup and molasses, and later margarine. The community was appreciative, but Professor Parker and his colleagues agreed there was nothing like the real thing.

Vera and Eleanor Osgood heeded Isabel Parker's call for volunteers to help out at the Red Cross blood-donor station downtown. On Wednesdays Charlotte Russell put on the starched uniform of the Gray Ladies and prepared to visit the sick and wounded in local hospitals when, inevitably, the casualties came home. Katherine Oliver and her classmates rolled bandages in the function room of the public library one afternoon a week. When the United Service Organization opened on the Common downtown, Bea Norton, in a fit of pique at her husband, who would certainly not approve, was among the first to volunteer.

Once or twice, Bea spied Mrs. von Kempel on the subway into town looking too smart in her navy blue suit with her fox fur piece gripped at the neck, the little snout of the animal nestled in his tail. Mrs. von

Kempel filled in as a greeter at the same USO center where Bea worked as a hostess. They nodded to each other on occasion, but as if by mutual agreement, they did not say much, and Bea worried if she should tell someone that Mrs. von Kempel was a divorcee and had been married to a German. When she told her stories about the darling young men and their funny dance steps over a drink with the Russells, enjoying the disbelief on their faces, she did not mention Mrs. von Kempel.

From the beginning of the hostilities Margaret Graham had been concerned about the impact of the nation at war on the Parker Farm School, as one by one, the young male teachers signed up. Mr. Upton told his math students he'd always wanted to be a pilot, leading the older girls to speculate how handsome he would be in blue. Mr. Johns returned in army uniform to say good-bye to his sixth grade, looking unfamiliarly wise and protective. Mr. Ely, the shop supervisor, went into the merchant marine, leaving Mr. Dooley in charge, the only male figure left at the school except for the elderly Latin teacher. The school seemed diminished, the students and staff anxious and undirected. Tempers flared, and the headmistress was at a loss on how to encourage a sense of participation. Then in May, the West Ivers school committee accepted the mayor's request to sponsor a city-wide paper drive. Since high school students were contributing to the war effort as plane spotters and bandage rollers, the committee voted that middle-schoolers from each district be responsible for the drive during Youth for Victory Week. Miss Graham announced in assembly that the Parker Farm School was proud to join with the public-school children in this "valiant egalitarian effort."

During the summer, while commercial farmers were feeding the Fighting Forces, Mr. and Mrs. America were urged to dig in and plant their own vegetable gardens. Vitamins for Victory. When the governor was photographed hoeing a row of early radishes, the mayor of West Ivers put on his overalls and joined the spaders on the Common. On Parker Farm Road, Bea Norton put in early lettuces for the children before they went away to their grandmother's for the summer, and Charlotte Russell tried a trellis of peas across the back of her perennial bed. Harry had Dominic lay out a full vegetable garden along the backyard line. The wind carried the smell of rotted manure through the open window of Professor Parker's study, reawakening memories of boyhood summers on the Island, when he used to help in the kitchen garden. With the help of his English Rose he turned over the lawn behind the conservatory and felt quite rejuvenated as he contemplated the planting. Tomatoes and beans, but first he must have two or three rows of onions. He paused in his grand design to consider what would complement them. Carrots and "good old spuds." The Maine farmer's flat twang echoed cheerfully over the decades. He took the last of Hilda's potatoes in the pantry bin and cut them in pieces, each with an eye. As he set them gently in the trench, despite his wife's dire prediction of the rationing to come, he savored the thought of the early little ones slathered with butter or the hearty stew Hilda would simmer in the autumn.

Richard enlarged his tomato and bean patch to include carrots and beets, and tucked in some Hubbard squash seeds by the garage. Even the Russells' Nora dug up a strip along the clothes-yard fence, perishing for the vegetables the well-to-do always scorned. Just a row of parsnips and the lovely cabbages. Sure they'd be grateful to her later on, she said to herself, not knowing that she would not be there for the late harvest.

Despite the first Allied victory at Midway in early June 1942, it was a troubled summer on Parker Farm Road. Along with the war news, the rhythm of things seemed to move faster; the unexpected became the norm. Opportunity was everywhere, and wages were sky high. Cynics said that if the war went on like this, a fellow might even get out of debt. It was rumored the Nortons' Katy had gone to California, alone, to make big money in the booming wartime economy as a riveter in an airplane plant. Brassy young girl. Gas rationing left everyone irritable. An "A" card allowed only 3 gallons a week. It meant that Ed Russell had to travel to Buzzards Bay by train and Vera often rode the streetcar to the Back Door Store. Of course, Isabel Parker, as a Red Cross emissary, qualified for a priority card, entitling her to more than the rest of them. And that Harry Lewis, who had kept the wartime money-maker, the die-making investment, for himself. He had enough gas to drive all the way out to Framingham to his industrial plant seven days a week.

Even Margaret allowed herself an intolerant thought. Worried about stretching anticipated income over a new school year of rising prices and shortages, and ever mindful of Harry's threat about the physical plant, she decided to go over to the school one Sunday after lunch to look at the books. She just missed the trolley car at the top of her street and so she set out on foot. The walk took longer than she expected, and she grew tired and irritable. As she turned up Parker Farm Road, Harry drew alongside in his comfortable Packard and offered her a ride. She looked at his priority sticker pasted on the windshield and said the walk was good for her, then immediately regretted her decision. Finally, settling down at her desk to go over the ledger sheets, she was exasperated to see Harry's initials as treasurer over his correction on her books. On closer look she saw that she had been wrong and he was right. Did Jews really have an instinctive cunning for finance, she muttered angrily to herself, and was immediately filled with remorse at such an ungenerous thought.

"I'm dropping the Lewises from my Christmas card list," Charlotte Russell announced to Bea Norton. "The gall of Harry Lewis, snatching Nora out of my kitchen to work in his little munitions factory. I notice he's not carrying off his own help." Her teacup rattled as she set it down. "It's unbelievable, a Jew trying to match Wellington Brass. My grandfather would turn over in his grave."

Bea, tempted to be standoffish in the light of all the criticism she had taken of late for actually enjoying her job at the canteen, suddenly remembered Harry tipping his hat to her when he glimpsed her with an airman in her garden. "Well, you know how nosy they can be."

"Ed says Harry Lewis thinks he's the Messiah." Charlotte raised her eyebrows. "I wonder if Vera Oliver still thinks he's God's gift to school boards and refugee shops now that he's after her cook."

While Vera didn't take it personally when Mary gave her two weeks' notice to go to work at Izrael and Son, she couldn't help but be upset. She knew Richard would be pleased; he'd come to resent Mary's increasing insolence, something Vera quietly enjoyed when it was directed toward him. But she felt disappointed for herself. In another week or two she would be back in the kitchen, where she had started. And this time, it would be without the company of women talking, no mother, aunties, schoolmates, certainly not the neighbors. For a moment, she wanted Harry to smooth the ragged edges of her life, as so often had happened before, but of course, he was just the nice neighbor down the street, a fellow committee member, a friendly person who did not take umbrage if an Irish maid asked him for a job.

She thought of Jenny, too, who loved the maid so

voraciously. Sometimes more than she loved Vera herself. She consoled herself with knowing that the crush would pass. But even so it tugged at her heart. Now, she must break the news to her daughter when she came home from school.

"She'll come home at night," Jenny said.

"No, dear."

"Mr. Lewis does."

"She and Nora are going to live together in a rented apartment nearby their new work. Lots of working girls are doing it. It's an opportunity for them."

Jenny could feel her whole body draw in on itself, lines gathering across her forehead like Mrs. Parker's old mother. When her mother reached out to embrace her, she ducked away and moved toward the living room doors.

"You told her to go," she screamed as she fled up the stairs. "I think Mr. Lewis stinks." She slammed the door of her room.

Vera went back into the living room and sat down for a moment to collect herself. The staggering mobilization of the country that allowed the Marys and Noras of the world a new chance in life, and the good news from North Africa and Russia had renewed national resolution and brought back hope to the country. It was ironic. In the early years of the war, in response to human horror and tragedy abroad, it was Harry who helped Vera build up the Back Door Store, and together, they had mapped out the air-raid shelters for the school. Now things ran so smoothly, she was no longer needed. Even sharing the depressing war news used to bring her together with Richard, but she tried not to think about what he was up to now. A wartime fling. Maybe just a natural attraction. She still went back and forth in her mind almost daily. Angry, vengeful, frightened, rational, resigned. But Richard was right, she never intended to divorce him. She would sit it out like a sensible woman. Trying to keep her feelings from exploding or seeping out in public like a slow leak. Putting a good face on things. Anything else would leave her alone. And worse, a pariah. Her world did not tolerate scandal.

The void she felt was visceral, as painfully hollow as if she were ravenously hungry. She took her handkerchief from the sleeve of her cardigan and blew her nose. She was worse off than even her spinster aunts, with their jobs in the mill and community of workers. She raised her fist to the memory of her mother. She was as unsettled and overwhelmed as she had been years ago when Margaret first asked her to join Isabel Parker's committee.

To fill up her time now, she volunteered more hours at the school, typing up minutes and reports, taking a turn at the switchboard now that the regular operator had gone to a job attaching steel snaps to assault gas masks. Sometimes Vera envied the women who earned good wages in the defense plants. But a lady like herself didn't do work like that. She was gratified that people at the school had come to depend on her, but it felt like a step back into her mother's dream for her, when she had already been to loftier places. The truth was that everything depressed her.

And Richard came home late, harried and distracted. "On the run," he said. She always wondered whether to believe him now when he said he had an evening meeting that promised to be long and contentious. But she was mollified this evening. For the first time in days he suggested a quick drink together before supper. While Richard mixed himself a very dry martini and poured Vera a glass of sherry, she told him the news. He laughed. "Poor Lewis. It won't be long before she's telling him how to run his plant." Just as he sat back to take his first sip, Mary announced dinner.

"In a moment, Mary. I hear you're leaving us," Richard said and saluted the maid with his cocktail glass.

Then, the telephone rang. It was Katherine to say she would be staying with Christina Grew again tonight. Late choral practice.

"Late choral practice every night, Vera?" Richard asked. "When I was in college we were expected to do a little studying now and then."

"They're preparing for the fall concert, dear." Vera tried to sound soothing. "And Katherine has a fine voice." But Vera was uneasy herself. Ever since her first weeks as a freshman at Boylston, there was a new Katherine emerging from her chrysalis. Secret phone calls. Heels to class. Showy red lips that reminded Vera of Miss Sperry.

"She'll need more than a nice singing voice to stay

in college," Richard said, shaking his head. "She'll have to settle down to her studies, Vera. She's always been a fine student."

Vera sighed. "I do worry about her spending so much time at the university. The square is full of servicemen, and as a local student, she shouldn't even be in the dormitories at night until she's a junior. When I pointed out that she and Christina were breaking a wartime regulation, she said everyone does it."

Richard took a gulp of gin. "People like the Philadelphia Grews always think they're above the rules, but that's no reason for Katherine . . ."

"I can't keep it hot much longer, Mrs. Oliver," Mary said from the hall.

Richard looked at Vera and shook his head. "That's what I mean about her. She might as well stand out there and holler 'Soups on.'"

He stood up wearily and made his way into the hall as Jenny came down the stairs. She glared at him. "What's the matter with you, young lady?"

Jenny scrunched up her nose and went past him ino the dining room.

"Mary," Vera whispered.

"Mary again," he said, annoyed. "It's just as well she's going, Vera. Both the children seem to have gotten out of hand while you've been out of the house looking after the rest of the world."

"I enjoy it, Richard."

He raised his eyebrows and looked over his glasses. She felt very sure of her ground. At least he didn't oppose her any more.

Jenny left the table without asking to be excused, and Richard looked at his watch several times. Immediately after supper he hurried into his study to make a telephone call and reappeared in the hall in his hat and coat. He bent to give Vera a peck on the cheek. "Sorry, if I'm a little irritable, Vera. Overworked, that's all. "

"Good night, Richard."

Neither one of them mentioned how late he might be anymore.

Vera lit an after-dinner cigarette. Nothing on the surface had changed. Only Richard rarely mentioned Miss Sperry anymore. Vera was still ashamed of the fuss over the bracelet, not because she was wrong but because she had lost control, lost the advantage. Richard had been so rational, so calm, never dignifying Vera's accusation that he had lied to her. But doubt had flared up again when she saw her husband's secretary helping out at the paper drive last summer. Miss Sperry was no longer a young mouse eager to please. This woman was a city cousin, a modern young woman, her cheeks rouged, nose powdered, comfortably chic in a casual cotton frock and pert summer hat. Her smile, her manner with the boss's wife was assured and unconcerned. The only sign of insecurity had been her eagerness to please Jenny. Vera still suspected that Richard slept with Emily Sperry despite what he had said.

She recalled the awful night that had followed the scene in Richard's study. Locked in her room, in between bouts of tears, loving Richard or hating him, she had not been able to escape the truth of a wife's dependence on her husband. Money had the upper hand. Mrs. Parker, of course, had her own inherited income, and Vera had always wondered if that was the great leveler between the Parkers. Richard paid for everything: the house, the maid, the car, the children's school bills. Richard's name was hers, and without it, she would not be welcomed by friends and neighbors. Look at Mrs. von Kempel. Think of the children. The shame she felt just imagining such isolation had brought on a new flood of tears. Against a lawyer like Richard, even if she were to brave divorce, she would never get a good settlement. And in her position, she could hardly seek her fortune like the Nortons' maid or the receptionist at school. She had gone into the bathroom and put a warm washcloth across her tired eyes. Opening them into the dark rose of the terry cloth, she had told herself there were worse marriages.

She lit a second cigarette off the first and blew out a plume of smoke. She had been understandably upset that night, she did not blame herself for her hysteria. Since then, she had tried to concentrate on the comfortable compensations of marriage. House, maid—for two more weeks. The social status marriage gave her in the community. Men in important positions had come to depend on Richard. Often someone from New York or Washington would telephone, seeking his advice. When she picked up the receiver and heard, "The White House calling," that was when she was proud to be Mrs. Richard Oliver.

But then . . . Her mind was on the spin again. She was driving herself crazy. Torturing herself. She stamped out her cigarette so forcefully the stub broke open, spilling tobacco out of the little Limoges ashtray. As she swept the tobacco shreds into her palm, she resolved one last time to continue to strive for a respectful calm between them, remembering the lesson of her childhood: a woman kept a husband by letting him think his concerns came first. They were older now, their bodies full and comfortable with middle age. The sexual ineptitudes and disappointments of their youthful naiveté didn't matter. If Richard had strayed, it was almost to be expected. He was a man.

She turned out the lights and parted the blackout curtains to look out into the shadowy night. The cold weather had curled the rhododendron leaves and she could barely make out the frozen clumps of dead grass heaved up in the lawn. Along the fence, the skeletons of Richard's tomato plants stood sentry near the outline of the hawthorn tree that he had planted for Jenny. It was only a matter of years before Jenny would step into her own life, like Katherine. Then she and Richard would be alone. Suddenly, painfully, her mind betrayed her again. With time, she had finally learned to meet Richard's sexual needs, and she had welcomed the pleasure and power it had given her. Now Richard's desire for another woman had withered her. In the darkened window glass, she could dimly see the gathering lines in her face, the sagging cheeks, little pockets of flesh under her eyes. Suddenly, she felt as if middle age had swept her aside. What was left was a yearning for something of her own, a devotion beyond her family to take her out of herself.

The atmosphere in the house for the next week was one of battle readiness. Jenny was determined never to forgive her mother. When she came through the door, she left the schoolgirl at the stoop, dripping like a wet coat, and stepped into a icy shroud of studied indifference. She refused to acknowledge any well-meaning overture—"I saw Miss Graham today. She says your choice of props for the Christmas play is just perfect"—and gained strength from criticism. "Your mother and I have had enough of this, Jenny. You will leave the dinner table right now and go to your room until you can behave rationally." But on secret forays into the kitchen, she whimpered and sniveled, clutched and sobbed, until Mary gave up stroking and joshing—"I'll be back to see you. We'll have a grand time." Pulling out of Jenny's angry embrace, she went back to scraping the carrots. Over the past few days the house collected a grieving silence

The morning of Mary's departure, Jenny refused to go to school. She wasn't being bad, she just felt forlorn. She'd been crying through the night, and she was limp with fatigue. When Mary went to finish packing, Jenny, still in her pajamas, left the breakfast table. Her mother didn't argue.

"After I take Mary and Nora to the train station,

I thought I'd do a little shopping," her mother called after her. "I want to talk to Frank at the meat market to see how far our ration will go, now that Mary is taking her book with her."

Jenny went up the stairs in heavy silence.

"I thought I'd pick up an ice cream log as a treat for dessert tonight. Daddy will be out to dinner."

Her mother waited, but Jenny had nothing to say.

"Or I could come right home after I drop them off. Would you like that?"

Jenny shut the door of her room quietly.

Later, she heard footsteps in the hall, but her mother must have thought she was asleep. Would her mother take Mary off without letting Jenny say good-bye?

And then it was time for Mary to go. Her mother called up the stairs, "I'll be back as soon as I've done the errands."

Jenny opened the door instantly and came down the stairs, sad and sullen. Her mother was just putting on her hat and coat. Without speaking, they went into the kitchen.

Mary stood by the back door beside a battered cardboard suitcase. She wore a pair of serviceable brogues and her Sunday black, bought in Cork for the first leg of her journey to independence. She looked young and uncertain, like a girl hiding in her grand-mother's overcoat. Even Jenny peered at her as if she were looking for someone she knew. The only touch of the Mary who had sometimes ruled too boldly was the purple snood she wore to capture her wavy, dark hair. It looked ridiculous.

Jenny's mother smiled gently at the young woman. "My goodness, Mary, won't your head be cold? What happened to your new hat with the feather?"

"Oh, I won't be needing that." Mary slipped a finger sheepishly under the lattice work of heavy cotton thread across her head. "It's all the rage, you know, and Mr. Israel said if we think we're up to doing a man's job, we'd better keep our hair out of the machinery when we're on the lathe. The hat's on the peg there for Jenny."

"Oh," Jenny cried, lunging to hug Mary, "I know you really want it." Mary reached for the hat and set it on Jenny's head. It sat tumbled to one side. "How do I look?" Jenny asked.

"When the little people come out of the bog, they'll recognize one of their own."

As Jenny watched the Buick go down Parker Farm Road, the two Irish maids in the back seat, she thought about the trip with Pearl to Mr. Lewis' factory. The lap robe across her knees, lunch in the diner, the empty machine shed and the crates of new lathes for Mary and Nora. It had been a glimpse into a world beyond imagining. She pressed her nose to the window glass and waved until the car was out of sight. Then she curled up on her bed and cried herself to sleep.

Chapter Sixteen

Vera didn't pretend to be much of a cook, but it didn't
bother her. She didn't need to be admired for her cooking; she just tried to be good-humored about it. When
Richard was home, she rushed from kitchen to living
room, climbing out of her apron and grabbing her
timer, to join him for a glass of sherry. It was almost
too comical, this dual role, the madam and the maid.
Joking about it lifted her spirits. "Won't you have a
cheese cracker, Mrs. Oliver?" "Yes, thank you, Vera,"
she quipped as she took a cracker from the plate she
was carrying. She made goulash and ham with mustard,
spaghetti sauce with the summer tomatoes that Mary
had put up, and then she added shreds of beef that she
sliced from the corner of Sunday's inevitable pot roast
and put through the grinder. When she braised the roast
in the old stew pot with a broken handle on the ancient
and unpredictable gas range, she wondered sheepishly
how Mary had put up with it. Vera stuck to her small
successes, and now and then, when she was alone in the
kitchen, sometimes she felt a sense of purpose.

But Richard's dining club on the first weekend in May was something else again. While there were certain things she didn't do if she could help it, like carry the tray of drinks to the living room or put the barrels out for collection, and Richard had finally learned to put up with the laundry service doing up his shirts, this was an occasion when the success of the evening would reflect on her. The speaker was a financier from New York and adviser to the president. The members had been delighted when he accepted until Richard read them the letter at last month's meeting. "I hope you will oblige me by including Mr. Harry Lewis, one of your fellow citizens of West Ivers, on the occasion," the expert had written in his acceptance letter. "He's a rare friend and the kind of financier with the entrepreneurial talents I'd like to see more of in this country." Richard hadn't been bothered by this request, speakers often brought guests. He told Vera he went on record as saying he liked to be in the company of successful men, "and Harry Lewis is certainly that." There were some in the club who were less sanguine, but they were unwilling to ruffle the speaker's feathers. The latest and youngest member to the venerable old club, recruited in the search for new blood, was Ed Russell. He asked that the minutes record that for personal reasons he could not attend. Richard told Vera this statement led to too much whispering-behind-the-hand speculation. Vera shook her head at such childish behavior among distinguished men. She knew Harry was used to this kind of thing, but more than ever, she was determined to make the evening go smoothly.

She had been hoarding coffee and skimping on the newly rationed meat stamps for weeks, and the butcher could promise her a nice rolled roast. She had also engaged Mrs. Wright and her helper Mrs. Pierce to do the preparation and cooking, but she was stymied when she learned that Mrs. Pierce would serve and do the dishes, but she did not set up. Such help was almost impossible to find nowadays, and cost an arm and a leg. Katherine was busy, of course. Finally Vera settled on Jenny and Rosemary.

On the morning of the dinner party, Vera woke up determined to banish her anxieties in favor of a brisk and purposeful modus operandi . Richard left the house early, despite it being a Saturday. "Don't forget your umbrella, Richard," she called after him, "it's going to rain again." She supervised Jenny and Rosemary as they carried the two center leaves of the dining room table up from the cellar—"Careful you don't scratch the finish on the banister there"—and reassembled them. She dismantled her squatter's space, carrying her files and lists from the corner of the dining room to the pantry, where she squeezed them into the cupboard with the flower vases. She shoved the collapsed card table behind the coats in the front hall closet. Then, with the help of the girls, she unfolded the heavy white damask tablecloth and set out eleven matching napkins. In the pantry, while Vera arranged the cocktail glasses on the silver tray, ready to be carried into the living room, Rosemary laid out the dinner forks. Jenny followed with the knives.

"Which way do they go?" Jenny asked.

"In," Rosemary said, turning the knife nearest her so the blade faced toward the fork. "So no one gets stabbed." She ran her finger lightly down a blade. "Wouldn't hurt a flea, let alone a big booby," she said derisively.

"You saw the Beasty?" Jenny picked up a fistful of soup spoons.

"Don't get fingerprints all over the silverware, Jenny," her mother said as she passed through the dining room.

Rosemary pointed at Jenny's mother. "I'll tell you later," she whispered. They followed each other around the oval table again with the salad forks and dessert spoons. When the telephone rang in the hall, they strained to hear as they placed a wine glass at the tip of each knife. It was obviously Katherine calling. Rosemary was just hoisting herself up to reach the water glasses off the top shelf above the flower sink when Jenny's mother poked her head around the pantry door. "That's not safe, Rosemary, you'd better get down. I'm going upstairs to the other phone. I'll be back in a few minutes with the kitchen steps to help you with those goblets." The door swung shut.

Rosemary finished her climb into the sink and stood up. "The Beasty was peeking in the window at us," she began, glancing down at Jenny standing before the sink looking up at her.

Jenny sighed and looked away. "Us" meant Goatfred, of course. And the window, uncovered now after the blackout was lifted, looked into the playroom of the Parkers' basement. It was recessed below ground, and there was a grill to stand on while crouching out of sight against the side of the brick enclosure. Jenny knew. She'd seen them herself.

They were sitting with their backs to her, side by side on the piano bench, their shoulders touching. Suddenly, Fred rubbed his nose against Rosemary's. Then she kissed him. It was the most disgusting thing Jenny could imagine, Rosemary touching her lips to blubbery ones like Fred's. Even so she couldn't stop looking, or wondering what it felt like. "What were you doing?" she finally asked.

"Nothing. Eating crackers and jam. Playing chopsticks," Rosemary said lightly. "Of course, Fred flew at the window in one of his rages, and the Beasty got stuck trying to get out, and Fred started stabbing the air with the spreading knife and yelling, 'Kraut monster, moron, slob'"—Rosemary was waving her arms now—"and the Beasty screamed, 'Jew, Jew, you touched her.'"

"I thought you said you weren't doing anything."

"We weren't doing anything bad." Rosemary flashed her smile.

"I saw you," Jenny said triumphantly.

"You horrid sneak." Rosemary stamped her foot on the copper sink. "You spied. You're just like that dumb Beasty."

"I am not," Jenny protested, thinking of her

mother screaming "divorce" and bursting into tears. "You're my best friend and now you like awful Fred better."

"Cry baby bumpkin," Rosemary sneered, reaching behind her for one of the glasses. "You're so immature." She held the goblet over the sink.

"Oh don't, Rosemary. I'm sorry, I won't do it again, I promise. Don't, please. Mummy will . . ."

"You're just jealous." Rosemary opened her hand and dropped the goblet. It lay at her feet in the sink, severed at the neck like a broken figurine. Years later, Jenny would notice that Emily Sperry had upended the fluted bowl of the broken glass like a dome over a tiny cutting of a plant she was nursing along in the south window of the living room.

"Oh, Rosemary," Jenny's mother said, coming through the pantry door. "Why didn't you help her, Jenny?"

"But Mummy . . ."

Jenny's mother picked the broken glass out of the sink, her forehead creased with exasperation. She held the two pieces together. A chunk was missing from the stem.

Rosemary bent over to pick it up. "Sorry, Mrs. Oliver."

"I remember when I first saw these goblets in the shop window. I thought I'd never seen anything so beautiful." Lovingly, she set the broken pieces at the back of the dish cupboard. "The next time you two think you can manage something like this on your own, please think again," she said crossly. "Now go make yourselves some sandwiches. There's deviled egg in the refrigerator, and use the margarine. I'm saving the butter for the dinner party." She sighed. "Make one for Katherine, too. She's changed her plans, today of all days. She's on her way home. Just as well, she's supposed to be living here, not on the floor of a dormitory room. Oh, do get down, Rosemary."

"You want a sandwich, Mummy?"

"I've lost my appetite," she said, shaking her head.

"R is really mean." Jenny wrote later in her diary. "She dropped one of the goblets on purpose because of Fred." She drew a picture of the broken goblet. "R says I'm like the Beasty! Is it because his mother is divorced?" She started to put away her pen, then added, "Poor Beasty."

The dinner party got off to a good start. From the top of the stairs Vera could hear Richard greeting his guest as they arrived and Mrs. Pierce took their raincoats. While the guests were having cocktails in the living room, Vera checked the table. Thank goodness Ed Russell didn't come; there were just enough water goblets to go around now. When the men were seated at the table and dinner had been served, Vera peeked through the pantry door as Mrs. Pierce refilled the wine glasses or passed the platter of meat for the second time, and for a moment, she forgot her uneasiness about Katherine, who still hadn't shown up. The conversation at the table was lively and easy, always a good sign. The race of the British across North Africa and the impending defeat of the Axis, recounted by the military man among them and embellished by others, like a Greek epic. The amazing feat of shipbuilder Henry Kaiser, a ten thousand ton Liberty cargo ship finished four days after the keel is laid. Harry praised the wisdom of the president's anti-inflation order last month and the implications of the pay-as-you-go tax plan in congressional committee. Richard agreed and said how much he had come to admire the president, no doubt raising a few eyebrows, Vera imagined. Each man had a special expertise or a piece of inside information to contribute, and as she listened she thought wistfully, not for the first time, that men led more interesting lives. As Mrs. Pierce served the almond cake—half a pound of real butter, a cup and a half of precious sugar, a skimpy four eggs—Vera hurried up the kitchen stairs to change out of her shirt-waist dress.

She had agreed with Richard that it would be appropriate for her to put in a brief wifely appearance to pour the coffee, before the brandy and cigars and the serious business of the evening. She was flattered that he wanted her there, and she thought she'd look her best in the green cocktail dress she bought a few months ago, for the party on the Hill to celebrate the hasty marriage of a socially prominent law partner's daughter to an Army captain. She had worn shoes dyed to match the dress and a little black hat. But now Richard shook his head.

"Several people told me how nice I looked," Vera protested.

"I'm sure," Richard said, "just right for the Lawrences. But it's too showy for the club."

"You were the one who told me to get something smart. It's not easy to find a good dress nowadays."

He shook his head again.

"The gray chiffon?" She was disappointed.

He nodded. "Much more in keeping with the occasion."

But when Vera saw the respectable gray dress hanging on the back of the closet door, ready to put her in her place, she reached for the cocktail dress. She felt buoyed up. When she looked into the full-length mirror, she smiled at the radiance of the rich-colored taffeta, almost iridescent in the overhead light. It set off her dark hair and the blush of her skin. Richard would notice again how nice she looked in it. Then she wondered about the vanity V of lace snapped in at the neckline. No, leave it, she scolded herself, and went into the children's bathroom to get Katherine's rouge. Before the mirror at her dressing table, she reminded herself the important thing was not too much. Then she patted on loose face powder to hide the shine on her nose and lightly applied a bright red lipstick. Perhaps she would try a little Vaseline over her lipstick to give a glossy look. A last look in the mirror. Recklessly, she unsnapped the lace, exposing the hint of the hollow between her breasts. She felt quite giddy.

At the top of the stairs, she could see Richard

smiling up at her, but as she continued down the staircase a look of dismay froze on his face. "Vera!" he said
sharply, then softened, "dear."

Vera stopped mid-step and put her hands at the
plunge of her neckline.

The gentlemen in the living room were rising to
their feet. "Yes, Richard?" She stepped past him, and
he took her by the elbow and began the introductions
around the circle of men. She gave each one a wom-
anly smile. Their respectful good manners and cheerful
salutations brought the flush of success at her cheeks,
especially when the honored guest, a small, round man
who looked as though he always ate well, compli-
mented her on the rareness of the beef. She sat down
on the sofa in front of the coffee urn and tried to rein
in her excitement before beginning to pour. As she was
handing a demitasse cup to Mrs. Pierce to pass with
the cream and sugar, Harry suddenly stood before her.
She looked up into his face.

"Thank you for a delicious meal, Vera,"

"I wanted everything to go well tonight."

He bowed slightly. "You always amaze me, Vera."

"Do I, Harry?" She smiled.

"You look radiant."

The tears welled up in her eyes and she turned
away, her chin trembling. When she faced him again,
he was smiling down at her.

Upstairs, she laughed and cried away the thrill of
her triumph. Harry's gratifying admiration. Richard's
surprise. The tears warmed her, but she was careful not

to let them rekindle the foolish longings for Harry on a summer evening years ago or to dwell once again on her doubts about Richard. She went into the bathroom and washed her hands and face and changed into her house robe, then settled into a biography of Florence Nightingale while she listened to the delicate tapping of rain against the windows. Glancing at the frontispiece of the book, which depicted a temperate-looking woman, Vera was reminded that it was not the nurse's sexual allure that had brought her distinction and respect, but her administrative skills. And again, she longed to lose herself in something outside of household and family.

Suddenly, she sat up on the bed and looked at the clock. Where was Katherine?

Was she interested in someone besides Charles? His letter from the naval base in San Diego was still lying unopened on the table by the front door. A pinprick of suspicion exploded into panic. She had cautioned Katherine several times. Men forget themselves, even gentlemen. It is up to the girl to say no. She read the same paragraph in her book over again. Oh, why wasn't Katherine home?

When the phone rang about ten o'clock, she picked it up quickly. But it was Margaret calling to ask Vera to meet her at the school tomorrow. "I'd prefer you didn't tell anyone about this," Margaret said, when they had set a time. As if I'd run downstairs and tell Harry, Vera said to herself, revived by her role as insider. It must be another error in the books

she wants straightened out. And on a Sunday morning. Sometimes Vera agreed with Richard. The woman
takes herself too seriously.

It was almost midnight when Vera heard Katherine
come up the back stairs and go into her room. Relief
gave way to anger. She sprang out of bed and slipped
into her mules. Marching across the upstairs hall, she
burst through the door of Katherine's room without
knocking. "Really, Katherine, I don't think of you as
thoughtless, but this takes the cake. I've been worrying
about you all day."

Katherine lifted her head off the bed where she had
flung herself, still in her raincoat. "It's all so unfair,"
she cried out. "Teddy and George have been thrown
out of officers' training. They made an example of
them. They're sending them to Florida."

"Are you talking about Teddy Russell? I thought
the Navy would straighten him out." Vera advanced to
the edge of the bed.

Katherine sat up and grabbed her mother around
the waist. "I don't know how to tell you, Mummy.
I know how proud you were of me, and now you'll
never forgive me. That's why I didn't come home. But
after Christina got on the train to Philadelphia . . ."

"What's happened?"

Katherine looked plaintively up into her mother's
face. "We got caught."

Vera's mind blurred. There was a moment of silence between them. Then Vera said, "You don't mean
to tell me . . ." She stopped and held her breath.

"There's a new proctor. Teddy and George got away before the housemother came, but the night watchman saw them coming down the fire escape. I know you'll never forgive me, but I'm . . ."

"You're pregnant." It was as if a bomb had exploded through the roof of Vera's brain. How had she let this happen to her daughter?

"I'm not that stupid, Mother," Katherine said defensively. "I am not pregnant."

"Well, what is it?"

"I've been suspended from the university."

Vera didn't know whether to laugh or cry.

"As her father I must deal with this, Vera."

Vera had never seen Richard so angry. This was more than the look of exasperation that came over his face when he had to spank Jenny for sassing or throwing a stone through the garage window. Or his displeasure when he came into the bedroom after his dinner party last night.

"A plunging neckline is not appropriate at a club dinner." He tossed his jacket and vest on the chaise. "More suitable for the bedroom."

Vera smiled. Was this some kind of recognition of her attractiveness? "Well, you don't have to worry, Richard, I didn't disgrace you. The other gentlemen at the party thought I looked just fine."

When she told him the bare bones of Katherine's transgression, his disappointment turned to reproach. "Oh my god, Vera, where have we gone wrong?" This morning, he had the rigid calm of a sentencing judge.

She herself was alternately sad and alarmed, her throat swollen with rage. How could the girl be so silly as to ruin her life, cheapen herself and any chance of marriage, for Vera still believed men chose virgins as their brides. Vera herself had been over twenty when she received her first kiss. She shuddered to think what Katherine had experienced.

Of course, Jenny would know something was up from the sound of Katherine's weeping and her father's muteness. Vera worried about how to shield her younger daughter from the knowledge that her sister had been intimate with a man. It might whet Jenny's curiosity and frighten her all at once, like the time Katherine and her seventh-grade classmates visited a horse farm after a class picnic in the country. A few of the girls questioned poor Miss Osgood and she had no choice but to explain that the stallion was trying to insert the enormous red organ dangling at his belly into the mare. That was seven or eight years ago—Vera had accompanied the group as grade mother— and the horror she herself had felt at the sight was like a pain in her abdomen. And at thirteen Jenny was so susceptible. In the end she told Jenny only that Katherine had been suspended from the university. Jenny accepted the enormity of the offense with genuine understanding. She went directly into the kitchen where Katherine was huddled over yet another cup of precious rationed coffee, waiting to face her father. They sat quietly together for a few minutes before Jenny bounced out the back door to carry the news to Rosemary.

Vera stood in the doorway of the study, where Richard, in his courtroom pinstripe on a Sunday morning, had temporarily settled in the armchair across from his desk. The hot seat, Vera thought. His collection of pipes hung neatly in their rack on the bookcase, a reminder of innocent furtive pleasures. She understood his grave disappointment in the Katherine they had both cherished for her diligence and common sense. But Vera was concerned now for the reckless, foolhardy, rash, immature Katherine.

"It has to be the influence of Christina Grew, she's been so spoiled," Vera said, desperate to minimize the blame. "And, of course, that treacherous Teddy Russell." She looked at Richard's rigid face, but nothing cracked. "Richard, Katherine's really a nice girl. I'm sure she's learned her lesson."

"It's Katherine's responsibility, and she will take the consequences like anyone who has broken the code of decent behavior, not to mention university rules."

"Yes, of course," Vera said sensibly, "but she'll need our help. Remember she is our daughter."

"You don't have to remind me."

"Well, sometimes you tend to go from one extreme to the other without considering the in-betweens."

"In-betweens!" He paused a moment. "Can you imagine, Vera . . . I can't bring myself. If I ever get my hands on the witless scoundrel I'll . . ." He wrung his hands savagely. "And that father, so self-righteous because a Jew gives his maid a decent paying job while this is going on." He undid the top button of his vest. "What about her record at the university?" He slapped his palm down on the side table, knocking the ashtray with his pipe ashes to the rug.

"She and I will be meeting with the dean of women tomorrow morning," Vera said, stooping to scoop up the ashes into the ashtray and knock them into the wastebasket. "We'll know more then."

"And you carry on about Jenny," Richard said unfairly, but Vera knew he was running down. His misery would temper his brutality.

She reached down tentatively to touch his forearm. "If anyone had suggested Katherine would make such a mess of her life, neither of us would have believed it But the war seems so risky and urgent to young people—exciting, until they're faced with unforeseen consequences."

He looked up into her face. She could see the pain stretching along the lines of his brow. He squeezed her hand for a moment, then stood up to go to his desk. "Ask Katherine please to come in, will you?" His voice sounded tired and small.

"Don't go overboard, Richard, please."

As she left Katherine in the study, Vera heard Richard begin coolly, "Your mother tells me . . ."

Chapter Seventeen

Vera closed the front door behind her and opened her umbrella. Only a slight drizzle this morning. The neighborhood looked unusually lush, as if even nature was in a hurry. As she stepped into the road, she could see the yews at the corner of the farmhouse grown huge and menacing over the years as poor Professor Parker seemed to diminish. Despite the easing of the blackout he still patrolled the streets in his civil defense helmet, head bowed as if he were scanning the ground for something. The war had taken its toll on that household. The eldest son a prisoner of war, another in the army, the daughter in the WACs. And they had taken in Rosemary as well, but she was something of a comfort, at least to the professor. Across the street, the Lewises' well-clipped forsythia hedge was like a wall now, a few tiny trumpet clinging to the leafed out branches. Harry used to hover over the spindly plants like a brooding hen. Now, it was cost sheets and quotas of wartime production.

And suddenly, Vera recalled his helping hand at

Katherine's fireworks party four or five years ago and the confusion she had felt in his presence. Katherine and her friends had danced like nymphs that evening, fresh and untouched. A simpler time. Gone now. It's the uncertainty, Vera thought, the pictures of war dead in the magazine and movies, guns firing broadside, bodies in the water, lying in the mud. It was as if Katherine's generation did not have time for the old rules of prudence and decorum. The threat of death had added recklessness to the natural exuberance of youth. Vera drew in a deep breath and slowly sighed it out. Well, the younger children were still safe in their innocence, she told herself, and hurried on down Parker Farm Road, skirting the puddles, sidestepping and ducking the branches of shrubs and trees. As she passed the Nortons' house, the tall, erect blue spruce reminded her that Tom Norton was reported to be "having the time of his life" in Europe somewhere, while his wife carried on none too discreetly at home. Vera could think of another wartime hussy, carrying on with her boss, and suddenly Richard's helplessness in the face of domestic crisis seemed pathetic.

But then, she looked across at the lilacs fronting the Russells' house, heavy with their perfumed flowers about to burst, and she thought at least Katherine's not pregnant. It was not only the humiliation Vera had feared, but the decision she would have to make: a daughter's chance at a future and the back-alley death of an innocent. And despite herself, she tried to imagine her daughter's smooth-skinned young body yielding to Teddy Russell's—and could not, any more than she had ever been able to think of her parents in an erotic embrace. That's when you know they don't belong to you or you to them, she thought miserably, her heart pounding now. She ran a few steps and stopped before the entrance to the school to catch her breath.

The smell was overwhelming. Foul and pungent and repulsive. With all the rain she should have guessed what was on Margaret's mind. The cesspool had overflowed again.

The headmistress was standing at the window when Vera stepped into her office. "I smelled it out on the road, Margaret. Too much this time."

Margaret turned around to face her. "That's the least of it, Vera. I was sitting here at my desk while Mr. Dooley was laying the drainage pipe over to the ditch by the cemetery, away from the Russells this time. All of a sudden, a figure streaked by the window. When I went to look out, I could hardly believe my eyes. It was the von Kempel boy, so tall and scrawny now, chasing a couple of dogs around the common, out in the rain without his shirt . . ."

"They're all so free," Vera broke in. "Sassy and defiant. Not like we were, Margaret," but the headmistress spoke right through her.

"The big German shepherd was trying to get up on the smaller one, you know what I mean. Perhaps such things are confusing for a boy like that. I opened the window to speak to him, but he drove the dogs onto the field, splashing the muck all over Mr. Dooley."

"Poor Mr. Dooley can only do so much," Vera said.

"It's too late anyway." Margaret's voice was suddenly flat. "The other dog was Mrs. Russell's Airedale."

Vera groaned. "The Russells." She sat down. "They'll report it this time."

"Tomorrow morning. She was almost incoherent. Her husband's away. Teddy has been unexpectedly ordered off someplace. I apologized, of course, for any inconvenience and said we were dealing with the problem, but it made no difference. She said she would ring the authorities first thing Monday morning. I'll need your help, Vera, when the inspector comes. Moral strength."

"The person you need is Harry."

"I hoped Isabel would be willing to lord it over the inspector, for the sake of the school, you know. Play Mrs. C. Cyrus Livingston Parker II, hold the inspector at bay until Mr. Dooley and I can come up with something better. But Isabel wouldn't be a party to it. Said she was shocked that I would think of such a thing. So sanctimonious. What she means is people can't be intimidated anymore." Margaret shook her head. "But I can't go to Harry Lewis. You were at that meeting."

Really, Vera thought, bemused, everything's askew. Katherine abandoning all caution. Richard giving in to his misery. Now Margaret Graham worried about looking like a fool. And the awful thing, Vera had to admit to herself, was that somehow it made her feel better. "What about Eleanor? She knows more about the school than I do."

"Eleanor's no good at wheedling things."

And I am? Vera was astonished. "What can I tell the inspector? That we're not concerned about a public health problem? That it's not in our budget? I suspect most city officials consider the school outrageous enough without us trying to hoodwink them. Harry was right, Margaret, and we need him."

"He'll have a good laugh behind my back," Margaret wailed.

Vera was reminded of Jenny's histrionics, but then a visionary like Margaret was not accustomed to such inglorious defeats like being wrong and dealing with sewage. It was up to Vera to be practical, to get something done. She felt the energy fill her the way water expands a hose.

"We'll make temporary arrangements. We'll move the classrooms into the neighborhood basements," Vera said, thinking of the air raid shelters. "It's only a month until closing. Then we can get the problem fixed."

"The war. There are no materials," Margaret said, like a child giving her despair a good run.

"I'll talk to Harry. Maybe there are priorities for things like this."

"I knew you would, Vera." Margaret stepped forward. "But be sure to caution him about the publicity. It could be nasty."

"There's a war on, Margaret. No one's going to care about what happens to a precious private day school."

"Is it precious? I wonder." Margaret sat down hard on her desk chair, pushing the nosepiece of her eyeglasses up to settle them in place. "I never thought I'd say it, but I hope you're right. Nobody cares what happens here." She looked up at Vera. "Nowadays, sometimes I feel I'm in over my head."

The inspection was set for Thursday morning. When she called Harry, Vera confessed she had too much on her mind. Family responsibilities. And now the sewage problem and the threat to the school, just as he had predicted. Harry did not ask indiscreet questions or act vindicated; he just suggested that he join in the inspection tour. He knew the inspector, a Mr. O'Brien, through party politics. He and Vera agreed to meet briefly with Margaret at the school before the ten o'clock appointment.

When the day came it was something of a relief to get away from the house and the overheated atmosphere of incrimination and remorse, and the weather was mercifully clear and sunny for the second straight day. But the job at hand would involve a trip to the waste area, and there might be sludge still standing. Vera felt like the milkmaid in a barnyard novel in her dark cotton dress and Katherine's rubber boots which she had borrowed to be on the safe side. She could see Margaret's old galoshes tucked away in the corner of her office. When Harry came into the room, she thought anxiously of his perfectly polished shoes and the hem of his light gray trousers

Margaret shook Harry's extended hand. "Good of you to come today," she conceded.

"It's important that we don't appear to have tried to hide something," he said pointedly. "I can smooth the way."

From the indignant frown on Margaret's face, Vera could guess what was going through the headmistress' mind: Where Mrs. Cyrus Parker fears to tread. What gall!

Vera smiled to herself, then turned to Harry. "I just worry that Mr. O'Brien will penalize us because . . . well . . ." She paused, searching for the right way to address her doubts. She could hardly use the word snobby in front of Margaret. "He'll think us too high and mighty, as my mother used to say." She gave a little self-deprecating laugh.

Margaret looked aghast. Harry was saying, "I understand what you're driving at, Vera, but Frank O'Brien is a reasonable man. He won't use his position unwisely."

"I should hope not," Margaret muttered.

At ten sharp, cap in hand, Mr. O'Brien appeared in the doorway of the office in his two-piece suit and mucky workmen's boots. He stood at the threshold like a farmer who knows from experience the lashing out he'll get if he tracks manure on his wife's kitchen floor. "How d' you do, ma'am."

Margaret stepped up to greet him, mindful that he seemed to know his place. But were his hearty hand-shake and the showy smile meant to intimidate her? Then as she began the introductions—"Mr. O'Brien, this is Mrs. Richard Oliver"—Harry grasped the man by his elbow, shaking his hand vigorously. "Hello there, my friend."

"I wondered if you might be on hand, Harry." Mr. O'Brien gave Harry a poke on the shoulder. "I came early to have a look-see. Someone's tried to lay a pipe down the slope by the ball court to the ditch by the cemetery. That would be a serious violation, but the caretaker said he's there to sweep the floors, clean the blackboards, doesn't have much experience with this kind of thing." Mr. O'Brien addressed the headmistress directly. "You've got a good company man there."

"We appreciate Mr. Dooley's loyalty, Mr. O'Brien," She answered carefully, but she looked panicked by the implied threat.

The inspector turned back to Harry. "I would say that what you got out there is an old fashioned cesspool, and it's on heavy overload. I'm surprised this hasn't happened before." He looked at the headmistress. "I've been saying for years the city should inspect everything, not just city installations." He shook his head. "This should never have happened, Harry."

"I'm the villain, Frank." He paused for a moment, but apparently Margaret would not risk the truth. She remained silent. "We discussed the possibility of overflow in committee meeting a few months ago," he went on. "Miss Graham is a keen believer in the children's health and safety, we all are, of course, but I was hoping we could get through the war . . . restrictions, and so forth," Harry concluded.

"The war's already an eternity, Harry." Mr. O'Brien slapped on his cap. "Let me show you what's got to be done."

The three of them followed the inspector out of the building, Margaret grabbing her galoshes and rushing ahead to lead them along the side of the common green to the safest route out onto the field. Those students near the classroom windows paused in their work to watch the single file of grownups go by. It was no secret that there was trouble at the school. The smell lingered on, the field and dodgeball court were off limits at recess, their parents whispered about it at the dinner table. When the posse reached the fence around dodge ball court, Margaret stopped to lean against the chain link. Vera waited for her to pull on her galoshes over her brogues. Then they hurried to catch up with the two men where they stood in a row on boards that Mr. Dooley had thoughtfully laid down. Vera must remember to remind Margaret to thank him. The drainage area had dried up somewhat, but it was still damp, the grass visibly smeared. The smell hung heavy on the air. "This is the area . . ." Margaret began.

"There's no denying what you've got here," Mr. O'Brien announced to Harry, inching his way left. "There's no place for the goddamn filth to go."

"You two stay here," Harry said abruptly to the two women and moved gingerly after the inspector. Around the curve of the field further along, the men stopped, tracing the landscape with their outstretched arms, Harry leaning sideways toward the shorter man. The face of the inspector seemed to redden. The tone of his voice was harsh.

"I can't make out what they're saying," Margaret said.

"We're not supposed to."

"They'll shut down the school," Margaret said. "I know it."

"From the look of it—all that sludge drying on top of the grass-—how could you think otherwise? It really is disgusting. And the smell! Perhaps it would be sensible to let the lower school out early this year. We could have a little ceremony in someone's garden." Vera was taking over.

Margaret put a heavy hand down on Vera's shoulder like an old woman seeking support. "I have always taken pride in my school, Vera. It's my spiritual home. Here I could do only good." She paused. "Until Harry joined the committee."

"He's only trying to save the school."

"So much has changed, Vera." Margaret sighed. "I'm worn out."

She looked it, too, Vera thought, studying the older woman. She seemed smaller, bowed. Her eyes were sunken and streaks of gray had faded her hair. Suddenly, Vera felt sorry for Margaret. "Don't worry, we'll manage," Vera said, protectively. But the men were coming toward them and Margaret recovered herself, thrusting her head back, readjusting the bone hairpins at the nape of her neck. As they waited for the verdict,

Vera remembered again the first meeting of Isabel
Parker's committee. Margaret Graham had seemed the
goddess of wisdom and moral strength then, striding
up the road like Pallas Athena.

Before All Else Be True. The headmistress had
always epitomized the school motto. Everyone said
so. But over the past few days, so full of contraditions,
Vera had caught glimpses of a private woman far more
defenseless than the imposing public figure, defender
of truth and champion of forgiveness.

Mr. O'Brien closed the school for health violations
but agreed to give the permit for construction top
priority. When the headmistress asked what construction exactly, the inspector shook his head and asked,
"What are two ladies like you doing dealing with
things you don't know the first thing about? Holding
tanks, leach fields. Just understand that if you want
to open the school next fall, you've got to have a septic
system. Materials and labor won't come cheap or easy
with a war on, and time is running out. Cement dries
out in hot weather." Then his tone softened. "I'll keep
an eye on things." He gave the headmistress a pat on
the shoulder. "Don't worry yourself, ma'am."

Vera could see Margaret burn with resentment at
the man's patronizing ways—they were schoolgirls
playing with privilege—especially when he went on
to add, "You take my advice. Put the whole matter in
the hands of Harry Lewis here. You don't know how
lucky you are to have him on your side."

Now, Vera was often busy with school business. Phone calls, lists, trips down the street to consult with the headmistress or a teacher. She tried to get her work done in plenty of time to make dinner, and she kept her working papers in the silver drawer in the sideboard. Richard didn't seem to notice much, but sometimes Jenny's nose was out of joint. "It's like it's your school now, not mine."

Vera put down her pen. "I'm just helping out a little, dear. They're short-handed with the war."

"It's the smelly rot in the field from all the toilets, isn't it? We won't have any ninth grade next year, will we?"

"Mr. Lewis will take care of the trouble long before opening day. We are so fortunate to have him on the parents' committee."

Jenny groaned. "Oh, not Mr. Lewis again, Mummy," she cried and flounced up the stairs. Followed by the familiar slam of her bedroom door.

Vera quickly organized a lower-school Closing Day ceremony in the side yard of the farmhouse, where there was enough space for the first and second grade rhythms group to perform the scarf dances they had been practicing all spring. The morning of the event, she arranged to have Mr. Dooley bring the folding chairs and mats up from the assembly hall on a dolly, while Hilda, the Parkers' cook, and the accompanist pushed the piano to the window in the music room and opened the top. Professor Parker escaped to his office at the university. Then Vera arranged to have the upper classes move into neighborhood playrooms and living rooms. She did not ask Mrs. Russell if they might use her house, and Mrs. Russell did not offer it. For the few remaining weeks of school, by unspoken agreement, Jenny and Patsy avoided each other, unwilling to risk learning more about what might have happened between one's sister and the other's brother than they could already comprehend.

The upper-school closing, in the same garden setting, went smoothly enough, except that the Beasty was suddenly spotted crouching with his dog at the base of the huge yews, but nothing bad happened this time. Miss Graham talked about the high cost of victory at home and abroad and chose Alfred Lord Tennyson's "The Charge of the Light Brigade" for her reading. The Russells went away immediately after school closed, but over the course of the summer it came out that Teddy had been sent as a seaman second class to the Pacific. Before Katherine joined the Women's Land Army in Maine, she told Jenny in darkest secrecy that Christina Grew had to "get rid" of her baby. Jenny was so scared of what that meant that she was afraid to ask any questions.

She didn't even tell Rosemary.

Harry began the thankless job of seeing to the new septic system. It was a Sisyphean task. It wasn't materials; it was machinery and money. Finally, he made a deal with one of his workers who had been in construction before the war and could get his hands on

an old steam shovel. That was a beginning. There was
no priority on cement, and he could get the rest of the
materials through his company with a little bargaining
with Ari Izrael. A small crew of men from the factory
could do the job in four or five days. But when it came
to paying for the project, he really had to put himself
on the line for the money. There was a small sum still
left in the budget that Margaret had hoped to use for
a weeklong summer program for poor city children
at the school. Of course, that was out of the question
now. A fund-raising letter to a select group added a
certain amount, but not enough. At the final meeting
of the parents' committee held at Vera's house, after
much debate, Harry offered to make up the rest of
the cost with a personal loan at half a point below the
going rate of interest. After the committee had taken
Harry up on his offer, Vera overheard one member
whisper to another, "I have to say, with all the profits
he's made while our boys are out there getting slaugh-
tered, you'd think he'd give us the money."

Vera was shocked. "He's already given a substantial amount through the campaign."

"I only wish he'd seen fit to invest as well for the
rest of us as he has for himself," the man exclaimed.

Vera noticed the frown on Harry's face. She
remembered the first meeting at Mrs. Parker's and
wondered what he would do. Then she overheard him
say, "I heard that, Rufus. Let me remind you. You told
me you weren't interested in a company like Izrael and
Son." Vera smiled.

Adele Lewis felt differently. "You go right on bailing these people out, and then they're so critical, so ungrateful. I've said it many times, you bring it on yourself. I'm fed up with that school. Sewage on the playing fields. Classes in the basement. Is that what knowing all the right people is about? The special education for your children that you're paying for? I've been looking into the Hebrew school in Riverside for next year."

"Oh Adele, that's just another kind of elitism. Our children will be moving into a different world from the one we knew. There'll be a place for them."

"Yes and no, Harry," Adele answered, standing before the mirror in the bedroom. Harry put his arms around her. She laid her cheek against his and stared at the reflection of both of them in the mirror, dark and aquiline. "We'll always be on the outside, Harry. It's our history." As she lifted her arms to unclasp the ruby brooch at her neckline, his hands went to her breasts. She nuzzled him. "Maybe we like it that way."

"No one likes to be on the outside, Adele."

"At least people on the outside know who they are. You're like one of those little lizards the children bring home in a box from the circus."

"A chameleon? Blends in with the landscape. I wish I could."

"You know what I mean. You're everybody's patsy."

"Just as long as I'm yours." He kissed her behind the ear.

Chapter Eighteen

The wonderful camping-out feeling that came with going to school in people's houses spilled into June and the summer activities of Jenny and her classmates. Now that they were turning fourteen and would be next year's graduating class, they had that heady feeling of being almost beyond the reach of the rules. While the school was off-limits, of course, because of the shut down, they moved seamlessly from the driveways and backyards of Parker Farm Road onto the forbidden paths and fields, on scouting parties of two or three, prowling, peeking, dodging the occasional sight of an adult or the pale-fleshed Beasty, skulking along, brandishing his weapon. He no longer alarmed them. Now their mockery of him bound them together when a disagreement or rebellion threatened corps solidarity, or when one of them was forced to defect to visit a grandmother or join a family holiday.

As evening approached, the long day's end shadowing their whereabouts, sometimes one or two couples would linger behind the trash shed by the eighth-grade building or crouch out of sight in the Russells' lilacs. On weekends, when they knew the school grounds would be abandoned, after they played Simon Says or kick-the-can up and down Parker Farm Road, the whole troop would streak through the parking lot at the edge of the swamp onto the school grounds. They played hide-and-seek among the familiar buildings or ran relay races across the playfield, stopping often at the edge of the condemned area by the dodgeball court to inspect the matted grass, dried up now. They crinkled up their noses against the smell, real or imagined. Or was that the stench of the abattoir across the river on the wind? The haunting lowing of the condemned cattle was like a counterpoint to the deep-throated tuba's slow funeral march as the corteges moved along the road, behind the row of maples that marked the far edge of the field and the cemetery beyond. Often, they waited to hear the three rifle shots, the sound of taps, then moved quietly back across the field, unsure for a few minutes about death and what came after. Sometimes Fred would yodel to break the mood. Then a new game would begin.

And then, the moment Parker Farm Road had been waiting for finally came. One Tuesday morning in July, the old steam shovel was transported in on a flatbed truck like an ancient and venerable warrior, shovel slung low, at rest, the boiler standing up at the rear like a sentry. Behind it, a dump truck hauled the cement mixer, the great bowl twisting as the wheels of the trolley bumped along. The children stopped their games and waved and danced, moving along side, the powdery dirt spinning off the huge wheels hot in their faces. Mrs. Parker got up from her desk and went to the window to see what all the commotion was about. Jenny's mother stepped out the kitchen door to watch the cavalcade go by. As it progressed through the school parking lot, the Beasty emerged wraith-like from the swamp path to join in the procession.

The flatbed scraped around the corner of the main building as it hulked along the narrow walkway, rutting and gouging across the common green, lurching left to skirt the short end of the rectangular field and sink at ease near the cordoned-off construction site beyond the dodgeball court. Mr. Lewis and the driver stepped down from the cab. As Miss Graham and Mr. Dooley came marching across the field, the children fell away, prepared to scatter.

"I have to say, Harry, I couldn't miss that entrance." Miss Graham turned to speak to the children who lurked behind the bulk of the steam shovel. "You children know you aren't supposed to be here."

But no one was listening to the headmistress. They were watching the steam shovel roll slowly down the ramp, the driver of the dump truck in the operator's seat, straining at the control levers to brake the momentum, keeping the shovel high. Once it was safely off the truck, a second man began to stoke the boiler, feeding the coal from the bin at the back to the paper and kindling already burning.

"Harry, look at the grass," Miss Graham exclaimed.

"It's too bad, but they couldn't go around by the shop, too swampy for a load like this."

The driver stood looking at the ruts, his hands on his hips. "The ground is pretty dry, missus. It'll spring back on its own, if you keep the kids off it."

Miss Graham tried again. "Run along now, children, the school is off limits. We don't want any further trouble, do we?"

Mr. Lewis said. "I'm wondering about some fencing around the site when the hole is dug, just to be on the safe side. It's not in our budget, but I'd be glad to . . ."

"Can't we just leave it cordoned off?"

"It might be worth the extra expense, especially if the job goes into next week."

"But you said you thought it would take about five or six days except for the seeding, and this is only Tuesday," Miss Graham reminded him.

"We're already behind. They had to meet a deadline at the plant yesterday, and it was a one hell of a mess—excuse me—bringing this load through traffic. There was a long line of supply transports just pulling out of the arsenal. Armored tanks, howitzers." He shook his head and combed his hands through his hair, wavy in the humidity. "The men will work the regular eight-hour day, but if we ask them to go over, we pay them for it. That's how it is at the plant. And since this is not a wartime priority, they don't work Sunday. That's the agreement."

The men nodded. "That's the deal with Mr. Lewis, ma'am."

"Oh really," Miss Graham said petulantly. She knew they'd do whatever Mr. Lewis said despite any deal they'd made with him, but then he would not ask more of them than they had bargained for. It wasn't going to be like working with Mr. Dooley. "I can't spend money on fencing, Harry. It's a needless extravagance when the school grounds are virtually empty in summer. I'm sure the rope cord will do very nicely," Miss Graham said firmly.

Mr. Lewis looked skeptical. "Well, Mr. O'Brien gave me a NO TRESPASS sign to post."

"And they'll be done by Saturday," The headmistress stated as if it were a fact.

"I know they'll do the best they can, but this heat may slow them down," Mr. Lewis told her. "Wet cement doesn't bond well with dried concrete."

"We'll be all right, Mr. Lewis. If we have to leave it overnight, there's plenty of burlap to keep the concrete damp. We'll need access to water anyway when we get to mixing."

"I haven't seen one of these monster in years," Mr. Dooley said admiringly. "I'll drag out the hoses."

"Take your time," the driver called after him. "We'll be a couple of days at digging by the looks of it."

"We'll leave you to your work." Miss Graham turned to go. "Come on, Rosemary, Jenny, you boys there. Fred, and you, too," she said pointing to the Beasty, who was making fencing motions at Fred.

"But Miss Graham," they sang out in a chorus.

"I'll keep an eye on the children while the men get

started, Margaret," Mr. Lewis said, unbuttoning his suit jacket and tucking his tie into his shirt.

The headmistress questioned the students with her look. "This is an experience, children," the headmistress said finally, giving her educational approval to something beyond her control. "But remember when you leave you are on your honor. The school is out of bounds." The children turned their backs on Miss Graham as she returned across the field.

"It's an amazing piece of old machinery, isn't it," Mr. Lewis said to the men. "When I was a boy, I'd have given my eyeteeth to run one of these."

"Now's your chance, Mr. Lewis," the operator called out good-naturedly.

"You want me to end up in the hoosegow for reckless driving, Jerzy?" Mr. Lewis laughed. "Why don't you kids help Mr. Dooley while the steam builds up." The children flew off like a formation of ducks, this time the Beasty in the lead.

By the time they returned, unrolling the garden hose across the field, pausing while Mr. Dooley screwed the pieces together, the steam shovel was hissing and pounding rhythmically, creeping into position. It belched and reached out to take the first scoop. Like a Greek chorus the children cheered.

Several times a day, they came around the swamp side by the shop, out of sight of the school offices, to wave at the workmen and watch the progress. As the hole became a pit and then an excavation, the rope no longer reached around the perimeter, and they could walk right up to the edge and speculate on how deep it was. Then they slid down the mounds of dirt piling up around the sides. When the wooden forms went in, they peered into the long, hollow rectangle like a fort, where the battery of old surplus reinforcing rods set in a floor of cement stood at attention. As the workmen poured in the cement, pushing the wheelbarrow across a board that acted as a bridge over the narrow trench, the reinforcing rods disappeared in a wall of concrete, until only a foot or two was visible, head and shoulders, reaching up over the top of the trench to catch sight of the enemy. Once they thought Miss Graham saw them as she came across the field, but they dashed back along the swamp side to the parking lot where she found them later playing hopscotch. The only part of their sneakiness that disturbed them was that they couldn't share their excitement at family dinner tables.

By Saturday, it was clear there was at least another day's work. There was still one side of the concrete box to finish off, and while the pieces of the top had already been cast and brought in on the flatbed, they had yet to be fitted. As the men tamped the last load of cement for the day and laid down the wet burlap, one said, "Maybe we can get the caretaker to wet it down, we won't be back until Monday."

"With a little overtime, we might be able to finish the pouring," the machine operator said.

The first man wiped the sweat off his brow with the back of his hand. "You better ask the schoolmarm,

Jerzy," he warned. "She don't want to spend no money, and I ain't working for love."

"We'd have to use up what we mix. Could take a while" another worker added.

When the foreman came to her office with the offer to put in overtime, Margaret thanked him but said it could wait until Monday. "I'll ask Mr. Dooley to come in first thing tomorrow morning to run the hose over those burlap bags."

As the man set his cap on his head, the principal noticed his massive hands, rough and knobby from his labor. She nodded to him pleasantly and picked up her pencil to return to the papers on the desk. But she could feel his presence and looked up again. "Is there something else?"

"There's no fence, miss. We don't want the kids messing with anything."

"I know they've peeked once or twice. The job is fascinating to them. But there won't be any construction going on tomorrow. Nothing to bring them to the site."

The man looked unsure for a moment, then finally said, "I'll relocate the sign closer to the pit and run the rope along the rods, just to mark them."

"Thank you again."

Before she left for the day, on the way out to the field, Margaret checked that the water had been turned off at the faucet by the dodgeball court. The sun was still hot in the long daylight hours, and the clover at the unmowed edge of the field was scorched. At the site, she could see that the men had tied some strips of dirty toweling at intervals on the rope stretching along the line of rods on the unfinished side. The rods looked old and rusty, but she supposed that was all they could get. The garden hose, curled up like a reptile, lay at the base of the slope up to the construction site, the nozzle resting in a pool of muddy water.

She went cautiously five or six steps up the slippery slope and looked into the excavation. It was like an underground mausoleum, cold concrete floor and walls. Something like the ancient Egyptians would build. And when it was all finished, lid on and the dirt graded over it and seeded, it would look just like a heroic burial mound. She'd try to remember that when the final bills came in. She turned around to look down the length of the field along the line of maples that paralleled the cemetery, and then across to the corner of the eighth-grade building. The field was like a long, broad avenue of approach, and she imagined the great funeral procession of a Pharaoh coming diagonally toward her from behind the eighth-grade building, the golden bier, carts of precious artifacts, attending ministers and servants who would be entombed to serve the passage of the soul. She had to laugh at her fanciful thoughts. The heat must have gone to her head.

She glanced back into the pit. The floor and walls looked unforgiving and the crest of the slop was slimy. She turned to go. Not very firm underfoot. Should she have listened to Harry? She shook her head vigorously; she would not tolerate the expense. She'd see that Mr. Dooley rigged up something when he came to water the burlap tomorrow. She eased her way down the slope. Nothing like a fence, just a few boards. On firm ground, she took a deep breath, then let it out slowly before walking back across the field. She very much looked forward to joining Eleanor at the Island after this whole ghastly business was behind her.

When Harry came home that evening and looked into the dining room, the table set for one, he was startled by the sense of aloneness that came over him. It was different from the loneliness he felt in the absence of his family, who had gone to visit Adele's mother again. He mulled it over in his head for a moment. This was not the joy of solitude he sometimes had when he could hole up in his study and read until dawn without Adele interrupting, her peignoir open, looking sleepy and tempting, to crush his momentary interest by reminding him crossly how irritable he was in the morning without a good night's sleep. No, it was a feeling of isolation, the segregation he recognized from childhood or college years, but he had no idea why it should sweep over him now. The construction site, he suspected. It had been on his mind all day that this was Saturday, and he wondered how far the men had gotten. He tossed his hat on the shelf in the front hall closet and started for the drink tray—a whiskey would help—but halfway across the room he changed his mind. "I'll be back in a few minutes," he called into the serving pantry to the maid and strode out the door and down to the school.

The field was dry and brittle to his tread, and here and there, patches of scorched grass gave it a barren unfriendly look. In the distance, to his left, he could see the steam shovel rising up like a skeletal monster. That meant the top had not been installed yet. As he got closer the row of reinforcing rods told him that the near side was unfinished. A dozen rods were still exposed, spiking up above the mound of earth surrounding the holding tank. He wasn't surprised; such a job took time, despite Margaret's prodding. The men would have wet down the burlap before they left, and he suspected Mr. Dooley had been persuaded to do the same on his day off tomorrow.

Harry climbed the muddy rise, slipping back once or twice on the smooth soles of his shoes, like walking an assembly-line belt. He paused at the top of the mound to survey the job. It looked pretty good, tight and neat. He was pleased with the work his men had done. But looking down directly into the unfinished concrete rectangle, he felt breathless and lightheaded. He closed his eyes, but the picture shone brightly in the darkness: low and enclosed, just high enough for the men or women to stand up, packed in like sardines. He had read about the death camps in one of the Jewish pamphlets Joe Izrael was always passing around the shop. He opened his eyes and pressed a hand to the side of his head as if to put the lid on his imagination. Like an old man, one foot tentatively before the other, he retraced his steps down the rise, reaching out for an imaginary railing. At the corner of the site, he clutched the top of the no-trespassing sign to steady himself for a moment before he set out for home. He did not look back, but on the way across the field he reminded himself to ask Mr. Dooley tomorrow if he had any old boards or makeshift fencing he could put up as a barrier, just until Monday, when the workmen would be back on the job. As he passed by the school parking lot, he could see the children at their games, and he thought of Pearl a thousand miles away playing hopscotch in her grandmother's driveway.

At home, he had a stiff whiskey and enjoyed his solitary meal. Grateful to feel himself again, he decided to postpone reviewing plant orders and accounts and spend the evening reading an entertaining book. He had just settled into *See Here, Private Hargrove*, when the telephone rang.

When they had finished supper, some of the children gathered in the school parking lot. After a desultory game of touch tag, Rosemary suggested they go to the playroom in the farmhouse and play spin-the-bottle. A nervous ripple ran through the crowd, but no one was enthusiastic. The only time Jenny had ever played, she was forced to kiss Jeffrey Malcolm on the lips, and she itched all over when she went to bed that night. She wanted to play Pounce or Go-fish, but Rosemary said no one could use her cards. So the gang drifted up the road to the tennis court, but the gate was padlocked and the grapes on the heavy vines were still green. As the other children followed down the passageway to the vacant lot and out to Great Hamilton Street, Rosemary decided to spy over the fence into the von Kempel side yard.

The dog raced out of the shed barking hard, but the Beasty just sat there, staring at her. Rosemary flashed her smile and wiggled her fingers at him. At that moment, Fred came back down the alleyway looking for Rosemary. When he saw the Beasty, he grinned moronically, waving his jackknife over his head. He stood beside Rosemary and draped one arm around her shoulder, leaning into her.

The Beasty stood up and stabbed an ice pick into the side of the door.

Fred jabbed the point of his knife into the fence.

"Really, Fred."

"He's a fascist *schwein*. He's after you."

"You're so possessive," Rosemary said delightedly.

"Come on, let's go." Fred grabbed Rosemary's arm and led her down the road.

Jenny went down the alley to join the others, then turned back. Rosemary might change her mind and look for her. She could hear the dog barking as she approached the Beasty's yard. The German shepherd was straining on his rope, and the door to the shed was closed. The others were right behind her now. They lingered at the fence to throw sticks at the dog as she stepped out onto Parker Farm Road. There was no sign of Rosemary and Fred. Too often, without warning, they were suddenly not there. She had tried hard not to care. But she didn't know how to not feel left out, and each revelation or discovery about Fred and Rosemary still felt like a betrayal.

She knew they had gone to the movies alone together; Rosemary told her they'd seen *For Whom the Bell Tolls*. For a week Rosemary spoke with a strange lisp. A Swedish accent was alluring, she said. Fred had been to supper at the farmhouse just recently. And then there was the cellar playroom, but Jenny didn't spy anymore. But she had no illusions about Fred. He was the same nasty boy the grownups fawned on. Wasn't he growing up to be handsome? How his English had improved. Weren't Fred and Rosemary sweet together? Two wartime casualties, they said, and smiled.

The gray wash of dusk was already seeping into the sky. As the others headed home, Jenny searched Parker Farm Road more thoroughly for Rosemary and Fred, invading favorite hiding places. The sharp bark of the dog cracked in her ears like a command, egging her on. They were not hiding in the giant yews at the farmhouse or behind the Lewises' wall of forsythias. As she passed under the streetlight, in the yellow glare, there were no shadows under the cone-shaped spruce tree by the Nortons, no sight of them in the lilac hedge in front of the Russells. She ran across the road and into the parking lot of the school—and stopped short by the utility room. Suddenly, she remembered the groundskeeper who shot himself because of Hitler when she was in the third grade. She pictured him closing his lips around the barrel of the gun, then squeezed her eyes tight to blot out the image.

She dashed along the walkway by the assembly hall and across the common green, following the ruts made by the flatbed, marching toward the playfield, plunging through the approaching dark. At the edge of the field she stopped. Across, to the far left, she could see the outline of the no-trespassing sign and the dark, pencil-thin lines of the reinforcing rods that marked the great concrete box.

Out of the corner of her eye, she caught a glimpse of something moving in the distance. It turned a right angle beyond the construction site and proceeded down the far side of the field, along the line of maples. When the moving mass was opposite, it split into two. She could just make out the line of Rosemary's braid down her back. "Rosemary," she called out, starting toward them. The two figures disappeared into one behind the trunk of a maple.

But a moment later, near the eighth-grade building at the other end of the field to the right, a third figure emerged. Frightened now, Jenny dashed across the field, calling out to Rosemary and Fred, "Wait for me."

When she caught up with them, they were halfway down the line of maples. They stopped and Fred said, "Guess who. It's the Odious Olivant."

"I am not an elephant." Jenny looked from Fred to Rosemary.

"Honestly," Rosemary chimed in, "can't you ever take a hint."

Jenny's heart was pierced.

"*Scheiss*," Fred shouted and set out steamily across the field toward the eighth- grade building.

Rosemary watched him go. "Oh Fred, don't be in a temper." She faced Jenny, hands on her hips. "Now see what you've done. Just because you can't get your own sweetie, you make my life a bloody hell."

"You're mean, Rosemary Bent-Wilson," Jenny screamed. "And stupid Fred always gets his way." She stamped her foot and turned to leave.

Suddenly, there were voices and then Fred's yodel, almost like a scream. In the diminishing light, a shadow emerged from behind the corner of the eighth-grade building, growing more distinct as it charged diagonally up the field. It was the Beasty. Open shirt flapping. Waving the ice pick above his head. Fred came tearing after him.

Jenny and Rosemary stopped short, watching. When the boys passed by, still running hard, they started after them. "Slow down. Wait up," they shouted. "Stop!

The Beasty slithered in the mud up the mound at the edge of the construction site, halting at the lip of the trench between the mound and the wooden pouring forms. He turned around to face them, the rusty reinforcing rods spiking up behind him like a row of spears. The bits of cloth knotted on the rope hung at his flank like pennants.

When they reached Fred at the bottom of the slope, he was carefully folding out the blade of his jackknife.

"You're a showoff, Fred," Jenny challenged.

Without moving forward, one looking down, the other up, the boys dueled their weapons at each other in the ten feet between them.

"Stop it," Rosemary whimpered. "You two are being such babies."

Miraculously, both boys held their fury, red-faced, panting, the alertness going out of them. Then suddenly, Fred stumbled up the mound, and the girls lunged forward, each grabbing one of his legs. They held onto Fred's ankles, cringing as they looked up the short slope at the Beasty.

But he stood his ground, grinning stupidly. The girls let go of Fred, and he got slowly to his feet, smearing the mud on his shins and knees as he tried to brush it off. He let out a yodel, then flipped his knife down. The point stuck in the ground. The game was over.

The Beasty stared down at Fred. Then he flung out his arms and began pivoting around and around, bowing slightly. "To the winner, to the winner," the Beasty called each time he turned and bowed again.

Fred reached down for his knife and closed the blade before he put it back in his pocket. "Made you nervous, didn't I." He grinned at Rosemary.

She looked at him scornfully. "You're daft, Gott-fried Goldstein. You like to frighten people. Come on,

Jenny, it's getting dark."

"He could have stabbed you to death, stupid Goat-fred," Jenny sneered at Fred. "He beat you. The Beasty beat you," she chanted. "The Beasty beat you."

"Come on," Rosemary hissed.

Fred started up the mound, hurling himself forward, his arms outstretched. As he shoved the backside of the victor, both boys began to slip back in the mud, Fred clutching at the flailing Beasty. The Beasty came down hard on his face. Jenny and Rosemary screamed. "I win," Fred snarled.

A great hoarse bellow devoured the air and hung there.

Fred lay still a moment in the breathless silence that followed, then scrambled back down to the bottom of the mound where the girls stood. "What happened?" Jenny cried out, but no one answered. She looked up at the prone figure a few feet away, legs lying down the curve of the slope,

"Get up, Wilhelm," Rosemary shrieked. The Beasty didn't move. All three of them went cautiously up the mound.

The body bridged the trench between the rise and the wooden pouring forms. The Beatsy's head hung suspended a few inches above the damp rags over the wet concrete. A reinforcing rod pierced through the eye socket and out the back of the skull.

The children stood paralyzed for a moment while the truth sank in. Then they ran screaming for help.

Chapter Nineteen

Nothing appeared to be very different about Parker Farm Road. The gang of children was gone, but the phlox still bloomed by Harry's gate. Richard had green beans coming in, but Vera was too busy to cope with them. The tomatoes on the vines up and down the street were finally apple-cheeked. Only the von Kempel house gave the neighborhood away, the draperies drawn across the long front windows, the back door boarded up. Even the shed had a padlock on it, and the running rope for the German shepherd trailed in the dust. There was a noisy stillness about the place that demanded the attention of a passerby, neighbor and stranger alike.

After the informal investigation held at the school, all of West Ivers could read the concluding statement made by the eminent local lawyer, Richard Oliver, in the newspaper: "It was determined that while no one participant is culpable in the regrettable accident at the Parker Farm School, all parties agree to bear equally the moral responsibility for the tragedy, extending regrets and condolences to the victim's family and the neighborhood and city at large."

For a week or so, the *Morning Bulletin* ran articles and editorials about the need for new sewage requirements and inspection. Safety regulations and negligence penalties. Or materials and labor shortages and the behind-the-scenes dealings of a local wartime tycoon. The questionable relationship between the mitigating lawyer and the Parker Farm School. As parents of children at the school, weren't both men guilty of a conflict of interest? Didn't a man shoot himself at the same school some years ago? Privilege has its darker side.

It was Harry—stunned by the grotesque sight of the impaled head—who lifted up the body, the torso limp across his arms, and carried it in the darkness over the field and up the road, the way his mother used to carry a newly ironed tablecloth. The head flopped against his chest, the face obscured in blood and flesh and seeping brain matter that stained into Harry's fresh white shirt front. The large adolescent ears were absurdly clean.

The familiar trek across the school common, out into the parking lot by the utility room, along the edge of the lilacs, beneath the outline of the blue spruce, this was Harry's atonement for the blunders that led to this moment, the lull before the onslaught. The lights in the neighborhood were already out by the time he finished his statement to the police and walked home from the von Kempel house.

When he tried telephoning Vera first thing in the morning, the line was busy. He did reach Isabel Parker, who seemed overcome by melancholy. "Yes, thank you for asking, Harry. Rosemary seems subdued but she'll be all right. I worry about Fred Goldstein. He's so excitable, but he became frighteningly silent at the sight of the policeman. The uniform, I suppose." She sighed into the telephone. "This war brings so many sorrows," she told him. "I wish I could have done something to prevent this one."

Margaret was on her way to church when he called. She was outraged. "A boy's life," she exclaimed abruptly, as if Harry had committed murder. "There should have been provisions for a fence in the construction contract."

There was a painful silence. "Yes, it might have been avoided." He could hardly say the words. "I should have just gone ahead and okayed the extra expense for a fence."

"It shouldn't have been extra."

"It's too late to argue, Margaret."

He finally went over to Vera's house. She was beside herself. "I search my soul, Harry," she burst out as she opened the front door. "How could we have let it happen?" She looked up into his face with pleading eyes. "The police sergeant wouldn't sit down. He stood in the doorway there. Finally, Margaret arrived in a fury. We had to go through the questioning again, but the children were really too upset to tell us much."

Vera hid her face in her palms. "The poor boy wasn't normal, Harry. We all knew that."

"Tell me what happened, Vera," he said gently.

"Jenny tried to explain about a chase across the field, 'like warriors,' she said, but all she could do was cry. When everyone finally left, she was afraid to be alone. She slept in Richard's bed. A fitful night for all of us." Vera rubbed her palm across her forehead. "Jenny's never been fond of Fred, but she doesn't want to speak to Rosemary either."

"Do you know what happened?"

"Rosemary said he slipped." Vera sat down.

"Can you . . ." Harry began soothingly, but Vera talked right through him.

"Fred was screaming when they came up the road. I heard this shrill wailing—you've heard that sound he makes—and I went to the door. They were all in tears. It was Rosemary who called out, 'There's been a frightful accident, we're ever so sorry, Mrs. Oliver.' The policeman wrote that down."

"Is Richard out of town, Vera?"

She nodded her head. "I finally reached him this morning. He says the important thing is to answer all questions simply and truthfully, but not to offer information. That's the lawyer in him." She gulped for breath. "I'm sorry to go on like this." She was silent for a moment.

"I have to take some of the blame, Vera. I should never have left the oversight of the construction in Margaret's hands."

"It was her responsibility, Harry. Will she admit to that?" Vera wondered aloud. "And what about the children?"

Walking back from Vera's house, Harry was almost ashamed of how relieved he was that his own children were away. It might have been Pearl who was involved in such an ugly tragedy.

Jenny stayed in her room on Sunday, the door ajar so her mother would know to leave her alone but remember that she was there. Downstairs, she could hear Mr. Lewis' low voice, warm like a blanket in the cold, answering the murmur of her mother's. Last night, in a double vision, she'd heard the Beasty's bellow as the rod pierced his eye at the same time the blast of the gun went off in the groundskeeper's mouth. She woke up screaming and had to spend the rest of the night sleeping in her father's bed, near her mother. This morning when she gagged on her toast, the stuff that came up into her throat left a bitter taste in her mouth. Her mother poured her a glass of water, but she couldn't even swallow that. She went to stand before the window, staring across the school field to the cemetery beyond at nothing in particular. Suddenly, she saw the Beasty race across the field, brandishing his weapon He seemed so pitiful, silly, sad. She saw the body sprawled face down in the mud. If only she hadn't yelled at Fred. She threw herself on her bed. This was the worst thing that she had ever done, worse than lying about relatives to Patsy and Molly. Was it all her fault? She was scared by how bad she could be.

On Monday, when the phone rang, her mother called from her bedroom, "It's for you, Jenny. It's Rosemary."

For a moment, everything seemed like it had always been. She dashed down the stairs to the telephone phone cubby so her mother wouldn't overhear. Then, as she shut the door, she was afraid to pick up the receiver. "Hello," she whispered.

"I thought you'd never answer," Rosemary scolded. "Aunt Isabel says Miss Graham called to tell her that the report says we shouldn't have been trespassing. That's all. I thought we might get blamed. Fred really. Wasn't it too awful? I couldn't even sleep."

"I had to sleep in Daddy's bed," Jenny said. "I keep thinking about the Beasty."

"But the Beasty didn't feel anything for long."

"Poor Beasty." Jenny began to cry. "It was my fault."

"Oh silly old bear, they said it was an accident."

The police report was straightforward. The construction site at the Parker Farm School was unfinished when the crew left on a Saturday afternoon. The earth was slippery where the fourth wall of the concrete enclosure had been tamped down for resumption of work on Monday. The workmen had strung a safety rope along the line of reinforcing rods. The site was posted against trespassing. The children were trespassing. There were signs of scuffling in the mud. The victim slipped. The rod pierced through the brain. The victim would have lost consciousness in seconds.

Death followed quickly. The only question unanswered was why an old ice pick was lying on the newly poured concrete floor of the holding tank.

It wasn't until after the funeral on Tuesday afternoon—there was no doubt about the cause of death—that the trouble began. Even though the reading of the Lutheran service for the dead was well attended, the heavy, dark space of the church itself overwhelmed the plain coffin before the simple altar. At the foot, in the first pew, sat the dead boy's mother, heavily veiled, slumped between the upright figure of the housekeeper and the starchy white presence of a nurse, the stiff band of her cap edged in black ribbon. Margaret was there, midway down, in the last row in the front section of the church. Beside her was Vera with Jenny, then Rosemary and Isabel Parker. They were close enough to the two principal mourners for their presence to be noticed, but apart from the regular worshippers.

Most of the members of the parents' committee were on hand. The men were seated in two pews on the right side, uniform in dark suit and tie. The headmistress had called an emergency meeting for this evening, bringing some of them back from their summer houses. It was the first time, but then even the suicide of the refugee groundskeeper had been nothing like this. This involved children. Some committee members felt the accident was yet another scandal on the premises that should never have happened; others viewed the circumstances of such an awful death as another metaphor for a war-torn world. "Could be a long meeting this evening," they whispered up and down the rows and thought of missing the scavenger hunt at the golf club or tomorrow evening's clambake on the shore. Eleanor Osgood, who also sat on the committee, slipped in silently at the end of their second row. She pointed out to the man next to her the Irish inspector and the Polish machine operator, seated together across the aisle. Bea Norton came in late, in an afternoon dress, ready for work at the servicemen's center downtown.

Harry stood at the back of the church behind the last pew, where Mrs. Goldstein sat with Gottfried. The bereaved mother, heavily sedated when Harry had visited her in her hospital retreat, had been sharp enough to tell him, before she turned her face to the wall, that she didn't want any murderous Jewboy coming between God and her son on his journey to eternal peace. Her look told Harry that she would like to include him too. He ignored it, she was distraught. But still, he had to explain to Mrs. Goldstein that Mrs. von Kempel blamed Fred for the accident.

Ada Goldstein was used to condemnation. Grim-faced, she told Harry that she felt obliged to be at the service for the boy, German or not. Harry was relieved when the Goldsteins chose to sit at the back of the church. In the end, he was sure that Mrs. von Kempel never noticed them.

After the ceremony, Mrs. von Kempel and her

companions vanished through a door to the left of
the altar. On the sidewalk outside the church, Harry
greeted some of his fellow committee members heading back to the subway and downtown offices, then
turned to offer the Goldsteins a ride, but they had
joined the other women and children at the curb.
He tipped his hat to the gathering, as the Goldsteins
stepped up into Vera's Buick. At the last minute, Jenny
slipped out of her mother's car and into the back seat
of Isabel Parker's Pontiac, and Rosemary settled in
the front beside her aunt. As Harry turned away, the
inspector caught up with him. They shook hands. "I
thought I might find you here, Harry."

"Dreadful, such a death, Frank. Good of you to
come." Harry paused.

"Common decency, Harry. I don't want any of this
to reflect on the city." Frank O'Brien placed his cap on
his head. Together, the two men watched the coffin being slid into the hearse.

"It's been a terrible time for everyone, Frank."

"I told you those women had no business med-
dling where they know nothing." The inspector shook
his head. "What a sorry mess, and a schoolmistress at
that. You'd think she'd know about children. I saw the
whole array of your school dignitaries on hand. You
know I'll be over there tomorrow, Harry." He raised
his hand to make a point. "There'll be charges. Nothing criminal, terrible accidents happen, but there'll
be a penalty for negligence." He paused. "Against the
school or the business, both maybe."

Harry heard the warning. "Can't be the company, Frank. Izrael and Son had nothing to do with it. A fence should be regulation," he pointed out, "but I blame myself."

"Regulation, maybe, but you? You saved their school. Why do you cover up for these people, Harry?"

Harry lifted his hat and combed his fingers through his hair. He was hot and tired. "They're where I live, Frank." He set his hat back on his head.

"You must be some kind of a saint, Harry."

"On the contrary. My children go to Miss Graham's school. That doesn't happen everywhere for my kind. In their way, they've taken me in."

"As long as it suits them, my friend."

"Now that the funeral is over, let's see if we can't get a few things straight," Margaret said, as she stepped into the entryway of Vera's house.

Vera took off her hat and gloves and set them down with her pocketbook on the dining room table. "Why don't you three children settle down on the sofa," she called into the hall. The girls did as they were told, but Fred hovered near the front door, close to his mother. "Margaret, take the Goldsteins into the living room. I'll go rustle up some tea."

Ignoring her request, Margaret followed Vera into the kitchen. "It's important that we treat this seriously, Vera. I need to hear what the children have to say without that policeman hovering over us."

"I think we'll all feel better with a cup of tea,

Margaret. It was a painful service and we don't want
to follow it with an inquisition. Even Rosemary has
not been very forthcoming. I wish Isabel Parker could
be here now, but of course she had to go back to her
work."

"Oh, no one listens to Isabel anymore, it's Richard
I need now. He'd have this cleared up in minutes,"
Margaret said. "I've told them we've nothing to hide,
they've seen it all, but still the inspector is coming to
the school tomorrow."

Vera lit the flame under the kettle and reached for
the teapot. "Tell the truth but don't offer information,
that's really all Richard can advise you, Margaret."
Vera reached for the silver tray. "Oh dear, look at this.
I can't keep up with the polishing." She hesitated a
moment, then set the cups down on the tarnished tray
anyway.

Margaret removed her hat and stabbed the pin
into the crown. "I'll need your help with details, Vera."

"Harry's the person to help you with any details."

"Did you see him talking with the inspector after
the service?" Margaret asked. Vera nodded. "I don't
want Harry in on this."

Vera was incredulous. "Without his help, there
wouldn't be any school this fall." She poured a little
boiling water into the tea pot to warm it, then poured
it out. She brought the water to a boil again, while she
spooned the loose-leaf tea into the pot. "He's done so
much for you, Margaret."

"He let that makeshift work crew of his walk off

the job at a dangerously crucial moment."

"They didn't 'walk off the job.' It was the end of their work week. You knew it might happen that way."

"They'd have done anything Harry said. He could have persuaded them to finish." Vera shook her head, but kept silent while she assembled the tea tray. When she was about to pick it up from the kitchen table, Margaret placed her hand on Vera's arm. She spoke in a softened tone. "The important thing now is that we look ahead and not get bogged down in a lot of blame and recrimination."

At first, if Jenny looked at anyone, she was afraid she would blurt out something, and she knew the most important thing was not to, that's what her father had told her mother. Don't offer any information. But then if she didn't look at someone, everywhere else she looked, the image of Beasty hovered before her. It was like the man's brains on the water pipes when she was eight. It followed her everywhere. Just a minute ago the Beasty was floating above the coffee table, the rod sticking out the back of his head. So after three days, mostly she could look at people. She and Rosemary even giggled about Mrs. Goldstein's painted eyelashes in the car coming home from the funeral. But she didn't want to talk about what happened. If she did, she knew she'd say the wrong thing.

Jenny snatched her feet off the coffee table as the headmistress came across the hall into the living room. She followed Rosemary's example, wriggling to sit up straight at the edge of the sofa cushions, pulling down the skirts of their good summer dresses to cover their thighs, crossing their ankles. Jenny propped her fists on her knees. Rosemary clasped her hands in her lap.

"Come along in." Miss Graham was beckoning to Mrs. Goldstein and Fred. "Do sit down, Mrs. Goldstein. Fred, on the sofa with the girls." But the Goldsteins chose two straight chairs under an ornamental mirror in the corner of the room. They settled at attention. Jenny's mother put the tea tray down on the coffee table. Mrs. Goldstein put her hand on Fred's leg.

The headmistress smiled. "You children have had a terrible shock," she began, addressing the three children, glancing from face to face. "We all have. Such a tragic experience. I know how hard it is to talk about it, but we have to face up to the truth in our lives." She leaned forward over the coffee table, frowning at the two girls.

Jenny looked down at her lap as Miss Graham walked the length of the living room rug and back again. "Now I must meet with the inspector, and I am counting on your help," she continued. "I know you've been over what happened Saturday evening with the policeman, but I want you to go through the details with me once more, slowly and clearly, in your own words. We're all friends here."

A cup rattled and Miss Graham paused again. They all watched the ritual: tea, hot water, one precious lump. The headmistress shook her head. Mrs. Goldstein also refused. Jenny's mother poured in a dollop of milk and put a gingersnap on the edge of the saucer. She set the cup down in front of Rosemary just as Miss Graham turned on her heel and leaned toward the sofa. "Yes, Rosemary, why don't we start with you."

"I did tell the policeman, Miss Graham. We knew we shouldn't have been there. It's just that Fred and I got separated from the others, and we thought they might be in the cemetery."

Jenny saw her mother's eyebrows shoot up.

"Did you often go into the cemetery in the evening, Rosemary?" she asked.

For just an instant Rosemary looked unsettled. "Oh no, Mrs. Oliver, that's forbidden. We just went to the edge by the maple trees. It was only a shortcut, going across the field. I'm ever so sorry we didn't obey you, Miss Graham. We couldn't find the others."

There was the faint ring of the telephone, and Jenny's mother went to answer it. "Don't say anything until I get back." They waited, Miss Graham tapping her toe.

"It's for you, Margaret. Harry Lewis. He has something he thinks you ought to know."

"He always has something he thinks I ought to know." The headmistress shook her head. "Tell him not now, Vera. I'll see him this evening at the meeting." She turned back to Rosemary. "Now, let's get back to business. The others, you say you were looking for the others?"

"All the other kids went down the passageway by

the tennis court," Jenny said. It seemed okay to say that much.

"Well then, Jenny, what were you doing at the school field?"

"I followed them," she answered sheepishly.

Rosemary spoke up. "It was just that we were on our way back, Miss Graham. You know, it might get dark."

"But where was the von Kempel boy in all of this?"

Rosemary looked over at Fred, but he wouldn't look at her. Jenny traced a flower in the damask fabric of a sofa pillow with her forefinger. Rosemary tugged at her braid and shrugged. "He came racing out of nowhere, you know, with that pick thing. He thrust it at Fred." Her voice quickened. "They chased each other across the field to the edge of the construction pit. Once Fred slipped in the mud, and we thought the Beasty was going to stab him, but Fred got out of his reach and . . ."

"That's not so. The Beasty didn't even try," Jenny interrupted.

"The short pants were very dirty." Mrs. Goldstein gave Fred a pat. He twitched her hand off his leg.

Rosemary went on. "Jenny yelled, 'the Beasty beat you' at Fred."

Miss Graham looked at Jenny disapprovingly.

"Even if the Beasty didn't stab Fred, he could have. So he beat him," Jenny declared.

Fred stared at the floor.

"When we saw Fred chasing the Beasty," Rosemary continued, "we raced after. We called to them to stop, didn't we, Jenny, but they wouldn't." She turned to look at Jenny.

Jenny nodded at her slightly, then collapsed back against the sofa cushions.

"Do you have something to add, Jenny?"

She shook her head from side to side. But then she said, "I saw him."

"Who, Jenny, the von Kempel boy?"

Jenny shook her head again. Fred's face was pale now.

Miss Graham said, "It would help, Fred, if you told us what happened next."

There was a long silence before Fred spoke. "He slipped."

"Where was he when he slipped?"

"He slipped. He slipped. He slipped," Fred shouted. His mother stood and put her arm around his shoulder.

Rosemary leaned forward. "He was on the mound, Miss Graham," she said breathlessly. "It was very slippery with the wet mud and all. He was looking down at us from right at the edge of the trench. The rods were behind him at his knees. I remember, they looked like a line of soldiers marching up out of the pit. He had that pick in his hand."

Miss Graham was surprised. "But if he was looking down at you, Rosemary, how could he fall on his face across the trench behind him."

"Well . . ." Rosemary started, then stopped abruptly. She was frowning. "He was sort of twirling around when he slipped." She clasped her hands in her lap. "That was all I saw, Miss Graham."

"Jenny, is that what . . ?" Miss Graham looked from the alarm on Jenny's face to Fred's glower. "Fred, do you have anything to add to Rosemary's account."

"No."

"Do you, Jenny?"

Fred crouched forward on his chair like an animal about to pounce.

Miss Graham said, "Yes, Fred?"

He shook his head and settled back in his chair. She turned to look at Jenny again. "You have something you want to say."

"No, not really, Miss Graham," she said tentatively. She could hear her voice getting smaller and smaller, as if were inside someone else. "Only . . . what was it Daddy said about the truth, Mummy?" she whispered.

Her mother looked puzzled. "You mean tell the truth but don't offer any information?"

"So you have to be asked?"

Now Miss Graham looked alarmed. "You have to be very sure about what you say, Jenny. The truth is not something you embellish."

"Daddy says there are as many ways of telling the truth as there are lawyers."

Jenny made a sudden bounce to the edge of the sofa, glaring at Fred for a long moment, steely-eyed, like her father when he wanted the culprit to consider the consequences of her crime.

"But the real truth is that Fred . . ." She pointed at him.

"*Mein Gott*," Mrs. Goldstein cried out.

"You pushed him."

"She tells lies," Fred yelled. "I got the weapon from him."

"You did not. The policeman found the ice pick in the pit. You pushed the Beasty, I saw you."

"I did not do what she says. She says those things against me. Ask Rosemary." Fred's voice was shrill.

"*Lieber Hertz*." Mrs. Goldstein clasped her breast.

"He pushed. Ask Rosemary."

Rosemary looked from Fred to Jenny and back, then sat up straight, smoothing down her skirt, ready to go on stage. Jenny's mother held her breath. Mrs. Goldstein clutched Fred's arm. Finally Rosemary addressed the headmistress. "I saw him . . . I was turning . . ." Her voice trailed off, her shoulders slumped. "Actually, I didn't see him."

A slow smile came over Miss Graham's face. "Ah, now I understand what it is, Jenny. We often think we see . . . Rosemary didn't actually see . . ."

Rosemary nudged Jenny. "It was a tackle, not a push."

Mrs. Goldstein began to sob.

The schoolmistress went on evenly, as if she hadn't heard Rosemary's last remark. "Sometimes we think we see things differently in the heat of the moment." She stared down at Jenny. "Is that it, Jenny, or did you make something up?"

"No. No." She looked at her mother. "Mummy, honest, I . . ."

"I understand, Jenny," the headmistress cooed at Jenny. "You might have felt a little left out."

"Margaret," Jenny's mother interrupted, moving to stand beside Jenny. "I think you should let Jenny explain herself." She leaned over to ask, "Do you want to say any more, dear?"

"I don't think that's wise, Vera," Miss Graham said quickly. "The children have had enough for today. This has been difficult for all of us, and tempers have run high." She looked at Jenny's mother. "I suggest we summon up the courage to forgive and forget."

"It's not that easy, Margaret. There's the matter of the truth."

"A good night's sleep will bring the whole thing into perspective for you, Vera. Consider the children. Fred . . . and your Jenny. What about her?" It was almost a threat. "A good lawyer like her father will know how to approach . . . Your job is to have Richard call me as soon as possible. This is an emergency." Miss Graham paused. "Now, I'm going to take the Goldsteins home," she went on. "I'm sure the committee will agree that the sensible thing to do is to see if we can't put the inquiry off until Richard can break away from his wartime duties to iron out this whole regrettable incident. Under the circumstances, he'll find a way." Miss Graham looked hard at the two Olivers before she called, "Come along, Rosemary. I left my car in the Parkers' driveway. You can walk home with us. It's getting late." Miss Graham never stopped talking as she hustled the others out of the house. "And Vera, we don't want to encourage discussion at the meeting tonight."

Mother and daughter stood in the middle of the hall and watched them go. Rosemary smiled over her shoulder, but Jenny didn't smile back. They returned to the living room and began to pick up the tea things.

"That woman. Wait until the committee questions her this evening. Harry will get to the bottom of this."

Jenny was surprised at her mother's anger toward someone else, but it made her feel safe, almost lighthearted. She picked up a box of matches and tossed it up in the air, then lunged but missed the catch. "Miss Graham has forgotten about the poor Beasty."

"Hiding behind Rosemary's silly dramatics. Implying all kinds of things" Her mother's voice was full of scorn. It made Jenny smile. "What was it you wanted to say, dear?"

"Nothing much. She didn't want to believe me, anyway."

"Only what suited her." Her mother began to stack the cups by twos on the tray. "I worry she's got something up her sleeve."

Jenny bent down to pick up the matchbox off the rug. "Don't worry, Mummy. Miss Graham doesn't really care about what really happened. I think she just wants a story to tell to the inspector when he comes to see her."

Her mother looked up at Jenny in surprise. "You know, I hadn't thought of that. It's not the truth she wants, it's a good story. This is getting out of hand." She handed the tray to her daughter. "Here, take this to the kitchen. I think I'd better try to reach your father right away."

Chapter Twenty

The meeting of the parents' committee that evening at the school began late. Called for seven o'clock, it cut short the summer cocktail hour in the garden, and for some of the men, it meant a pickup dinner since the maids had gone with the family to the country or were on holiday. For others, it meant no dinner at all.

As Vera entered the assembly hall, she looked up the long rectangular table where Margaret sat at the head, her folded hands resting on the top in a posture of controlled calm. There were no papers or pen, no clipboard laid out before her, only her rattan handbag. She's on edge, Vera thought. What is she planning? She caught Margaret's half-smile and saw her pat the empty chair at her side, but Vera pretended not to notice. Instead, she chose a seat at the far end of the table. She was not prepared to overlook the sacrifice of her child's integrity in order to smooth the way for the headmistress. In the past she had always sat as close to Margaret as she could, as secretary, she told herself. But the real reason was the protection Vera had once felt. She could take secretary's notes from any seat.

Vera glanced up the long sides of the rectangle at the suntanned faces and ruddy cheeks, sunburned scalps and bald spots, navy blue blazers, seersucker suits, woven leather shoes. How much this display of summer good looks said about the affluent in August. Not a trace of discomfort or anxiety or even wartime commitments when they stepped into their own vacation lives, only the fretful irritation of having been called away to sit through another meeting. Vera mistrusted the atmosphere in the room. Then, she realized that Harry had still not arrived.

Margaret looked at her watch. "It's twenty after seven. I really can't wait for Harry any longer."

"I'm sure he'll be here soon," Vera said.

Margaret looked around the table. Many of the expressions were already dulled. "I don't know what he has on his mind this time, Vera, but we need to move on," Margaret said. There were nods of agreement. "I'm going to dispense with the reading of the minutes tonight. This is not a meeting on regular school business; it is about the meeting with the inspector tomorrow. But I will ask the secretary to take notes so that we will have a record of our joint recommendations." She waited while Vera closed the book of official minutes and turned to a fresh page in her secretarial pad. "We all feel the shock of such a tragic accidental death of a young neighborhood boy." Everyone bowed their heads slightly as if a look of piety would hurry things along. "Thank you for interrupting business and pleasure to attend the service today. I thought it would look best if the committee were there. I know you understand that the reputation of the school depends on good relations with the town." The headmistress paused a moment. "And now, I want to be clear about what I will say to the inspector. I don't want there to be any misunderstandings among us." She paused again. "This is no time for blame and recrimination," she went on, dwelling on the words as if she were gently scolding a recalcitrant child. "We must look to the future, I'm sure you'll agree. For the sake of the children."

"We've heard too much about this sewage crisis from Lewis already," one of the committee members said, "but we have to ask, were there any safety precautions that . . ?"

"Oh, the inspector knows all about that, and he will have read the police report," Margaret assured the speaker.

There was the click of a door latch, approaching footsteps, then Harry entered the room. "Sorry to be so late," he said. "I was trying to reach . . ."

"Sit down, please," the headmistress commanded. Harry took the empty seat next to Vera and put his hat down on the table while Margaret went on speaking. "I was just going to say that this afternoon I talked to the three students involved, and I was impressed with how much more expansive they were without the policeman present. It's perfectly clear that the German boy was baiting them, particularly the refugee boy, Fred Goldstein, threatening him with an ice pick. At the construction site—in plain view of the no trespass sign—the German boy climbed up the unfinished side of the tank. The ground was muddy. He slipped and came down with such force that . . . Well, you know the rest." Margaret looked so holier-than-thou that Vera could hardly keep from blurting out the truth. But then the consequences to Jenny. Would the headmistress try to make Jenny a scapegoat? Make her out to be a hysterical teenager. Or worse, a liar. Vera wouldn't put it past her. She knew she must keep quiet, at least until she could talk with Richard. She returned to her notes.

Someone asked, "Isn't that what the police report says? It was muddy, he slipped."

"I imagine the inspector is just making a friendly visit to hear the story from the horse's mouth, so to speak." The headmistress laughed self-consciously. "But it's important that we all keep the details straight."

"You should hear me out, Margaret, before you go any further," Harry said.

Margaret faced Harry squarely. "What is it that's so urgent?"

"Frank O'Brien says he'll be meeting with you tomorrow."

"Is that it, Harry? Is that what you've been trying to tell me?" she asked. "Don't you think I know that?"

Harry held the headmistress's eye for a moment,

then answered her deliberately. "When I spoke with him this afternoon, he seemed very sure that there will be a penalty. It occurred to me later that the more we know, the better you'll be able to handle it. I've been trying to reach him on the telephone before you . . ."

"Penalty for what?"

"Negligence."

"Isn't he the one who provided the no-trespassing sign?"

"Against the school," Harry told her.

"The school!" The headmistress looked at Harry in disbelief. "I don't see why my school should be penalized."

Harry remained silent.

"As representative for the school I only followed your advice, Harry Lewis. You all know I'm no expert when it comes to maintenance matters." She turned to the rows of bewildered faces for confirmation, then back to Harry, the scowl along her forehead sharp and deep now.

"I advised a fence," he reminded her.

"You should have included it in your work contract." Her face reddened. "How could you let something like this happen to my school?"

But Harry kept to his point. "As representative of the school, you took responsibility and refused to include a fence because of cost."

"The cost. How can someone like you mention cost." There was a rustle of uneasiness. The slide of a chair leg, a cough, a clearing of throats.

"Margaret, you forget . . ."

Margaret made a fist. "I put my faith in you, Harry, but you let me down." She pounded the table-top. Eleanor Osgood reached to calm her. Softly, her breath coming more easily and in a biting tone, Margaret said, "I thought you were better than the rest of your kind."

"Margaret!" Vera threw down her pencil and glanced at Harry.

Heads turned up the table to the headmistress, red-faced and defiant. A quiet gathered and grew.

"I'm sorry, Harry," Vera said.

Harry cleared his throat. His face had slumped, long and grim, and he held his hat across his abdomen like a shield. He looked up at the headmistress until she turned toward him and finally he spoke. "It pains me to hear a woman I have admired for her ideals and integrity speak this way. I thought you were beyond such prejudice." He glanced around the table and took a deep breath. "I have grown complacent over the years." He stopped to clear his throat. "My father-in-law cautioned me once. He said people will always suspect you, if you're a Jew making money."

"Harry . . ."

"It's all right, Vera. I'm the only one here who can say it," he pointed out caustically. "I'm a Jew who makes money for investors who have money." He forced a thin smile and addressed the table. "And people like you are sure to want a good return, but most of you are afraid I'm doing better for myself.

326

That's because I take greater risks. Adele's father had something else to say. Look at yourself the way others do. Then you'll know where you stand. It was good advice, but I lost sight of it." He paused. "I'm resigning as treasurer of this committee."

Vera laid her hand on his arm. "You've always been a special friend, Harry."

"Thank you, Vera."

"To all of us," she added pointedly. There were a few nods among the stony faces.

Margaret Graham squared her shoulders and looked around the table. "These have been distressing weeks." Her eyes rested on Harry. "I hope you will forgive me, Harry, I forgot my manners. I can understand how you might want to resign in the heat of the moment. It's true, you and I do not always agree. But despite what you think now, I value your advice. Our job is to strengthen our hearts and stand together again. We need you to help us move forward. "

Harry met Margaret's gaze. In the long moment that followed, Vera turned away. She couldn't stand to look at them. Would he give in to her?

"I'm afraid I can't help you, Miss Graham. I've been living in a world that is not my own." Harry pushed back his chair and stood up. "I've appreciated the support of some among you," he said, putting his hat on his head. They watched him cross the assembly room and step into the hall. A moment later, they heard the heavy door close.

"Well, Margaret." Vera's voice was deep with disgust. "I hope you're proud of yourself. Driving out a decent man like that when he's done so much for you."

"I shouldn't have said what I did, and I apologize to all of you. It's the strain. But Harry chose to go, Vera. We would have been better off leaving the whole thing in the hands of someone like Mr. O'Brien, who spends his life dealing with . . ."

"Mr. O'Brien closed the school. He didn't offer to solve your problem. He said you were lucky to have Harry to cover up for you and find a way to clean up your mess at a time when most people wouldn't bother." Vera was almost screaming now. "Before all else be true. You'd rather find a scapegoat in Jenny or an outsider like Harry Lewis than admit your own part in this whole ugly thing." She stopped to catch her breath in a deep sigh. "The real truth of the matter is that Harry was right and you were wrong, Margaret, and you can't tolerate that."

Margaret looked directly at Vera, arms across her chest. "Are you quite finished?" She pursed her lips. "Everyone knows how much I care about the school, and I do what I think is best for it. Any implication in the death of a demented boy is serious business. You should appreciate better than anyone that what we need now is a good lawyer like Richard who will know how to approach . . ."

"Yes, Richard is a good lawyer, and for the sake of the school and the children, I'm sure he will see the best way out of this." Vera closed her notebook and stood up. "I won't resign from this committee. I wouldn't give you that satisfaction. But I'm not going to sit through any more of this spectacle tonight."

When Jenny heard the front door shut, she was startled. She hadn't expected her mother home so early. She rushed to the closet where she kept the phonograph to make sure she had privacy and took off the record. She didn't want her mother to know she was listening to anything as acceptable as a Brahms symphony.

Out in the hall, she hollered over the banister, "Daddy called. He's says he'll be home tomorrow night. He got the inspector to postpone the meeting."

"I've never said this to you before, but for the first time in months, I'll be relieved to see him," her mother said flatly. Jenny made a face at the ceiling. Didn't she know? She was always saying things like that. Her mother went on. "It was a terrible meeting. I left early. Margaret Graham is just as prejudiced as all the rest of them, and no one is interested in speaking the truth any more."

Jenny went down and sat on the bottom stair, rearranging the gaps between the buttons on her pajama top to cover up the tiny mounds of breasts. Nothing fit her anymore. She waited until her mother put away her pocketbook and white gloves. "Lots of people don't tell all the truth, Mummy. When Rosemary went to the Beasty's house, she told you her aunt knew. Well, she didn't. And the memory map in sixth grade. She got sick so she could trace it from an atlas she got from the Beasty." Her mother drew in her breath. Jenny rushed on. "She made me take the book back to him." She had to make her mother understand. "Or like you, Mummy. When Katherine got caught with Teddy Russell, you only said she was suspended."

Her mother flushed. "There are certain circumstances when all the truth won't change things, dear, and it may hurt someone."

"Is that what Daddy means? There are different amounts of truth," Jenny said, then paused a moment. "There shouldn't be, though. There should be just the plain truth. But there never really is," she added, unable to let go. "Well, maybe sometimes." She put her hand on her hip the way she did when she was thinking, and she watched her mother watching her. "I guess it depends," she said finally.

Her mother sat down beside her, and Jenny let her mother put her arms around her. "Maybe that's a way for you to understand the events of the last few days, Jenny. When Daddy comes home, he'll know what's best."

"But Fred pushed the Beasty. I told the plain truth, Mummy."

Her mother hugged her. "I know you did, Jenny, and you were right."

For a moment, Jenny wanted to hug her mother back, but she could feel the color rising on her cheeks, and she couldn't stand the sappiness. She broke free and raced back up the stairs, crashing open the door of her room and slamming it shut behind her. Then she

snatched the door open again. "Jenny!" her mother exclaimed, and she slammed it shut again and flung herself onto the bed, relishing the bounce in the springs.
"Mummy believed me." She gave a bounce. "I told the
truth, and Mummy believed me," she hollered at the
light fixture in the ceiling. "I was right." She raised her
fist. "I won."

She sat up abruptly. Is that what Fred felt like
when he shoved the Beasty?

Chapter Twenty-One

Richard reached home late Wednesday night. The train had been delayed. Something on the track in Connecticut.

Vera greeted him with relief. She gave him a peck on the cheek as he set down his briefcase and bag on the front hall rug. "The Merchants Limited has never been this late before. I was concerned."

"There was some kind of obstruction on the tracks." He set his hat down on a chair. "Ever since the saboteurs from the German sub were picked up on Long Island last year, the slightest disruption gives everyone the jitters." Vera didn't have the heart not to believe him. He looked deeply tired.

"I'll fix you a sandwich." She started for the kitchen.

"I could use a scotch and soda." He picked up his briefcase and moved toward his study. "How's Jenny?"

"I'll tell you in a minute."

They sat across from each other while she ran through the details of the tragedy, Richard in the hot seat where he could stretch out his legs, Vera at his desk, leaning into her account. He looked at her in weary disbelief, sipping the drink she had brought him.

"Margaret Graham chose to believe Rosemary, who said she hadn't really seen Fred Goldstein push the poor von Kempel boy."

"Are you telling me Jenny lied?"

"No, Richard, that's precisely it. Jenny didn't lie. She told the truth, but it wasn't what any of us wanted to hear."

They sat in a long silence, Richard staring off into space. Vera left him to his thoughts while she nestled the pencils in the desk tray by length, exchanging the inkwell and pen holder to sit in the appropriate grooves. He unbuttoned the jacket of his seersucker suit, kicking off each shoe with the push of his toe at the heel, and let his body slump. He was worn out from his journey. But more profoundly, he felt empty. As husband and father, he tried to be a good provider, but their sheltered life, out of harm's way on Parker Farm Road, had been invaded. A more complex and coarser wartime climate had spread everywhere like an epidemic. He could not protect his children from dangers and temptations that he and their mother had never known in childhood.

He set his glass down on the side table and reached to gather up his shoes. He spoke decisively. "I made a few telephone calls before I left Washington. From what I can gather, there have been a couple of veiled threats, but there's nothing much to investigate." He paused and looked into his wife's anxious face. "And it would be in the best interest of everyone to leave it that way, Vera," he said pointedly. She nodded. "I don't think I'll have any trouble tomorrow pointing out to the inspector that his department is as much at fault as any of the other parties involved," he went on. "The whole business of the construction has an under-the-table flavor to it, and there were no laws to break." He started to get out of the chair, then paused a moment. "When I reached Lewis, he was adamant. He would not be at the meeting with the headmistress. I was surprised. I always thought they had a special affinity for each other." Richard raised his eyebrows at Vera; she did not comment.

She watched him get up, slowly, his weight forward on the arms of the chair, shoes dangling from the fingers of one hand, and realized how much the war had aged him. "I think I'll take another drink upstairs. Helps me to sleep," he said. "Good night, Vera."

"I'm glad to have you home, Richard."

At the door of the study he turned. "I worry about Jenny sometimes. She doesn't seem to know when to keep quiet, look the other way. She'll have a rough row to hoe if she doesn't smooth off a few of those sharp edges."

"I know what you mean." Vera smiled to herself, a little proud of those rough edges. "But I'm sure she'll get over it. Everyone does."

The afternoon following Richard's meeting with the headmistress and the inspector, Vera spent waiting,

waiting for the chance to accidentally on purpose run into Harry—what a pleasant surprise to meet like this.

Around five o'clock in the afternoon, she changed into one of her better day dresses and began peeling tomatoes at the kitchen sink, peering out the window every few minutes. When Jenny came in Vera couldn't repress a look of irritation.

"I know, Mummy," Jenny said crossly. "I'm supposed to water the lawn. I was on the telephone telling Rosemary that Daddy said it was everybody's fault, but she already knew."

She came to stand next to Vera, stretching forward over the faucets to follow Vera's gaze up the road.

"What is it, Mummy?" Jenny asked impatiently.

"Nothing, dear," Vera said too smoothly.

"Miss Graham told Mrs. Parker that Fred ought to go away. 'O frabjous day! Callooh! Callay!'" Jenny twirled around the kitchen. "Wouldn't that be wonderful."

"That's not very nice, Jenny."

"Oh, mother." Jenny stomped to the kitchen door.

"I'll water the grass today," Vera said hurriedly. "You run along and take care of yourself." Jenny bound up the back stairs like a dog let off the leash.

A little later, Vera went out and unreeled the hose to the far edge of the lawn, then positioned herself at one of the dining room windows, where she could peek around the curtain. When she saw Harry drive by, she flew out the front door to water the grass. He caught sight of her, and she raised her hand to wave.

"Hello there, Vera. I didn't see you when I drove up." He tipped his boater to her. "You really are a slave to that lawn."

"It's Richard's pride and joy, you know, and we've had some hot days this week."

Harry smiled uncomfortably. "In more ways than one."

"It's all settled, no one's to blame."

"Richard left a message for me at my office." Harry set down his briefcase. "I'm grateful to him for stepping in."

"Oh, Harry," Vera said ardently. "I want you to know how much . . . please, understand we don't all feel that way." Tears came to her eyes, and she turned away from him to water a scorched patch.

"I know, Vera," he said gently.

When she turned back, she looked up into his face. "I've been thinking it over. I intend to resign from the committee myself."

He smiled down at her. "I appreciate the gesture, Vera, but I hope you won't."

"I don't see how I can face her now that I know what she's really like."

"Margaret Graham will regain her equilibrium. People like that always do. But the school will value you more than ever now, the voice of reason."

Vera blushed and dropped the hose. The water sprayed up in an arc before the nozzle burrowed into the ground. Harry stepped back and she lunged forward, grabbing his arm. "Oh, did I get you wet?"

"Just a little." They both bent over to inspect his wet trouser leg. As they straightened up, their heads bumped.

She put her hand to her forehead and laughed. "This is really Jenny's job. I'm only doing it so I can speak to you, Harry."

"I suspected as much." Now he laughed. "You know, I like you, Vera. I'm glad you never got over being honest."

Vera was smiling as she returned to the house. All evening long, there was a calm about her.

Fred wasn't in school when it reconvened in the fall. Boarding school was considered a great opportunity for him to develop his superior debating skills. Mrs. Parker was pleased to augment the scholarship Miss Graham had gotten for him.

"What debating skills?" Jenny asked Rosemary. "Miss Graham just made that up to get rid of him."

"Well, she had to say something, didn't she? But I don't really mind. He was so immature."

Jenny was thrilled. Everything would be the same again. Now they spent their afternoons secluded in the cupola, smoking Rosemary's Uncle Cyrus's precious Lucky Strike cigarettes, blowing the smoke out the window, so her Aunt Isabel wouldn't get a whiff. Jenny liked holding the butt, but the actual smoke choked her. Rosemary took deep draws and claimed she was inhaling. Then one day, a note appeared on the top of the cigarette carton in Professor Parker's desk drawer.

OFF LIMITS, it read in Mrs. Parker's elegant hand-writing. After that, they had to satisfy themselves with sips from the sherry decanter as they went by the lowboy in the dining room. Sometimes they did makeup with Rosemary's secret stash. Her Aunt Isabel did not approve of ruby red lips with exaggerated peaks at the bow or spots of rouge to highlight distinctive cheekbones on fourteen year old girls. Afterward, they dabbed on cold cream and scrubbed their faces until their skin was pink and sore. On Saturdays, they went to the double feature picture show at the University Theatre and strolled the university campus so Rosemary could ogle the good-looking soldiers and sailors. Jenny said it was cheap and pushy. Rosemary said Jenny was chicken. On the way home, when they passed the Beasty's house, sometimes they broke into a trot. Other times, they lingered to look in the windows. A new family had moved in. Jenny could see the curve of a grand piano and a plant in a tall stand. She imagined the Beasty sitting on the front steps the way he used to or prancing through the swamp that time when she was eight.

"Do you believe people go to heaven when they die?" she asked Rosemary.

"Of course, that's where my brother will meet his make, so he'd better behave himself."

"You don't really think that?"

"That's what Mummy tells Ian. Heaven is for bad boys and old people."

"I thought hell was supposed to be for bad people." Jenny paused. "The Beasty wasn't bad really."

For a long time Rosemary was silent, running her finger along the top of the fence, and Jenny wondered what she was thinking. Finally, she spun around and flashed her smile at Jenny. "No, not really. He was just a pudgy giant cabbage worm."

Jenny glanced down at her sneakers. "Poor Beasty."

In December, Margaret Graham announced that she would be leaving the Parker Farm School to organize relief workers for the Unitarian Church as soon as the parents' committee could find a replacement. The community hardly had time to absorb the news before the committee announced the appointment of Vera as the administrative director. The position was to be temporary. Eleanor Osgood would be in charge of curriculum. As it happened, together they ran the school for sixteen years.

Vera felt so certain of her ability to do the job that she had accepted on the spot, without discussing it with Richard. So as not to overwhelm him Vera referred to her new position as her "little job." Richard was dumbfounded. He was duty bound, he said, to object. But with time, he could not help but be impressed by the check deposited in the savings account each month.

Vera's first meeting with Margaret after her appointment was not easy. They had not been alone together since Vera had walked out of the meeting room last summer.

The headmistress did not look up when she said, "I have to tell you, Vera, I was surprised when the committee made a hasty interim appointment." They were seated across from each other at the headmistress' desk.

Vera could see the tightness in Margaret's shoulders as she thumbed her way through a sheaf of papers. A little generosity might smooth the way. "I think the committee understood how eager you are to take up your new assignment, Margaret, and wanted to accommodate you."

Margaret looked up. "Yes, it's an opportunity to do important work. I imagine I'll be sent overseas when the hostilities die down."

"It's a feather in your cap."

"Yes, I suppose it is." The headmistress smiled and leaned back in her chair. "Well now, let's see. I have office matters pretty much in hand, as you can see, and you have some familiarity with procedure. I'm sure that's why they made the choice they did, but I think you'll do all right."

"Of course, Margaret."

Vera let the silence between them linger.

"I'll miss the school, it's been my life's work, the only home I've known really." The headmistress laid her hand on the pile of papers in front of her. "There are always challenges in wartime. The tragedy of the groundskeeper. The refugees driven from their homeland. The evacuee children. But everyone is always welcomed into our community. Tolerance and trust, these are our most basic values, Vera."

"Harry Lewis and the German boy," Vera said quietly.

"I often think of the boy, unbalanced really, such a pity." Margaret paused, then said, "I could see the danger when I visited the site the afternoon before the accident. I was going to ask Mr. Dooley to erect a barrier when he went in the next morning after Mass to moisten the rags on the cement."

"Did you ever tell Harry Lewis that?"

The headmistress stood up and stepped over to the window. "I haven't spoken to him since he stormed out of that extraordinary meeting last August." After a few moments, she turned back. "I'll leave you to begin going through these files and accounts, while I attend to some things in the outer office. Call me if you have any questions." At the door she paused. "Don't worry, Vera, the school will pretty much run itself until they find the right person."

Vera carried the books and files over to the conference table and spread them out. She pulled up a chair and opened the first file. The nerve of that woman, she muttered to herself. The arrogance, never out of step, always right, the guardian of truth and honor. And not an ounce of gratitude to people like Harry. Or me, she added, as she thumbed down the index tabs.

When the Lewises moved to Riverside early in the new year, Jenny and Rosemary watched the men load the moving van. Mrs. Lewis and the children had already gone on ahead with the maids to spend a few nights at the Statler Hotel downtown, and Pearl and her brother were probably skating on the Common. Mr. Lewis locked the front door of his house for the last time and stood on the step for a moment. It had begun to snow again. The rhododendrons were hunched up in the cold. The forsythia hedge looked old and dark and shriveled against the white of the ground. As he came down the walk, Jenny's mother appeared, bundled up in her good navy blue overcoat. She was bare-headed, and the snowflakes rested prettily in her dark hair. Mr. Lewis took off one glove and they shook hands. Then he went to open the door on the driver's side of the Packard, pausing to look over the hood at her. There were tears in his eyes. "Good luck, Vera. I told you the school needed you. You'll do a wonderful job."

"I'll miss you, Harry." She put her hands to her face as she ran back into the house.

Jenny and Rosemary waved as Mr. Lewis drove off.

Closing Day 1944 at the Parker Farm School was on a Tuesday, June 6th. As a member of the graduating class, Rosemary got to recite the Twenty-first Psalm—because she had such a nice accent, Jenny's mother explained when Jenny objected to Miss Osgood's choice. But Jenny was one of the singers in the "Dona Nobis Pacem." It was twenty-four hours before they knew what else had happened that day. D-Day.

That fall, on the morning she was to travel to New York to board the transport ship that would take her away, Rosemary walked with Jenny to the car stop on Great Hamilton Street, where Jenny would take the trolley to her new school. Despite the Indian summer heat Jenny had on the reindeer jacket that Rosemary had given her the evening before. Rosemary wore a new reversible, plaid coat, a going-away present from her Aunt Isabel. They had already exchanged addresses and pictures and stolen lipsticks. There was nothing left to say except, "I love you," but of course girls didn't say that to each other. When Jenny saw the streetcar coming, she felt sick to her stomach. "Write me." "I shall." Seated at the window, Jenny pressed her nose against the dirty glass and made a face at Rosemary, waggling her fingers held up to her ears. Then she turned away and cried herself to school.

Epilogue

Jenny excelled in high school, where she had no legacy, no perfect Katherine to live up to, no praise for her admirable mother. It gave her the anonymity and freedom to became one of the brainy group—good in math and English, indifferent in art and gym. She thoroughly enjoyed being noticed. She sang in the glee club and joined the school newspaper to editorialize about the shocking lack of workable locks on the stalls in the girls' bathroom and ask why football got more attention than music. Parker Farm School seemed precious and far behind. At home in the evenings during supper, she held forth on such topics as Iron Curtain diplomacy and anti-semitism in America, fired up by her current events class. She stuck up for President Truman and called Republican Senator Taft a stuffed-shirt isolationist. Occasionally, her father expressed an opposing view or tried to temper her argument, but she knew she had her parents cowed.

After graduation Jenny turned down Boylston University, her parents' choice for her. She went instead to a progressive college in the middle west where, much to her mother's consternation, she declared herself an agnostic. "It seems so unnecessary," Vera wrote. "You've never been a member of a church. I've always regretted that I did not insist that you and Katherine attend Sunday school at West Ivers Episcopal." Jenny put this down to her mother's habitual hand-wringing and wondered if she wasn't really an atheist. In her senior year, she joined the college chapter of the World Federalists where she met her husband-to-be, Joe Stern, a semi-invalid veteran who had lost part of his bowel in the war. When her anxious parents suggested a long engagement, Jenny knew they hoped she would change her mind. She told them that he was entitled to happiness just as much as anyone, maybe more so.

Vera tried to console Richard by dwelling on Joe's maturity. He was no fly-by-night lightweight. Richard got up from his chair to get another drink. As he left the room, she heard him mutter, "I'd take any one of Jenny's other causes over this one." The couple moved to upstate New York, where Joe went to graduate school and Jenny worked part-time as a file clerk, a copy editor, a Brownie Scout leader and started a family, straining all the time at the boredom. It was a hard marriage to find pleasure in. Jenny's energy choked Joe; his moderation kept Jenny in restraint. Each lost interest in the other's welfare.

Almost by mistake Jenny learned her mother had breast cancer. It was still a time when mentioning certain parts of the body was unseemly. A brain tumor might have been public knowledge. Jenny was home for a late spring visit with her two daughters. She felt calm and in charge, a grownup in her childhood setting. And over the years her mother's position at the Parker Farm School had become a leveling influence that had established some equality and calm between her parents. It was a pleasant occasion to be having drinks on the back terrace.

"Who would want to be anywhere else," her father said, scanning an oval bed of tea roses where lawn used to be. He set down the tray of drinks on the table.

Her mother looked up at him. "It is nice, Richard."

Jenny had to smile. Years ago, such a statement would have brought at least a frown or a quick move indoors on the pretext of getting a cardigan to throw over her shoulders. Jenny looked more closely at her mother. Her hair was pepper and salt, no-nonsense short. She had a little bit of a jowl. She looked pale, almost gray.

"Would you like your cardigan?"

"Oh, that would be nice. It's on the chair in the hall."

When Jenny put the sweater around her shoulders, her mother reached up to capture Jenny's hand and hold it for a long moment. Her mother's expression was one of serious calm. For a moment, Jenny felt like a child again. "You all right?" she blurted out.

Her mother rubbed her upper arms to show how warm she was, wrapped in the sweater. "Thank you, dear." It was her mother's too-smooth tone. Jenny scowled and let it pass.

Her father passed around the drinks. They discussed the perfect weather, the little girls asleep upstairs in Katherine's room. Katherine's remarriage. A doctor she'd met at the California hospital where she was a nurse. They'd only met him once, but he seemed very nice. The inevitable question about Joe's lingering PhD thesis. And the inevitable answer. It was coming along. Her parents seemed more than calm, they seemed resigned. Old before their time. Well, she couldn't tell about her father, but her mother? Something Jenny had never considered before.

Jenny picked up her martini and wandered out to inspect her father's vegetable garden. She knew he would follow.

"What happened to all the beans?" she asked.

"There're only the two of us now."

"You used call up from Washington or wherever you were and ask about them. Mother would tell you how delicious they were, then we'd stuff them down the incinerator to get rid of them. We couldn't keep up. 'Not beans again!' we'd scream." Jenny laughed at the memory.

"She never told me that." Jenny was glad to hear the irritation in his voice. A little bit of normalcy around here.

"So what's she not telling now?"

He looked down at his shoes, then put his free hand in his pocket and began to rattle the change

It was serious. "What? What is it?"

"The doctor says there's a good chance of catching

it all." He glanced away, guilty for spilling the beans. Jenny had never seen him helpless.

"Is it cancer?" she asked.

"You'd better speak to your mother."

"Just the left one. I haven't told anyone. We don't know everything yet. You know how news travels, and I didn't want to burden Eleanor. Better to have the surgery after Closing Day."

"But Mother. Sooner is better than later."

"It's all right, it's scheduled for next week. So hard on the little girls to have their grandmother under par. I didn't want to spoil your visit, dear. I was going to tell you and Katherine when there was good news."

"Oh God, Mother," Jenny yelled, stamping her foot. She went in the house, slamming the screen door.

When Vera died, Richard married Miss Sperry within a year, leaving Jenny and Katherine indignant on their mother's behalf, but also relieved. When he told them that the months without Vera were the worst time in his life, they believed him. They saw he was adrift, he could not look after himself.

A small inheritance allowed Jenny to get a divorce, after ten years of marriage, and she returned to graduate school while raising her children. She found the study of history full of drama, imagination, and character, people pursuing independence and power. But her students at the school in the Vermont town where she settled thought it dry: when, where, why. Facts and dates. The Declaration of Independence, July 4, 1776, that was easy, or the Emancipation Proclamation, 1863. That kind of thing.

Some years ago she began to teach twentieth-century history in a new way, in reverse. Starting with the present they explored historical events that the students recognized or experienced themselves. Then, they moved back decade by decade to explain and inform the years that they had just discussed. These times were often still vivid in the minds of the students' parents, who found their lives changed by the events their children were about to examine. As they traveled backward, Jenny tried to dramatize some of the important events by personalizing them. Did your father serve in Vietnam? A grandfather in World War II? Where was your mother when President Nixon resigned? When President Kennedy was assassinated? When she heard from a parent about a lively discussion at the dinner table or a student brought in a piece of memorabilia, an Eisenhower button, a glass milk bottle, a cloche hat to show the class, she knew she had reached beyond the textbook to bring events alive to have meaning in the present.

From time to time, Jenny read about her classmates in the Parker Farm School Alumni News. Patsy Russell married a lawyer, Molly Norton a world-famous polo player. Pearl Lewis became a circuit judge. After the war Gottfried Goldstein and his mother went first to Canada, then returned to Europe. He married and settled in Amsterdam to become a successful prosecutor, no doubt raising his fist at the enemy even as he moved smoothly through life. Jenny sometimes thought about Fred and the Beasty and the hatreds they inherited, or her own burning childish dislike of Fred because of the attention and pity he got and the experience of disaster that he had shared with Rosemary. She still wondered sometimes what would have happened if she had not jeered at Fred. Over the years, she'd felt unduly guilty, then dismissive, then unable to rid herself of the burden of responsibility. She even considered that Fred believed he was telling the truth when he said the Beasty had slipped. But like other images of that war, the look of terror on the face of the little boy in the Warsaw Ghetto or the gross-headed body of Mussolini strung up in the streets of Milan, the terrible scene of the Beasty's death did not fade.

Jenny thought about her friendship with Rosemary, as well. In a novel, Rosemary would have been the sly seductress. She had been everything that Jenny could not be: charming, deceitful, irresponsible in a way that gave her a kind of enviable freedom, the only person Jenny ever knew who lived unabashedly in the present. It was farcical, the power she'd had over Jenny from the love-at-first-sight moment. That's how Jenny always saw Rosemary in her mind's eye, coming down Parker Farm Road, red-cheeked with her long, dark braid down her back, her kit bag slung across the blue sweater jacket with the silver buttons and the reindeer. Jenny had hung onto that jacket for decades.

She had kept in touch with Rosemary, Christmas

cards, little notes to mark important occasions. And she'd seen her more than once, as university student, the mother of four, active member of the local conservative party, chairperson for the drive to restrict council flats. She was widowed a few years ago by the death of her barrister husband, but the last time Jenny visited she was happily ensconced in a garden cottage just outside of Gloucester on the Welsh border, near a married daughter. Jenny was coleading a junior-class trip abroad. The English teacher had taken the students to Tintern Abbey, and Jenny was glad to have time off. Plump and graying and cheerful, in a flowered print dress with a little bow at the kick pleat, in contrast to Jenny's sensible denim pants, Rosemary had replaced her disingenuous grin with a purposeful smile.

"We'll take tea in the garden, I think," Rosemary said. It was a soft late-June day.

Jenny hovered at the window. "Yes, let's. Your roses are lovely."

The two of them moved awkwardly from the kitchen through the dining room, Rosemary carrying the tea tray, Jenny trailing behind, steadying a plate of scones and the marmalade pot on her forearm as she tried to hold the door open for Rosemary. They might have been twelve years old.

"Your father grew roses, didn't he."

"He was still tending them up until his death."

Rosemary set the tray down on an ornate metal table. The seats of the chairs, with comfortable pillows over the metal web, bounced as they sat down.

"I remember a photograph that demented German boy took of me in a bathing suit in front of the hedge of roses by your garage." Rosemary was spearing a sliver of lemon with a tiny fork. She placed the slice on the paper-thin saucer and poured tea and hot water into an elegant China cup. "It did cause a ruckus. Your mother was frightfully upset." She handed Jenny her cup of tea. "But we lived such innocent lives in those times. You Americans hardly did without." Rosemary's voice had that familiar tinkly bell tone, but it was unusual for Rosemary to reminisce.

"Nothing is really innocent in wartime," Jenny said, then thought how pompous she sounded. If a student said that, she would ask for clarification, but Rosemary ignored her. Instead she pushed the plate of scones toward Jenny.

"You remember Gottfried Goldstein?" she asked ingenuously.

"Of course." Jenny straightened up.

"I saw him last summer at Glyndebourne." Just a flash of her Cheshire grin darted across Rosemary's face. She'd surprised Jenny. "My husband was a great opera aficionado." She said the word with a burst of air through her teeth. "I've kept up our support. Gottfried's name was listed in the program. Then there he was, standing next to me in the patrons' refreshment tent."

"I'm stunned," Jenny said, putting down her teacup.

"I knew you would be. When you wrote to say you'd be visiting, I thought I'd save the news." Rosemary laughed. "He was dotty about me, and he did so get on your nerves."

"What did you have to say to each other?"

"Nothing, really. It was amusing to see what he looked like. Stiff as a ramrod. A fringe of hair. Gray, of course. Frameless glasses. Not much fun." Rosemary paused to pout. After a moment, she brightened. "His wife was quite nice looking."

Jenny sat silent for a moment. This was too fleeting a dismissal. "Do you ever think about what happened? Our part in it?" She looked into Rosemary's startled face and hurried on. "I used to a lot, not so much now. But once in a while, my memory surprises me with an image. Fred's bony knees caked with mud, the ice pick at the bottom of the concrete tank, the spike poking through the head of the Beasty's body."

"Of course I don't think about it, it was fifty years ago."

"But our part in it?" Jenny persisted.

"Our part? Well, we called to them to stop."

Jenny said nothing, then got up to walk around the garden. The beds of lavender and campanula, delphinium and scabiosa were riotous shades of blue tempered with white. The phlox were ready to burst. A cluster of fruit trees formed a bower at the bottom of the garden. The lawn was dense and deep, closing in around Jenny's bare ankles as she walked. It was the perfect reflection of its mistress, bold, well tended, regenerative. On the terrace, Rosemary was putting empty cups on the tray. Jenny said, "You know Fred may really have thought he was telling the truth when he claimed that the Beasty slipped—that Wilhelm slipped." She dug the toe of her shoe into the earth. "Maybe he thought he didn't push him, but he did. In all these years, that memory has never wavered." She knew there was too much passion in her voice.

Rosemary stood staring at her. "For heaven's sake, what does it matter now?"

"It matters because it happened, Rosemary. It always will matter."

Rosemary shook her head and smiled. "You always were a silly bear." She turned to go into the house. "We'll have sherry in the drawing room, shall we?" Her tone was full of indulgent affection.

She just doesn't have a clue, Jenny thought crossly. Not the least idea that the truth matters. Never has. She picked up the half empty plate of scones and followed Rosemary across the terrace. Never will.